Anonymous

Western Texas the Australia of America

Anonymous

Western Texas the Australia of America

ISBN/EAN: 9783337313951

Printed in Europe, USA, Canada, Australia, Japan

Cover: Foto ©Andreas Hilbeck / pixelio.de

More available books at **www.hansebooks.com**

WESTERN TEXAS

THE

AUSTRALIA OF AMERICA;

OR

THE PLACE TO LIVE.

Must I remain forever here penniless and destitute? Is there no
spot upon this wide-spread earth whereon I could live and accumulate
a little to be called my own?

BY

A SIX YEARS' RESIDENT.

CINCINNATI:

FOR SALE BY E. MENDENHALL,

No. 10 West Fifth Street.

1860.

PREFACE.

To drop the plow, spade, ax, and the like, and travel over the earth until a country is found where these companions of the laboring man need not swing so heavily, where his task need not be so hard, where his condition in life may be easily bettered, and then write home and to all the world, in the shape of a book, and tell poor mankind of such discovery, is what men seldom do. Men may explore the remotest ends of the earth, and draw the heavens near for geographical, historical, and philosophical purposes, and they may crowd the world with their histories and important discoveries; they may write of love, of daring deeds and lofty purposes, and upon almost all the subjects that commonly suggest themselves to the mind; they may peruse the Holy Bible even, and write theological works enough to convert the whole world to Christianity; and yet the poor man may look in vain among all these writings to find how to get his bread and raiment, how the means to educate his children, or how his pecuniary wants are to be supplied, and his earthly career made more pleasant to himself and family.

The world is full of book-producers, but how few address themselves to the legions who are anxious to know where they can go, what they can do, and how they are to do it.

The following pages were not designed so much for the literary world as for the generality of men. Nor were they designed so much to delight as to benefit. They were written principally for those who are and may be looking abroad over the earth for another and better range of operation, or a more accessible grainery of life; and although by the "huge paw" of a working man, the interested reader will not stop to criticize, but will leniently consider that the writer is one of those poor but somewhat observing laborers, who has snatched a moment from time to tell the world of a field that only awaits the sickle to reap its golden harvest.

As I have said, these pages may be considered as having been written to benefit rather than to delight. If the object is attained, what matters it to the reader that the writer is a bungler or anything but an accomplished composer? So, if the reader is of those for whom this work is written, it is hoped that he may not stop to notice faults and errors, but read on and see if there is anything here suggested that may be to his advantage.

A portion of this work was written more than a year since, which will account for any seeming conflicting statements in regard to time

CONTENTS.

CONTENTS

INTRODUCTORY.

KIND READER, take, if you please, an imaginary flight over the densely populated portions of the civilized world, and consider how many there are who would do well to emigrate.

Ask, in your flight, the legions with whom you meet if they would wish to emigrate, and then calculate the number whose answer was "yes, but where shall I go?" No doubt such an answer, or one to the same effect, would fall from the lips of many thousands; and to many of those whose wish it is to find another and better country, the contents of this book may be somewhat interesting.

How often has the poor discontented man retraced the fruitless efforts of his past, looked around upon his unhappy present, and gazing out upon the dark uncertain future, exclaimed with feelings of anguish, akin to despair, "O, what can I do, or where shall I go? Have I left anything undone that I could do in this unpromising land? Must I remain forever here, penniless and destitute? Is there no spot upon this wide-spread earth whereon I could live and accumulate a little to be called my own?

Is the reader a poor man of family, whose house may be open and almost roofless, and whose children are poorly clad, and the cold blasting snow storms of another winter coming on, and do these shivering children stand around and cry aloud for a father's care? Well might the father say, "This is too much; but O, God, what can I do? Where, O, where shall I go?"

Perhaps the reader is a man of property, and having his credit too far extended, it would now take one
half he has got to answer the demands against him,
and he may say, "I am already as deeply in debt as
my merchant will suffer me to go. There is no hope
of making anything here; and if I were to make a des-
perate effort to dispose of my effects, settle up my
business, and start out in the pursuit of a more promising country, where my little balance might accumulate, where my efforts might be crowned with success,
where I might live free from debt and the angry de-.
mands of creditors, where I might make life more an
object and live out a peaceful decline of years, and
give my children a liberal and respectable start in the
world—where," he may ask, "shall I go to find that
country?"

Should chance open my book to the perusal of any
whose feelings or situations might answer such or a
similar portrayal, then let them read on. Methinks
the reader is a young man whose cradle of infancy
was no stranger to wealth; whose boyish days were
happy in the sportive play of school-mates; whose
youthful mind was ever elate with the brightest of
prospects, and the green meadows of his father's land
bade him smile, be joyous, and hopeful; but by the
vicissitudes of fortune he is now rendered poor and
unhappy, and would fly away from the taunts and
jeers of those who were once proud to be considered
his friends and equals.

It may be you are an orphan boy, whose ears are
unaccustomed to words of kindness, whose last bless-
ing fell from the lips of a dying parent, and, galling in
the chains of discontent, would get away if you but
knew where to go. If so, cease the mingling of tears
with thy sorrows, and read on.

Possibly you are the resident of some densely-populated country, where every trade, occupation, and pursuit is overdone, and where you can not continue to live with hope of success in any business that you may be qualified to carry on.

Are you the daring sailor, for whom the perils and hardships of the sea have no further charms, and having furled the sail and bid adieu to hoarse commands, would you now seek that peace and profit which the billows of the ocean have failed to give? Have the prayers of an anxious and loving wife, whose mind has already too long dwelt upon the watery graves of the deep, induced you to remain upon land?

Perhaps you are the friend of some one whose wish it is to leave behind the land of his nativity, and look for wealth, honors, or contentment in another? If so, please read on; and should you deem it worth your while, call the attention of your friend to this book.

Are you the laboring man of intellect, whose only want to render you worthy of your immortal nature, is leisure? Would you burst the fetters of poverty while yet in the vigor of life, in anticipation of declining years, and accumulate a little to smooth the roughness of cares in your old and feeble days?

Are you the emigrant from eastern or European shores, now landing upon American soil, and would you find a beautiful climate and most excellent locality for your future abode in this great land of liberty? Or are you the farmer's son, whose minor days are quite or nearly out, and would you now mingle with the tide of emigration, taking with you your habits of industry, to some distant country to work out your destiny of weal or woe? Be you who you may, if your future is unpromising,—if you have carefully looked around you and can nowhere discover anything that merits attention, or, in other words, if you would better your fortune, read on.

Be you who you may—Briton, German, Frenchman, American, or what not—whether living upon
the snow-clad hills of New England, the lake-washed
shores of the Canadas, the hights of the Highlands,
or in the valley of the Rhine—if you are discontented
with your present abode, and are determined to seek
a fortune or better your condition in another part of
the world, then patiently read on. It may be that
some of you will be interested. It may be that some
of you will be benefited.

> There is a land where the grass is ever green.
> A land where a beggar seldom is seen.

I would not create an unnecessary excitement; I
would not lead one single human being astray; I
would not induce the rugged son to leave the aged
and helpless parent to mourn the departure of his un-
dutiful child; I would not have any one believe that
anywhere upon the face of this wide-spread earth
there is a country the spontaneous growth of which
renders the labor of man unnecessary; but I would
have thousands and tens of thousands of human
beings believe that if they were in a country with
which I am acquainted and about which I am going
to write, they would be by far better off than they
now are or can ever expect to be by remaining where
they are. I have no newly discovered gold or silver
mines, no second California or Australian gold excitement upon which to enlarge, but I have a country,
dear reader, of which to tell you, where, if some men
could be, the prattling of their babes and the music
of birds would be sweeter to their ears; where the
frown upon their brows would involuntarily dispel,
and the tears of their children would no longer come
forth from the suffering of cold, nor mingle with the
frosts as they fall; a country where a man can labor

with the hope of some day being lord of the soil; where a man can be a man, not a dog; a country where now and for many years to come there can be a glorious investment of a small or large capital safely made; a country where, having myself resided for six long years, traveling it over and over, I have never yet seen a public beggar or a person who lived by appealing to the sympathy of others. It may be that others have; but I can safely say that such people are hardly known in this fortunate country. A country, in short, where to my knowledge there are plenty of men who are worth from ten to one hundred thousand dollars, and who, but a few years ago, had hardly a dollar they could call their own, and many of whom, had they remained in their native countries, would most undoubtedly have remained there forever poor, and at this time getting their daily bread with their daily labor, instead of being as they now are, among the wealthiest of this naturally great and delightful country, doing what they do at their leisure or pleasure.

Now, kind reader, unfold, if you please, the map of the United States, and upon its southern portion you will find a country or state that, for some reason or other, is called Texas. Here is the promised land; here is the Lone Star; here is the Australia of America.

WESTERN TEXAS;

OR,

THE PLACE TO LIVE.

IT may be thought that through views of advantage, for the gratification of fanciful display or some reason or other, the writer is overdoing the thing and placing this section of country far beyond any real excellency or advantages that it possesses over other countries or neighboring states; but it is not so. Upon my word and honor, and as God is my witness, I feel from the bottom of my heart every word that I have said, and shall conscientiously continue my subject, taking with me to the end majestic truth as the guiding meteor of my pen. O how I feel, not the want of sincerity, but the want of ability, to enable me to do it justice.

Texas! Man, with all his ideas of perfection, might look in vain for a land more favored by creation and the government of man than this; and yet, comparatively speaking, her habitations are mere dots upon her surface, while in many parts of the world people are cramped up for the want of room. Here the denizen goes forth and commits to flames the vast surplus of spontaneous growth, while the people of other countries are carefully storing up every blade and spear that the soil, pushed to its greatest capacity, is capable of producing. Here the minds of men, ever so free and easy in regard to the cares of life, are revolving in schemes of speculation, and around them their cattle are cropping the luxuriant grass the twelve-month

9

through, while in other countries the eternal routine
of laborious preparation in summer for the necessities
of tedious winters, render there, both, the minds and
bodies of men, forever enslaved; never dreaming that
these constant cares of their lives, necessary upon a
stingy and contracted plan, are robbing their very
souls of their beauty; and their minds forever enslaved for the requirements of the body, never drink
from the fountains of thought, which are boundless
and free.

Let me introduce to our shores a stranger from
across the ocean or the Gulf of Mexico. When landing, he is generally unfavorably impressed. He has
cherished an idea that soon the land of Texas will
stand up in ready relief to his anxious eye. He looks
around in vain for that of which he had dreamed, and
inquires of the country. Hearing its many praises, he
loses no time in preparation for some part of the interior. He starts out over, what seems to him, an
endless level. Soon herds of deer are bounding away
before him. He sees cattle in every direction, and
wonders at the immense waste of luxuriant grass.
Although not satisfied with this broad level so destitute of noisy creeks and shady groves, he begins to
be somewhat reconciled. Now the timely setting of
the sun, casting her golden rays upon the dark green
foliage of the earth, reminds him of the approach of
night, and that here, as elsewhere, man must rest, eat,
and sleep. Under the branches of a live oak or cluster
of trees, not far from a lagoon or pool of water, he
turns in to answer the demands of his nature. He
sleeps upon the ground, in the open air, 'neath the
dew-catching branches, and dreams of all things glad
and free. The music of the night, and the first greet-
ing of his ears at the dawning of day, are the ever
changing notes of the mocking-bird. He rises to wel-

come back the beauties of day, and, being refreshed,
starts on his way. The scenes of to-day are those of
yesterday, but toward night, in the distance, are signs
of elevation, and at the close of day, upon hill-tops,
from whence the view is delightful, that overlook the
travels of the day and the sublimity of the distant
plain; close by the music of dancing little waters on
their way below, lull our traveler to the sweet em-
brace of refreshing sleep. The arms of Morpheus
again relax their hold, and the traveler awakens to a
conciousness of the rich comings that must soon follow
the now gray lights of the east, happy tidings of day.
The glorious orb appears, and here are not only beauties for the eye, charms for the ear, and sweet fragrance for the smell, but a feast for the mind. Visions
of happiness and hopes of fortune are now playing
their parts around his joyful heart. Again upon his
way, the surface now being hilly and undulating, and
the traveler, divested of the last inkling of prudence,
is eager to drink deep of these moistenings of the soul.
Wondering on at the continued increase of natural
beauty, unconsciously, upon some elevation he is now
fixed, as it were, and naught but his eyes and inner
faculties are moving. He looks and looks, wonders
and wonders, and finally the tongue, ay, the very lips
of the soul, burst forth: "Can it be that these broad
unbounded meadows are perpetually green? can it be
that the sweet fragrance of these flowers, whose beauty
can only be seen with beauty's eyes, are unceasingly
mingled with the air as if forever to delight the breath
of man and charm the flight of the honey-bee? and
are these birds of so many colors forever so sweetly
musical? Is it possible that these herds of cattle,
horses, mules, and sheep, the swiny tribe and all,
live here the twelve-month out without the aid of
man? and could man live here throughout all the

variations of heat and cold, with only the trees to shelter him, and all this in the United States of America, the renowned land of freedom? Am I dreaming, or is this really so?"

Such words as these will give the reader but a faint idea of the surpassing beauty and delightful appearance of this country, from early spring until summer; and in the dead of winter the stranger, from a snowy country, would be equally delighted; although the flowers of the forests and prairies are not so plentiful and fragrant as in summer, yet he is here and can realize the comfortable sleeping out of doors at a time when he knows that frosty snows are covering the land of his distant home, and can see, as in summer, the cattle living upon the grass of the prairies uncared for by man. The traveler may go on for hundreds of miles, in different directions, penetrating the mountains, if he pleases, continually absorbed with the beauty, fertility, and healthful appearance of the country, and particularly carried away with the idea that the doors of wealth are here wide open to every one who will devote his best efforts to the improvement of the advantages that here lay before him.

It is sometimes amusing to look over and consider the extravagant paper calculations of new-comers in regard to what can be done in Texas at the stock-raising and farming business—*i. e.*, as they say, and with much justness, too, if men would only work one half as hard here as they do where I came from, considering themselves proof against the habits of idleness, or *Texas fever*, as the saying is here, to which many of the older settlers of the country have become addicted. The time was, and it is the case now in many places in western Texas, that men, by stepping to their doors or outside their camps, could shoot down a fat buck or doe, the meat of which is excellent, and the hides of which, by a simple process of tanning, with which all old Texans are familiar, make most durable clothes. So it is not so strange that old settlers here, who were once so nearly cut off from the older states by so limited a communication with them, should have contracted habits of idleness, since most all they could do that then seemed advantageous to them, was to kill deer and other game for their meat and peltry, and fight Mexicans for their independence.

For my part, I would withhold that severity of censure that the old Texan very often seems to deserve for his relaxation of energy and loose morality. I would say to the old veteran, "All honor to you for your services in liberty's cause, and happy may you live and die. But since such exertions as yours and your childrens' seem to prove inadequate to the development of the resources of the excellent country for which you fought and conquered, you certainly will have no objections to seeing this country inhabited by those who will turn its rich soil to the greatest advantage, and its extensive productions to the good of mankind."

. The state of Texas is a planting and stock-growing country; its western portion being better adapted to the growing of stock, and not so well adapted to the growing of cotton and the great staples of the south; the valleys or bottoms of its principal rivers, however, are fine cotton and sugar-producing lands, and a large amount of these commodities are now produced and exported from the state. Their production, however, is confined principally to eastern Texas or the bottoms of the Colorado, and portions of the state east of this river. Many of the river bottoms west of this, however, produce more or less cotton, and some of them a large amount of it. But it is more the southern and western portions of the state, generally, as well as the

2

stock-growing business of Texas, that are here to be considered.

CATTLE RAISING.

For anything like a real picture of many parts of this country, my pen might labor in vain. I can only wish that the reader might travel it over, as I have done, stand upon its elevations, and contemplate its beautiful form and the rich mantle that God has spread over it. How often have I wished that the farmers of the cold country, where I was raised, and the cold and snowy countries where I have been, could travel over western Texas, taking with them a knowledge of its climate and soil, its different kinds of grasses, and particularly a knowledge of the stock-growing business of the country. It is not so difficult for me to imagine how those lords of the soil, in summer, and snow-drifts in winter, would feel, or what the impressions of such an excursion, accompanied with vivid recollections of their frosty homes, would be, but to spread out upon paper words that would justly convey my ideas of those feelings and impressions, would be futile for me to attempt.

Would that the representatives of such feelings and situations as those that, in my beginning I attempted to portray, could only know how well this country would be adapted to their peculiar wants—and O that thousands of unfortunate men, women, and children could exchange their present unhappy abodes for a home in this bountiful and most delightful country.

Who that has a soul, or that can feel his accountability to his God, would not open the channels of alleviation to unhappy and suffering humanity?

There is, across the deep, a country that resembles much, in many things, the one about which I am going to write; the pursuits and productions of which,

to a great extent, are the same—Australia. She, like
Texas, is a great stock-growing country. She has
been more fortunate than Texas in some respects.
The first cattle taken to Australia were of English
breeds, and the constant importations from England
have since kept up and improved the cattle and other
stock of this most excellent grazing country. The
cattle of Texas are inferior to those of Australia; but
their vast, luxuriant range makes them thrifty and
profitable to their owners. I believe they are a race
of Spanish and French cattle—or I can safely say
that they are generally Mexican, Louisiana, and Missouri cattle. Although they are generally rough, and
not compact and heavy enough, they are large and
rangy, and are fine cattle upon which to improve.
But, withal, beautiful droves of beeves can now be
selected upon our Texas prairies.

The first sheep introduced into Australia were from
those countries where improvement in live stock of all
kinds has long since been a great object. Australia's
adaptation to sheep and fine wool growing was finally
discovered, and her importance as a great wool-producing colony soon demanded the attention of the
English government, and from its patronage and encouragement it is now the greatest and finest wool-
growing country in the world. But is there no country that is yet to be her compeer? Has America no
Australia to furnish her looms and enable her manufacturers to compete with those of England? Has
America no country where wool can be produced
sufficiently cheap and in such abundance as to place
it beyond the control of the speculator, and counteract, in its production and manufacture, the penny
labor of Europe? Certainly she has; and more than
this, she has a country that will soon furnish her millions of consumers—the poor, laboring men and all—

with excellent beef and other meats at reasonable rates;
a country to produce her mules—that most excellent
cultivating animal—so reasonably low that they will be
within the reach of all her farmers; and this country,
or part of the United States, is Texas, and particularly
western Texas.

There are now about two millions of cattle in Texas.
Their average value per head is about six dollars. The
raising of beef and veal cattle is an extensive and
profitable business in this country. At this moment
I am thinking of a man, an Irishman, who has twelve
thousand head of these cattle. He lives upon the San
Antonio river, and the bulk of his cattle range between that and the Mission river, or over a range of
country, probably, about thirty miles square. This
man, I am credibly informed, not many years since
followed the business of saddle-tree making, and has,
by continued good management and economy, increased his stock of cattle from a few head to this
large number. He has, of course, bought cattle, but
they were bought with the proceeds of his beef-cattle
originating from his first little beginning of stock that
he made at the saddle-tree business. He has also a
large amount of other property, all of which he accumulated from this small beginning of stock and the
proceeds of his saddle-tree business. He now thinks of
disposing of a share of his other property and putting
the proceeds thereof into cattle. Should this be done
within a short time, he will have about fifteen thousand
head of cattle, and other property necessary for their
management to the amount, probably, of ten thousand dollars. I say necessary, as it will eventually be
required,—probably three thousand dollars worth of
horses, lands, etc., would enable this man to carry
on his business at this time, giving all necessary
attention to his cattle. I will venture to say that if

this person were asked what would have been his situation at this time had he remained in Ireland, his answer would be, a poor laboring man. He last year sold about five hundred beef-cattle, principally at eighteen dollars per head. He has this year sold eight hundred head of beeves at sixteen dollars per head. He will brand this year (1859) about three thousand calves. He probably would not take less than eighteen or twenty thousand dollars for his next year's increase. Not one of this large number of cattle does he ever feed a spear of hay or anything else, nor has he any of them inclosed in pastures. His cattle are scattered over a large range of country, with the cattle of other stock-growers, and outnumber those of any other brand in his range. Stock men in this country, for the purpose of marking and branding their calves, collecting their beeves, and working with their cattle generally, go together on horseback in numbers sufficiently large to enable them to work to advantage. It is not unusual here to see as many as three or four thousand head of cattle brought together in one bunch for the purpose of selecting out such as may be wanted.

Let the reader imagine himself upon a broad prairie, covered with scattering cattle as far as the eye can reach, and from twenty to thirty men and boys, mounted upon Mexican horses, swiftly surrounding thousands of these cattle, bringing them together with the cracking of whips and hooping of voices, or Indian yells, and when together the clashing of horns, roaring and fighting of bulls, and the dextrous riding maneuvers in separating such as are wanted from the main herd, make up an interesting and exciting scene. These are everyday occurrences here in Texas, saying nothing, at present, about the lassooing of wild horses, cattle, and other animals.

Men having large stocks of cattle are not particular about bringing them home. There is generally
company stock-pens built over the range, and they
brand at the first convenient pens, private or otherwise, anywhere within the range, and turn loose, and
collect, again and again, until their trip is made or
their work completed. On returning home, however,
from a stock-hunting trip, there is generally a goodly
number brought to the ranche or headquarters of the
business for the purpose of branding or haunting, particularly if the drove be made up upon the outskirts
of the range. Should a large stock-grower find his
animal out of his range, or beyond certain boundaries,
if he does not take it home, he works it back within
these boundaries before turning it loose again.

Men of small stocks of cattle are generally more
particular about keeping them near home, and sometimes those of considerable stocks have them haunted
to a small scope of country. Having myself, last year,
bought, for a shipper, the beeves from a stock of about
fifteen hundred head, belonging to a man who was
living in the valley of the Nueces, I am knowing to
the fact of his having his whole stock of cattle, except,
perhaps, about twenty head, brought together in one
herd in less than four hours' time, and this, too, by
three or four Mexicans on wages of trifling amount.
Probably the branding of this man's increase of stock
and the whole care of his fifteen hundred head of cattle, does not cost him more than two hundred and
fifty dollars per year, and his stock will turn off one
hundred three and four year old beeves, annually, at
sixteen dollars per head right at home. The owner
of these cattle is not able nor does he pretend to work,
nor is there any necessity of his working, for his cattle will make him rich, besides supporting his family
and paying for all the attention they require.

Now, Mr. lord of the snow-drift of New England, Canada or anywhere else, do you think that this man would exchange his fifteen hundred head of cattle and place of residence for the best farm that could be found in any cold country, with the understanding that he should go and live upon it? No indeed, he would not. Although his fifteen hundred head of cattle are not worth ten thousand dollars, and his house a picket hut, stuck up on land belonging to some one else, he would not exchange them, with the advantages of the range they have, and his residence, as humble as it is, for property of five times its value in a cold country, where he would be compelled to house up from four to six months of the year, to avoid freezing. He was raised among the destitute of Europe; he has experienced the frost-biting and snow-beating winds of the north, and is thankful that he has found a better climate and country. His expression is, "I am sorry for the poor devils of those cold, snowy regions."

A person having a small stock of cattle, or even eight or ten hundred head, need not pay out a dollar for hire, if he has a mind to ride and work with a stock-driving company. In fact I know a person who has fifteen hundred head of cattle, and by riding and working in company with other stock-growers, he accomplishes his entire branding without paying out a dollar for hire; and other stock-growers, I know, who depend entirely upon hired help to work and manage their cattle. Others let their cattle and give a share of the increase or pay by the head for their branding. The usual share given by stock-growers for branding their increase, is every fourth calf or a dollar per head for each and every one branded. Not a few, but many, men in Texas have made fine beginnings and are making snug fortunes by branding and managing stocks of cattle for the fourth calf or a dollar for branding each and every increase. A crowd of stock-boys, when hunting upon the prairie, look out for each other's cattle, and all their brands and provisions are packed upon the same horse or horses, cart or wagon, and made hot by the same fire.

When a herd of cows and calves, collected by and belonging to different individuals, are taken to a pen for the purpose of branding the young, those designed for one or two brands, according to the number of apartments in the pen and the number of hands to work, are cut out from the main herd, those for each brand by themselves and placed in these apartments, and the branding-irons already hot in the fire, handy by, the throwing of ropes and jumping of fences soon begins. Although these Texas cattle are generally quite easily managed on horseback, yet many of them, when hemmed in a pen and run about for the purpose of roping or lassoing the calves, until they are heated and maddened from the bellowing of their young, etc., will dash furiously at the roper, and he is obliged to retreat or take the fence for a moment until the fighting cow returns and mingles with the bunch, when all hands are at their ropes again catching and throwing the calves, marking their ears, trimming them, and scorching their hides with red hot letters and figures, or whatever characters may represent the brands of the different owners.

There are many men in Texas who had, but a few years ago, their brand upon but from one to five cows, who now have fine little stocks of from fifty to five hundred head of cattle, and in many cases such stocks have grown up, altogether, from such little beginnings. It is often interesting to hear some of these wealthy stock men relate the history of their business. They will tell you that a few years back, in 1840, perhaps, " I had but two or three cows, a few pigs and chickens, an old mare or so, and if my debts had been paid, I would n't have been worth a dollar in the world. We lived in that old shanty, and many a comfortable evening have I seen by the fire in that old fire-place. We had no land, but lived and cultivated most anywhere we pleased. We were often without much of anything to eat in those days but venison or wild meat of some kind. But my trusty old rifle was sure to knock down a plenty of that. The hundreds of cattle and horses that you now see around me and scattered over the range with my brand (diamond, ◇, or ⊙, perhaps,) on them, are mostly all from these few old animals and their increase."

How often have I heard them say that to get rich in Texas a man has only to buy a few animals and then lie down; but it takes a little more to get rich. He must brand up his increase in good season, and see that they do not stray off, or are not driven out of their range. A person having a start of fifty to a hundred head of cattle, will soon grow them up to a fine stock of several hundred or a thousand head, if he is careful to *haunt* them to a good range, and attend to them properly, which haunting can generally be done in about a year's time. After being well attached to a good range, near to one's ranche or place of residence, they require but little attention, further than the branding of the increase. It is well known that if a poor man in western Texas can get a start in the stock business, however small his beginning may be, he is sure to get well off with but little exertion, and this beginning is so easily made that a person of the least capacity or money-making qualifications, who is disposed to go into the business, is sure to make it. In the first place, he need not expend a dollar for land, if he prefers not, and if he be economical and at all inclined to work, not a cent for

3

lumber. The broad, luxuriant prairies are open and free to him for his cattle, and the timbers, in many places, at his disposal for the building of shanties, log houses, and the making of rails, or whatever rough improvements he might see fit to make for the present, until he should be able to purchase land of his own. I have known a person to own four or five thousand head of cattle in Texas, without owning a foot of land in the state, turning them loose in almost any range he might see fit, and building his ranche upon unoccupied lands.

Others, I know, having thousands of cattle in Texas without an acre of land, who give a share of their increase for branding and the attention their cattle get, or pay by the head for branding, etc. The better way, however, for a man of small beginning, is to purchase a homestead, of a few acres at least, as soon as he can, as the lands are cheap and fine for cultivation. A man of any industry can improve a little farm, the proceeds of which will support his family or self while his stock of cattle are increasing to a number that will of itself support him in a few years, and eventually make him rich. His stock should, from the beginning, however small it may be, turn off a few beeves every year, that is if his first purchase was made up of an average lot of stock cattle. An average lot of stock cattle, of different ages, in Texas, are cows and calves, yearlings and two years old, male and female, as they may run, including all females in the stock, but no beef cattle older than two years, and of course of the usual size, breed, and condition; which breed, etc., along a wide scope of the coast of Texas, is pretty much one and the same thing. Back from the coast, among the hills, mountains, and timbers, and in more northern Texas, the cattle are generally more compact in body, and pretty, not so wild, and of course more easily managed by an inexperienced hand. But the breed and condition, or unkindness of cattle in western Texas, should not govern the purchaser of limited means so much when buying for stock-raising purposes, upon the principle that the child must creep before he can walk. For instance, in the purchase of a stock of cattle in western Texas, the purchaser will get, for six dollars, cows that will raise calves which will sell for as much at six months old, for veal and other purposes, as will the calf of the same age for the same purposes, that may have been raised from a cow worth fifty dollars. And the new beginner might find himself under the necessity of parting with his calves and yearlings in order to get along.

If the beginner of quite limited means and new to this country, should undertake the business with improved or imported cattle altogether, he might find his little means exhausted before he should have fairly commenced, and long before he could have acquired a sufficient knowledge of the country to make his fine stock business profitable, and consequently subject himself to the danger of shoals, which, if the reader will follow me up, he will hereafter plainly see.

In the purchase of cattle, the new-comer or beginner in Texas should aim to get as many beeves, of good age, in his purchase as he can, provided he gets his stock at the customary average price per head. I have known stocks of cattle to sell here for five dollars round, including a fair average of three and four year old beeves. And again, I have known stocks of cattle to sell here for seven dollars round, exclusive of all beef cattle older than two years. The first mentioned may not have been so gentle and easily managed as the last, but to the experienced stock-grower this difference in the condition of the two stocks was of little consequence in comparison with the difference in price.

I am here only trying to impress the idea that to make a successful and anything like a rapid beginning with cattle in western Texas, the man of quite limited means should not be so particular about the kind of cattle to commence with. Let him buy anything of a Texas cow that will bring a calf, and get her as cheap as he can. After he is well set up in business, he can improve his cattle, if he wishes. I have known men in the northern states to buy old, superannuated ewe sheep for the purpose of getting a start in the sheep business. After getting a crop or two of lambs from these old sheep, they would begin to drop away, and would soon die out. But the purchasers got them for a trifling amount, and were thereby enabled to commence the business, which they could not have done, to any extent, by buying young and expensive sheep of the same quality of wool.

The stranger, with a plenty of money or a few thousand dollars, may come on with his fine stock in small or large quantities, according to his means. But he who brings improved stock to Texas, should understand the country beforehand, or have some one in advance of him who does: otherwise he should pay particular attention to what the writer shall hereafter say in regard to the importation of northern or European stock into Texas. I said, a little back, that the new-comer should purchase a homestead, etc., as soon as he can. But the man of small means should be very careful about putting his money into lands. He should first make sure of his stock, of whatever kind it may be; and as soon as he finds himself able to make a small outlay for lands, let him do so, and improve his place as best he can. Of course he should know, before getting his stock, where he is going to keep it; but it does not follow that he should have expended any considerable sum for lands or a place to live. *Vice versa,* the moneyed man who embarks in the stock business in western Texas should have his lands and place of business beforehand, particularly if it is his intention to raise fine stock or improve the stock that he may purchase in Texas.

One great advantage of this country to strangers, is that they may come here with a little money and put it into live stock without making an outlay for a home or a place to keep that stock; which outlay would of course take up their little capital, comparatively, in an unproductive way, where it could not afford that easy means of support, and at the same time be accumulating in a compound manner, as money does invested in stock here in Texas. A person can, in this climate, pitch strong and durable tents, or erect temporary picket or log dwellings, upon unoccupied lands, sometimes with and often without the consent of the owner. This enables him to invest his little capital as above set forth, and gives him time to look up a place for a permanent residence, and a range to suit him for his cattle or stock, also time to get ready to make a payment upon a place when and where it may suit him to buy. I must not forget to say that it is, in one of the broad prairies that I know of, expected by stock-growers there that a new-comer will purchase a quantity of land in this prairie before turning loose a stock of cattle upon it. But no one, so far as I know, regards the expectations of these people. I am knowing to the fact that men from all parts are turning loose their cattle in any range they please in western Texas, whether they have lands or not. But the better way, as I have said, is to get a little land as soon as possible, as it costs but a trifle, and can, as a general thing, be bought upon most favorable terms. If you are a man of quite limited means, put your money into stock, and then get your land on time. Should you then find yourself pushed to make your payments, sell out your male-cattle, of any age, your yearling mules or mutton sheep, etc., to the best advantage you can, and keep your females and best producing stock, which will fetch you out all right.

I will here say that the best way for a working man, of small means, who comes alone to the country and is unacquainted with its peculiar ways of stock-raising, to commence the cattle or horse and mule raising business in Texas, is to look up some stock-grower already in the business, in whom confidence can be placed, and not only consult and advise with him upon the subject, but work your stock with those who work his stock, if you can. Whoever comes to Texas to engage in anything pertaining to the stock or farming business, should move slowly and carefully at first. The difference in climate and the flattering appearance of the country, is apt to carry a stranger away with some foolish notion, and too often it takes him a long time to recover from the effects of his folly in the beginning. Strangers in this country should remember that there are already many settlers here, and that they are not all lazy and wanting in good sense, and that it would be well to find out a little how others do before "pitching in" too strong. The cattle business, as it is now generally carried on in Texas, requires a vast deal of horseback riding, which is hard work, at first, for one who is unaccustomed to this kind of exercise. But after following it for one season, almost any man will endure a day's ride or work at the business with but little fatigue. As hard as it may be, when compared with the splitting of rails, hoeing of corn and potatoes, mowing and pitching of hay, cradling and binding of grain, etc., etc., it might justly be considered pleasure-riding. The hardest work attending the business of cattle-raising in Texas, is the marking and branding of the increase. But there is a kind of excitement connected with this part of the business, as there is, also, with the riding part of it, which makes it, what the writer would call, laborious amusement, in which every little boy and thrifty young man seem eager to engage and participate.

When stock-cattle change hands, to be kept in the country, the original brand is generally put on to them again, which is called counter-branding, and the brand of the purchaser is also put on to them. The brand of every stock-grower must be recorded, to enable him to hold it in law, or in case of dispute. Men having large stocks of cattle generally have their brand recorded in several adjoining counties. They also like their cattle to go some ways from home, for the purpose of changing range and crossing with other cattle, which is conducive to health and thrift. The opposite course of hemming them into coves and bends of rivers, upon islands, etc., has a tendency to degenerate and run the stock down to puny, inferior animals. A person can keep his stock near home, however, and avoid all this by changing bulls, which costs him nothing, and by driving his stock, occasionally, away from their old stamping-grounds; all of which, in time, with a little watching, are sure to return. This precaution, however, is entirely unnecessary until a stock has become very large, and has been kept upon the same range for a long time.

An immense number of the cattle produced in Texas are used for oxen, and many of them are driven north. There are many thousands of beef cattle now annually driven from here to Chicago and different markets north of Texas. It is a singular fact that an inferior beef is here grown to four and five years of age and then driven thousands of miles to a northern market, and this, too, at a profitable rate for the producer as well as the drover. New Orleans is, however, the principal market for the present great surplus of beef and veal cattle produced in western Texas, but the time will come when Texas will produce more beeves than is now consumed in all the great markets of the United States. In the opinion of the writer, the time is coming when the same extent of territory in no part of the world will produce more live stock of all kinds than will the present domain of Texas.

The man of means, it is needless to say, can at this time, and for many years to come, do more with his money in Texas than he can do in almost any, if not quite any, other part of the world, particularly at the stock business. With ten thousand dollars a person can buy in Texas a thousand head of cattle, a league of as good land as there is in the world, and establish for himself a comfortable and respectable home in the way of dwelling-house, etc., all of which property, in time, would be worth several hundred per cent. more than it would now cost him. Inclosing lands for pasturage is quite extensively commenced by men of means in some parts of Texas; but the stock business here, as a general thing at this time, could not be made profitable by inclosing the stock of the country in pastures. In fact, from the nature and present state of things, such a course could not be generally pursued, and therefore our broad prairies are to be open for many years to any and all who may see fit to turn their stock upon them. Eventually almost every stock-grower in the country will require a pasture, but the time is far distant when the great bulk of Texas range will be fenced up—possibly fifty and possibly a hundred years may not see this. The time is coming when the cattle and different kinds of stock in this country are to be generally improved, and the better grasses are to be cultivated. Then it is that fencing will come into general requisition. It will not cost any more to pasture a Durham bullock than a Texas animal, and the Durham, all things considered, is undoubtedly worth double the money. Who doubts, that if the present stock of Texas cattle were entirely of English breeds, it would be worth twelve dollars per head all round, instead of six dollars?

When a great central railroad is put through Texas, from New Orleans *via* San Antonio into central Mexico, then look out for improvements of all kinds, and the going up of property in these parts. The time for the building of such road of course no one can now safely predict, but that such a road will some day be built, the most natural appearance of things renders certain. There are already many miles of disconnected portions of it built.

HORSE AND MULE RAISING.

The stock man in western Texas has a wide field in which to operate. If he has a speculative disposition, there is, and is to be, a plenty of room for its gratification: while he can have some one look to his stock, they can be doing just as well as though he were all the time at home watching them. There are any number of stock men, merchants, and speculators in Texas, who have made fine fortunes by driving horses and mules from Mexico to northern markets, or by bringing them here to sell to northern speculators, and to our stock-growers, or the planters of eastern Texas. I have known boys of fifteen and sixteen years of age, to go on wages with old drivers to Mexico with the privilege of investing what little money they might have in horses or mules, and put them with the drove of the employer; and many men who have started in this small way have become wealthy and large operators. Many of these drivers, after selling out enough horses, mules, etc., to pay the entire purchase money and all expenses on their droves, have fine lots of mares left on hand, which they keep here for the purpose of raising horses and mules, which, by the way, is no trifling business in this country.

It is estimated that the horse kind in Texas now numbers about a quarter of a million, but the continual driving of this kind of stock from Mexico to Texas, and from Texas to different parts of the United States, renders it very difficult to come at any correct knowledge of the number of this kind of stock really belonging in Texas. I should suppose that the tax-list of the state did not cover more than three fourths or four fifths, at most, of the horse kind really belonging in it; and whether it does or not, the raising of mules and horses in Texas is an extensive and profitable business. I am now thinking of a Dutchman who has made a snug fifty thousand by buying and driving horses and mules from Mexico to different states of this Union, and by raising cattle, horses, and mules in western Texas. He is now settled down in western Texas, loaning money at such rates of interest as could be paid in no country but this. I have been told that a mare colt, for which he paid five dollars, in Mexico, he sold in Illinois, when grown, for one hundred and twenty-five dollars; and that a mare, for which he paid, in Mexico, five dollars, when on her way to Illinois, being kept over one season in Texas, brought him two colts, one soon after the purchase and the other the next spring, and all together brought him one hundred and forty dollars. Who wonders at his making fifty thousand dollars?

I am an eye witness to greater doings here in western Texas than I have just mentioned. I know of men who have mares that were thrown in to them for nothing, as sucking colts, when they purchased their mothers in Mexico, and some of these mares have had their fifth and eighth colt since brought to Texas, and bid fair to have as many more, and their keeping has never cost them a dime. I have a knowledge of men, and there are plenty of such here, who have made large amounts of money or property by driving horses and mules from Mexico, and selling out such as they deemed advisable, and keeping the balance, are now here raising mules and horses at such paying rates, upon the capital invested, as was never heard of, except in Texas. Not a hundred miles from my place of writing, there is living a gentleman who, not many years since, came to Texas with a small amount of means, and commenced the buying and selling and raising of mules and horses. I am told that he now has an increase of one thousand mules annually from his stock of mares.

Think of this, reader!—a stock of mares that will raise a thousand mules annually, running on the big pasture of Texas, and for nothing! The owner of this stock has recently built a domicil that has the appearance of being worth fifteen or twenty thousand dollars. He could probably build such a one every year without any strain upon his income. Here is a country wide open for others who may wish to take his track.

This stock, like horned cattle, find here the year through, more grass of spontaneous growth than it requires, and is managed with very little trouble and expense. I have known a man in western Texas having four or five hundred head of horses, mules, jacks, etc., without the help of more than one man to take care of these animals, and this help only a part of the year during the branding season. This man, not many years ago, worked not two miles from the cluster of trees under which I am writing, for a single cow and calf per month, worth at that time five or six dollars. He afterward went to Mexico with the old gentleman for whom he had worked, and invested his small earnings with him. He continued driving horses and mules in this connection for some time. It was but a few years, however, before this laboring man had got more property than his old employer, he proving the most active and expert at the business. He is now settled here in western Texas, upon a tract of twelve hundred acres of fine land, which he owns, in addition to several thousand acres besides, raising mules and horses almost exclusively as a business.

This is but one or two of the many instances that I might relate to prove this a remarkably good business.

A stallion or herder placed with a number of mares, and kept with them altogether for one season, will never after suffer any of these mares to leave his herd, unless it is from some accident. Mares are kept together in this way, in different bunches, for the purpose of raising mules; jacks not answering the purpose of keeping them together. Horses fixed and used for this purpose, are called herders, and it is amusing to see them lay their ears and whip their mares into the herd when they get a little scattered out, or when a person is approaching them on horseback or otherwise, and woe to the stallion or gelding that attempts to intrude or make his company agreeable to any of this bunch of mares. The herder whips him, if he can. They do not fight jacks, but are a benefit to the jack that may be placed in a herd with them. These herders are a great help to the business, and will continue to be so as long as horses are raised upon broad unfenced prairies. The fact of a single herder keeping together fifty or sixty mares, on a broad prairie for a whole year, without ever suffering one of them to leave his herd, should be sufficient evidence of their utility, and that they will do this for a jack—submitting to Mr. long ears as the king of the harem—is a singular and striking proof of their utility in this open country. Horses are more inclined to stay together and ramble less than cattle.

A person having twenty or even five good brood-mares, and a proof jack, by selling his mules at a year old and putting the proceeds thereof into mares, will soon get a fine stock of breeding animals on hand. A good average lot of yearling mules, from Mexican stock raised in Texas, will bring thirty dollars round; a lot of half breeds of this age would bring fifty dollars per head; a lot of common Texas mules, at three and four years old, from sixty to seventy-five dollars; a lot of half breeds of these ages, from seventy-five to one hundred and twenty-five dollars, right at home; and mules of three and four years old, from American stock, are worth from one hundred and fifty to two hundred and twenty-five dollars per head. A pretty good average of Mexican mares can now be bought at twelve to sixteen dollars here in Texas, without going to Mexico for them. There is a certain point in western Texas to which the Mexican horse trade tends. A person anywhere in this country wanting Mexican mares, jacks, mules, or horses, can go to the old town of Goliad, at almost any time, and there meet with Mexicans or speculators having such animals for sale. They of course can not always be bought there as cheap as in Mexico, as the men who bring them there generally do it for a profit; but frequently there are great bargains made out of the Mexicans at this point.

BREAKING OF HORSES.

The breaking of Mexican or our Texas raised horses to ride, is a wild and exciting business. When first mounted they are inclined to pitch, and a majority of them do their best to get the rider to the ground. Pitching, as I would describe it, is first putting the head down, then one end up, and then the other, advancing forward every up and down, sometimes inclining this side and that, generally with the fore legs straight and stiff, and the head always down, contracting or gathering at every jump,—a furious, rapid succession of motions that soon exhausts the horse or downs the rider. An experienced or professional rider is, however, almost certain to sit firmly in his saddle or hang on until the horse gives up from exhaustion. The saddles of this country are of peculiar make,—of course well adapted to the riding of these horses. The Mexican manner of subduing these animals is adopted, to a great extent, by the people of Texas and those who come here. These Mexican or unimproved Texas horses are to be useful, and I might say almost indispensable, in this country so long as the stock of the country is left to range over unfenced prairies. There is no other kind of horses that would answer anything like as well for the stock business. Many of these Texas horses are beautiful pacing ponys, and of a variety of colors. When well broken, they make fine riding horses for ladies and children; and we, in Texas, think they are first rate riding horses for men.

STOCK DRIVING.

The driving of stock in this country is a peculiar business. All the native stock, even sheep, are liable to *stampede*. Stampeding is the sudden starting and running of a drove of animals from being frightened; and no driving manager, however careful he may be, can always avoid a stampede. Things will very often happen to stampede a drove of Texas cattle that can not be foreseen—such, for instance, as the unexpected raising up of a man out of tall grass in front of the drove; a first and unexpected quick clap of thunder and flash of lightning; or jumping up of a hog near to or in the midst of the drove; also many things, that watchful and attentive drovers can avoid, will sometimes stampede cattle and cause them to run a long way before stopping. A drove of cattle once well frightened and hard run, will afterward start without apparent cause. So it behooves the drivers to be cautious, for there is no regular rest with a drove of Texas cattle after they have once badly stampeded, until they are well quieted and broke in again. These remarks apply more to droves of beef cattle than to · stock cattle; although Texas cattle, of all kinds, will stampede.

I was told an amusing circumstance by an extensive stock-manager in this country. He says he once took a new-comer, a northern man, on a driving trip with him. Their cattle having stampeded in the night, every man jumped for his horse. The green man, who was an active, zealous fellow, mounts the first horse which he comes to, which was one that had been hoppled when turned out in the evening, when the day's work was done. After rounding in the cattle, and running their horses, now and then, to the best of their speed, for two or three hours, to hold the cattle together and get them where they wanted them, the crowd of drovers all got together, and the verdant *vaquero*, who had gloriously done his part, tells them that the horse he was riding had the d— gaits of any horse that he had ever ridden, and from his description of the gaits, some one of the crowd suspected that Yankee's horse must have been running with his hopples on. It being dark, the suspicious man gets down, and, upon feeling, sure enough the fore legs of Yankee's horse are tied together, which accounted for the awfulest jumps, as he said, his horse had been making all night long. Of course the jug of *Dexter's best*, which had several times passed around camp during the evening, had nothing to do with Yankee's case.

CAMPING AND STORY TELLING.

The stock-drover's camp is generally replete with stories in regard to horsemanship, lassoing maneuvers, wild horse and cow catching, etc.; and when in camp with these gentlemen of the pitching art, I always try to keep my end up. Upon one occasion, when in company with about twenty of these good-natured fellows, after hearing several well-colored stories in regard to mustang riding, etc., I came out with a story in regard to an old Dutchman and his son *Hans*, who lived not far from where I was raised, and who were in the habit of raising horses, or, in other words, *kept Dutch dairy*. Hans was in the habit of going out in the summer to work on wages, and in the winter would come home and help keep hot fires, drink cider, and break colts. Hans, one day, took a colt from the barn-yard, and after leading him, with the bridle, out into the deep snow, without a saddle, of course, mounted him, and, after repeated efforts, could not ride the colt to his satisfaction, turned him back into the yard. The old man, seeing this, comes out in bad humor, and interrogated Hans: "What for, Hans, you don't sthick to dish golt?—he musht pe proken, und might as vell pe proken to-day as any dimes." "Vell, dad, he ish te difle himself; I can do noting

mit him." "You vagapont, Hans, you mus'dt dink
zider gost noting. Tish mighty fine to vorm yourself
py mine fire, und to notings for your grubs. Get te
pridle, you *musht* ride him, Hans." Getting out the
colt, Hans succeeds in riding him, but can not get the
colt to go ahead as it should. The old man coming
up says: "Hans, I has von contrivance by vich I can
make dish golt go ahead. I vil get on to de gold, and
you go long town pehind dat sthump, and when I
rides long py dare you trow your hat and halloo boo!"
The old man with much difficulty reaches and is pass-
ing the stump, when here comes the hat, with a frightful jump and "boo!" from the top of Hans's voice.
The colt, of course, with a tremendous jump, keels
the old man heels over head and buries him in the
snow. Hans, quickly approaching and shaking him,
says: "Dat, am you kilt?" "*O no, Hans; put dat
vas too t—n pig a boo for a little golt!*" It is needless to say, after this, I was called upon until my fund
of stories was exhausted.

MUSTANGING.

Mustanging is among the wildest and most excita-
ble games of the country. I have been told by different individuals that they have seen as many as fifteen
hundred or two thousand mustangs together upon a
western Texas prairie. Mustang pens, for the purpose of catching these wild animals, are built in almost all the extensive prairies of western Texas.
These pens are strongly made, to the hight of ten and
twelve feet, and sometimes with wings from a half to
a mile in length. They are built where these animals
frequent, and, if possible, over their extensive trail,
among bushes or behind timber, where they can not
see their danger, when approaching these pens, until
they are too far within the wings of the pen to retreat,

4

unless it is by running directly back upon their pur-
suers, which they sometimes do when coming in sight
of the pen; but generally, when this far, furiously
take their cage, and not unfrequently with such force
that the foremost ones, unable to stop from being
pushed on by those behind, are smashed down,
striking the fence, and, like a train of cars in col-
lision, pile upon each other, until some of the hind-
most flounce along on the pile over the top of the pen.
When once in the *correll*, and the gap safely secured
with cross-poles, ropes, etc., boisterous work begins.
Here the *vaquero* can display his skill to his entire
satisfaction.

About twenty miles from my place of writing, there
is a family of young men who, several years ago, built
a mustang pen which I have several times seen.
These young men, having *correlled* several little
bunches of horses, and having made several ineffect-
ual attempts to pen a certain valuable gang of mustangs running in their prairie, had abandoned the
idea for a time, when, soon after, there came news to
them that a couple of little neighboring boys, on horseback, had accidentally come upon this very lot of
mustangs, on the old trail, in the very mouth of the
wings of the pen. Dashing upon them and bravely
pursuing their advantage, these boys forced them into
the pen, and securely closed the gap behind them.
Immediately all hands are on tiptoe, and soon, with
a preparation of ropes and lassos, revolvers, clogs,
hopples, blinds, etc., away they go to catch and sub-
due the valuable ones, which are the mares and colts,
and shoot down the worthless, which are the old stallions—worthless from being too obstinate and head-
strong to pay for breaking, and when broken, disagreeable animals. I believe there were about forty
mares taken from this bunch and gentled, which sold

for twelve dollars per head, after they were manageable in a herd.

The gentling of these wild animals is a wicked business. It is often done by tying one fore foot of the animal to a block of wood or a weight that they can not take away, and then left to feed upon grass, being led with a Mexican halter once a day to water, and worked with in this way until sufficiently gentle to turn all together with clogs and hopples upon their feet. When manageable without the clogs, etc., they are taken off, and the herd gently and carefully worked in order to restore the flesh they have lost in the hard and tedious operation.

CATCHING WILD CATTLE.

There are forests in this country where horned stock, from being neglected, have run wild. Crowds of stock-boys sometimes go, with their dogs, and hunt these cattle out of the timber on to the prairies, and catch or shoot them down to prevent them from tolling their gentle stock away into these forests. I know of stock-boys who are in the habit of going upon moonlight nights, with a plenty of help, each man with several ropes to his saddle, and as still and adroitly as possible get between these cattle and their hiding-place, when they are feeding on the edge of the prairie, and rush suddenly upon them and push them in a body far out into the open prairie, and hold them all together, if possible, and if not, when the captain of the crowd shouts, "Rope, boys!" every man secures his animal and ties it down, and if he has time ropes another before they reach the timber. All being safely tied down they are left until morning, when a gentle herd of cattle is driven to each one and they are let up and into the herd and driven away to be branded, according to a previous agreement of the crowd of adventurers.

There is another way of getting hold of these wild fellows, and that is by tailing them, which is a lively business. I was once with a crowd of stock-boys when we came, unexpectedly, upon a bunch of wild cattle, some distance out from their thicket or place of hiding. The boys made after them, and one of our number caught and threw, by the tail, a fine heifer, and, getting quickly down, put a fore foot of the animal over one of its horns, marking its ears with his jack-knife, for in case it should get up and run off it would be his. Mounting his horse he dashed away and overtook the frightened bunch just in time to tail another before it made the thicket. This one was thrown to the ground, but for some reason or other it got away.

This tailing business is nothing more than riding up behind an animal and catching it by the tail, and sometimes giving it a twist around the horn of the saddle, and, driving the spurs to the horse, he jerks the animal to the ground with such velocity that frequently it will not attempt to get up for several minutes. The faster an animal is running the more easily it is thrown to the ground. When driving stock-cattle, if an animal is not inclined to drive well and is continually breaking out of the herd, some driver takes after it and gives it a fall by the tail, after which it generally drives peaceably along.

THE KIND OF MEN FOR THE BUSINESS.

Now in regard to the kind of men who are calculated to carry on the business of raising horses and cattle in this country. Upon opening the subject of stock-raising in Texas to men of the northern states or European countries, they would most undoubtedly

give one to understand that they consider themselves
entirely unfit for a country like Texas, where the cows
and horses are wild and are to be caught by throwing
the rope or lasso, and managed of course by men who
are acquainted with that art. *But this would be a
mistaken idea.* There are men here from all parts of
Europe and America, who are engaged in the stock
business, and it is hard to say who are the most expert with the lasso or rope, or who are the best managers and workers with the stock of the country. I
can say, however, that I have seen a plenty of men
here, both from Europe and the northern states, who
could throw the rope with more certainty than any
Mexican I have ever seen, whose business it always is
from his childhood up. The knowledge of roping and
managing the different kinds of stock in Texas is
easily acquired. In proof of this it is sufficient to
say that most of the men of Texas are from those
states and countries where the use of the lasso is unknown, and where all kinds of stock are gentle; and
these are the men who are raising cattle and all kinds
of live stock here, and succeed so remarkably well.
"Where there is a will there is a way." I have heard
old Texans remark that from those countries where
cattle are driven by men on foot, come the best drovers
and most prudent managers of Texas stock. I do not
say the most expert in every respect, but I might say
the most profitable. They are raised to know the
necessity of working carefully and mildly with stock
of all kinds. To be patient, attentive, and industrious
with cattle or stock of any kind, in any country, is
essential, and for this reason those men who come to
Texas from those countries where cattle are gently
and kindly managed, will help to moderate the roughness, wildness, and carelessness of the country in the
management of its stock; and furthermore, it is

through these new-comers that its stock is to be generally improved and made valuable. I would not lead any one to suppose that they can come and manage our Texas cattle and horses without adopting the ways of the country to some extent; and these ways, as I have said, are easily acquired by the stranger, particularly the Americans and most Europeans. I am well aware that my accounts of wild doings in Texas would have a tendency to deter some men from coming here, if they were otherwise disposed to come; but I must here do away with wrong impressions. To carry on the stock business in Texas, there is no necessity of a person engaging in the business of wild horse or cow catching unless he prefers so to do. He need not brand his own increase even. There are always plenty of stock men who are ready and willing to brand any one's cattle or horses at a reasonable price, and sometimes unreasonably low. He can also, as I have said before, work his cattle with other stockmen, and, if he is determined, can become very well qualified to manage his stock in one season. What one man can do, generally speaking, another man can do. There are many people in many of the over-populated countries of the world who would be glad to emigrate, and would do so were it not that they look upon themselves as unequal to the emergencies of the undertaking. Thousands of men never know their capacities from the simple fact that they never try themselves, and consequently live a life of comparative nothingness. Is it not right for any vigorous young or middle aged man to believe that if away off yonder people are living and doing wonderful things, he could there live and do just such things? It is right for a person to give away off yonder matters a common sense looking into, so far as he conveniently can, at least. If the news of a newly-discovered gold region

reaches his ears, might he not say to himself, "What
are the prospects? how extensive is this region? what
proportion of the men there are making anything, and
how much are they making? Is it a risky lottery of
one chance in a thousand? Do a majority of the men
there dig for gold or for nothing? and am I not as
able to dig and go hungry, and endure as much hardship and deprivation for the sake of gold as any one
of my inches? Pa and ma are good people, but am I
always to stay at home with them and all the children?
Who knows what I can do until I try? So in regard
to Texas. If men are there from Ireland and Germany with more property than a thousand such men
would have ever made where they went from or where
I am living, why could I not go there and make money
as they have made and are making it, although the
cattle there do require roping? If in one season this
art can be learned, and I could manage my cattle by
working with others in the mean time, or as stock-
men there work with and help each other, why could
I not do as well there as any one? People are there
from Great Britain, Germany, France, New England,
and all the world, and am I not as smart as an Eng-
lishman, Dutchman, Frenchman, Yankee or anybody
else? Why should I not be benefited by the spontaneous growth of that beautiful country, and my cattle
live upon that waste of grass, since it would cost me
nothing?" Or another might say, "I have a fine
capital, and could go there and buy cattle and pay for
the attention they might require; speculate, in company with some experienced person, in mules and
horses, wool and hides, and other products of the
country; look up bargains in those leagues and immense grants of unoccupied lands; and live and enjoy
myself in that delightful country, where a man can do
more as he pleases and not live subject to so much

criticism, slander, and restraint, as in this old, worn-out country, where people are too nervous, too meddle-some, too artificial and unnatural for my purpose."

I will here say that a person, if he wishes, can buy in western Texas small stocks of cattle and horses, which are as gentle as they need be, or as much so as they are in any country where they are not stabled and fed with hay and grain. Many stock-men in Texas get up a large share of their calves and milk the cows for a little while, for the purpose of gentling the calves and keeping the cows near home, which has a tendency to keep the stock from scattering. I have known men to milk several hundred cows during the season a short time each, and it is not an unusual thing to see five hundred or a thousand head of cattle with bunches of mares and mules among them in front of the stock-grower's pen or place of branding, congregated there from off the prairie for the night; and the reader can judge something of the wildness or gentleness of these animals when I tell him that he can walk among them all, and put his hands on many of them, and some of them, when lying down, require kicking to make them get up out of his way. The reader must not think, from my remarks, that it is all wildness here. It is as much the way of managing the stock of the country, whether wild or gentle, that would be new and curious to the stranger as anything else. The ways of the country once learned, the cat-tle and horse business is many times as profitable, and a thousand per cent. easier, than in any snowy, cold country in the world.

HOG RAISING.

My remarks upon the stock business should have continued directly on from horned cattle and horses to other kinds of stock, without going off upon seeming irrelevancy, but from the fact that other kinds of stock can be managed here without the lasso or rope, and that a person from any part of the world can manage it to advantage from the beginning, if he knows how to manage it anywhere else.

Raising hogs and making pork in Texas is a business that many men would prefer to any of the stock-raising branch. There are vast portions of this country that are covered with different kinds of oak, pecan, and other producing timbers, and many are the thousands of hogs that come to the call of the horn out of these timbers and the prairies around for their bate of corn. It is contended by many that there is nothing so profitable as the raising of hogs in Texas. It can be done upon a small or large scale with equal success. In this business it is necessary to raise a field of corn for the purpose of feeding your hogs sufficiently to keep them haunted wherever you may want them, and for the purpose of feeding the sows when their pigs are young; although some people pretend to raise hogs in this country without ever feeding a kernal of corn or anything else. But frequently calling them by the sound of a horn or the voice to particular places, and feeding sufficiently to keep them gentle and from running away, is by far the most profitable; and unless the love of ease in the shade has overcome their inclination to work, men will always raise corn for tolling their hogs, at least as the most agreeable and easy way of managing them. As I am not in a hog-raising section of country, and as my personal acquaintance with the business here is not very extensive, I will close the subject with a few remarks. I can say, however, that I have been well acquainted with the business in other countries, and have seen enough of it here to enable me to say much more in its praise than I shall take time to do. To

5

relate the best I have heard as having been done in Texas in the way of raising hogs and making bacon, I fear might injure my cause, for I know it could hardly be credited by those who are unacquainted with the country. The constant emigration to the country, and the labor and attention that this business requires more than other stock pursuits, and the fact that other kinds of meat are so easily raised or obtained, occasions the neglect of this branch and renders pork in great demand and at extremely high prices. Although there might be the greatest abundance produced in the country, at fine paying rates to the producer, yet there is a vast amount of bacon, pork, and hams imported into the state. Owing to its convenience, palatableness, etc., this kind of meat is generally preferred by the mass of people, laboring men particularly, to any other kind of cured or salt meat; all of which insures a good home market for the produce of those who may see fit to engage in this business and make such meat as is fit to eat. And I believe that there never was better pork or bacon than is made upon Texas mast. It is no more like northern or western beech-mast meat than a hard head-stone is like a soft brick. The mast-fat pork of this country, when boiled, does not half shrink away, nor, when fried, does three fourths of it go to oil. It is more solid and firm, like northern corn or mush-fed meat, and is very sweet.

New and extensive markets will continually open for the producer of hog meat in Texas. When the great (is to be) railroad shall have penetrated into central and western Texas from New Orleans, then that great city of the south may look this way for her supply of fresh pork and mutton, as she now does for her beef and veal. Working men can go into good hog-raising sections of western Texas and make a glorious beginning with but little capital. How often have I thought, when traveling over different portions of this country, that many farmers of the northern states and the cold Canadas, and many other countries, would be overjoyed to know what they could do here at this business. If men of small capital or limited means would interest the right kind of laboring men with them and come to western Texas and engage in this branch of the stock business, they could make everything around them smile. In the first place, the land that would be required to make a respectable beginning at the business, would cost but a trifle, and could be bought upon easy terms. A stock of hogs could soon be raised from a few breeding sows, which would cost but little. I know of fine stocks of hogs, numbering several hundred, that were raised in a short time, originating entirely from a few head of pigs, that cost nothing but the trouble of taking them wild from the timbers and taming them. Dwellings and improvements, that would answer the purpose for a beginning, could be made of timber handy by, with a little labor, and without the outlay of money; and soon the settler could blow his horn, when hundreds of the swiny tribe would come at his call, and in seasons of plentiful mast, fine droves of fat hogs could be turned off to advantage, or perhaps salted smoked and packed away to better advantage. I know of a gentleman who sold out of his smoke-house, a year or two ago, fifteen hundred dollars worth of bacon, all of which was grown and fattened upon the mast near to his premises. Others I know of here in western Texas, who carry on the business much more extensively than this gentleman,—I might say five times, perhaps, and not be far out of the way. Should a person be determined to go into the business upon an extensive scale, and raise corn for the fattening of his hogs, he can do so with the most complete success. Early planting generally insures a good crop of corn in Texas.

In the selection of a location for the hog business exclusively, a person should of course be somewhat more particular than when looking for a range for cattle or horses. This country seems, by nature, to vary in sections, each being adapted to a particular kind of stock; although any or all kinds of stock will do exceedingly well in many sections of western Texas. The reason why men of capital should interest or bring laboring men with them to carry on the hog business, is that labor of the kind required is hard to get in Texas. This is unlike other stock-raising in this respect, as it is in almost all others. Mexicans and white men, who are ready and willing, can be hired to work with horses and cattle, and Mexicans can be had at a low rate for the purpose of herding and working with sheep, another kind of stock the raising of which in western Texas is considered by many the most profitable and agreeable of anything that can be done in the way of stock business.

SHEEP RAISING AND WOOL GROWING.

I might as well say at the beginning of this subject that, although Mexicans are good herders of sheep, and work at low rates, northern men, Scotchmen, and Europeans generally, who understand the management of sheep, can do well here as managers, herders, and laborers with this kind of stock.

The rapidity with which the sheep business is going ahead in this country is sure to make a great demand for labor of the kind required at the business, and northern men and Europeans as herders and laborers with sheep would be preferred to the Mexicans, whose ways are too wild to suit those who are to be the great wool growing community of Texas. Another advantage that the northern man would have over the Mexican is, that his language is the same as that of the generality of wool growers who are to occupy the country. Germans are to be wool growers to a great extent in Texas, which will give an extraordinary demand for laborers at this business of the German tongue. Americans and all countrymen are glad to employ Germans as herders of sheep or for anything else.

The growing of wool is to many a most interesting business, and one with which the writer is well acquainted. I have a knowledge of the wool growing business of the northern, eastern, and western states of the Union, and of different parts of the world, and my opinion is that nowhere can this business be made more profitable and pleasant than in western Texas. Years ago there seemed to have been a want of acquaintance with the business as adapted to the country, which, by degrees, has been and is now being rapidly acquired; and there are already many instances of success in western Texas that can hardly be equaled in any other country. I will here introduce extracts from a publication in the Texas Almanac, written by a gentleman who has had a good deal of experience in the sheep business in this country. He says:

"In preparing a second article upon sheep-raising, in this portion of Texas, I find that I have but little to add to the experience I gave you last year; my success has continued most flattering since September, 1857. The winter of '57–8, although very wet, was passed without any loss worth mentioning; two ews only died, and both from extreme old age rather than from any disease. At any time during the months of December, January, February, and March, nine out of ten of my wethers, although running without shelter and with no other food than what they could pick or crop upon the hill sides and in the prairie valleys, were in better condition for the butcher than stall-fed animals ordinarily are at the north, and since spring set in the greater number have been too fat for the shambles. 'Try and find one poor enough to kill,' has been the common request for three months past, whenever I have wanted mutton for my table.

"As an evidence of my success for the two past years, or since the first of May, 1856, I will give a short statement of the increase in the number of my sheep, and in the amount of wool sheared. I doubt whether a greater degree of good fortune ever attended the efforts of any one engaged in the business. In May, 1856, I had some eighteen hundred and fifty sheep and lambs, all told. Had I not sold or killed any bucks or wethers, I should have been able to count over four thousand at the end of May of the present year (1858). From this it will be seen that I have more than doubled the number of my sheep in two years. Meanwhile, the increase in the amount of wool has more than trebled, as the following will show:

In 1856, I sheared - - - - - - 2,800 lbs.
In 1857, I sheared - - - - - 5,100 lbs.
In 1858, I sheared - - - - - 9,000 lbs.

And this, after selling and killing nearly four hundred wethers, and without purchasing a single animal. When it is taken into consideration that the quality of my wool has been materially improved by breeding from no other than pure Merino bucks from the best flocks of France and Vermont, it may safely be set down that, while the quantity of wool has more than trebled in two years, its value has fully quadrubled. Am I not right in saying that so great a degree of success has never attended the efforts of any one engaged in the same business?

"I can not reasonably hope for a continuance of such unparalleled good luck or fortune; yet I can see no reason why so great a degree of mortality should visit my flocks in future as ordinarily prevails among sheep in Ohio, Pennsylvania, or Vermont, at all times. Here in the mountains of Comal and Blanco counties, I believe it to be impossible for two great scourges of flocks, almost the world over, to be generated and spread. I have reference to the foot rot and the scab. Nor do I believe that that worst of all epidemics among sheep—the liver rot—can ever cause much loss to our flocks in this high and dry region. Not a case have I seen in two years, nor can I point to any causes in the mountains to give it a foothold. We might as well look for a visitation of the yellow fever in a region where even the lightest bilious attacks are almost unknown, and where physicians are compelled to resort to other callings than their regular profession to gain a livelihood; and if we are to go on and escape the diseases I have enumerated, we have undoubtedly the best region for sheep in the wide world. In proof, I would state that good grazing lands can still be purchased at from one to two dollars per acre, and that the cost of watching, salting, and caring for a flock of a thousand head, does not exceed two hundred and twenty-five dollars, or twenty-five cents for each sheep per annum. How can the northern and western wool growers compete with us on lands which they value at from twenty to sixty dollars per acre, and where it costs eight or ten times as much to feed a single animal a year? As well might they attempt to raise sugar and cotton with the hope of gaining the profits made in Louisiana and Mississippi, as to raise wool as cheaply as we can produce it in Texas.

"Attracted by the heavy profits made in this region during the two last years (for it may safely be set down that those engaged in the sheep business have cleared from sixty to eighty per cent. per annum on their investments), quite a number of gentlemen have started off this spring and summer in search of flocks, and others will doubtless soon leave. Some have gone to Arkansas and Missouri, others to Mexico. I am confident that those regions will be completely swept of all the surplus sheep they have to spare, and at prices at least twenty-five per cent. higher than ever paid before."

Thus writes an intelligent wool-grower of western Texas, a Vermonter, I believe, by birth. Although this gentleman does not publicly ask people of any section or part of the world to come to this country and engage in the sheep business, he does, if I am rightly informed, privately advise and even persuade his particular friends, wherever they may be, to come here and embark in it as the very best thing that they can do, or as the most safe, profitable, and interesting pursuit in the world. It is an old and favorite idea with him that he had rather witness his innocent, playful lambs dance, caper, and run about, than to witness the most beautiful theatrical or dramatic display. He has a taste for this business, he loves it, and he makes money at it. He has seen much of the world, but admires the country in which he lives, and not only appreciates it as it is, but sees its coming greatness.

And why should he not advise his friends to participate with him in the profits of a most interesting pursuit? Why should not his heart swell with emulation when he thinks of his cold, frosty, native region, in comparison with the mild and most inviting one of his adoption? It is but a short time since I met a young gentleman in Texas, on his way up the country with a flock of sheep. He told me that Mr. K. was the cause of his coming to Texas with those sheep; that he, K., was a friend of his, and that he knew he would not advise or persuade him into anything out of the way. It would be a fortunate thing for thousands of cold countrymen if they were the friends and acquaintances of this gentleman, Mr. K., whose remarks I have taken from the Texas Almanac.

But in the absence of such friend or adviser, may not the writer's remarks be of some service? He has himself had in charge six or seven thousand sheep in this country, though under most unfavorable circumstances. He was raised at the stock and farming business, far north of this, and has an extensive practical knowledge of not only sheep and wool-growing in the north, but all kinds of live stock, and having been nearly seven years in constant contact with Texas stock-growers, managing sheep, buying, driving, and shipping beef and veal-cattle, branding and working with stock-cattle and horses, and, to a certain extent, with hogs, he ought to be well acquainted with and able to give a pretty good account of her stock-raising and farming business and capacities.

To continue the subject of sheep and wool-growing in this fine country, I will introduce the operations of an acquaintance, living not far from my place of writing. Some years ago I spent a week with him at his sheep-range. About the year 1840, he commenced with twelve head of Mexican ewes and a buck of common stock. In the year 1854, the increase of these few animals numbered nearly thirteen hundred head of beautiful sheep. That year the storm that blew down Matagorda, a town not far from where these sheep were raised, and proved so destructive to our coast, by the merest accident killed about seven hundred of this flock. This accident was their getting on an elevation that was afterward surrounded by

water, and, when swimming off, the larger half of
them stuck in a quantity of flood-wood and drowned;
but the increase of the four or five hundred that sur-
vived the storm have since brought the number of the
flock up to somewhere near sixteen hundred head.
This flock has been gradually improved, and now
yields a good quality and fair quantity of wool, and
produces the finest of mutton. The owner of these
sheep is an old sailor by profession, who was born
and raised in the state of Maine, and I was going to
say he would not give his flock of two thousand sheep,
together with his five thousand head of horned cattle,
lands, and place of residence, for his entire native
state, and be compelled to go back there and live out
the balance of his days, but I fear this would be too
extravagant an assertion to make without first con-
sulting the old sailor upon the subject. Had not this
flock met with the accident of 1854, it would now,
probably, number four thousand and more. This flock
of sheep was not raised upon such lands as are generally esteemed good for the business, nor in what is
considered a fair sheep-raising section of Texas, and
the old sailor has told me that for weeks together his
sheep were left entirely to themselves, and always
without a herder. They were raised, however, upon
a peculiar spot, otherwise they must have been herded.
This spot, the reader, if he pleases, can take almost
any map of the United States and directly see. It is
on the Gulf of Mexico, a narrow neck of land or peninsula, extending from opposite the town of Matagorda
down to Pascavallo, the entrance to Matagorda bay.
The grass of this range was eaten down years ago by
cattle, which made it better for sheep, and it being
narrow and nearly surrounded by water (consequently
having no wolves upon it), the sheep were suffered to
go for weeks together unlooked for, and the only herd-

ing they got was at occasional times, when some one or more would go up the peninsula and bring them down for the purpose of working with them or to keep them from getting too far away from home. This neck of land is now fenced across, *I believe;* and it is my impression that there is no live stock property in these United States or anywhere else, all things considered, that is paying a better interest than is this flock of sheep, numbering, as I said, nearly sixteen hundred head, and fenced into a pasture where they require no feeding, herding, or sheltering from one year's end to another. I don't know but the thirteen head of sheep that commenced this flock would have reached its present number, or the number it would have been without the accident, in some other countries with due attention, but to have been turned out to shift for themselves, winter and summer, as were these few head, it is doubtful whether they would have done as well anywhere else on the face of the earth. The old sailor told me that his sheep would have done much better had he been more particular about having his lambs come at the right season of the year. He says he has known many of his lambs to die from being dropped in the chilly, rainy weather of winter. The best protection that his sheep ever has is the banks of the beach, which, in places, are high enough to break the wind to some extent.

Now in conclusion about this flock of sheep. If such work as this can be done in western Texas, upon lands which, for the sheep business, nobody pretends are to be compared with the undulating, hilly, and mountainous portions of its interior, is there not good reason to believe that this country is to be second to none in the world for the raising of mutton and growing of wool? and does it not deserve the attention of those who are looking for new countries most suitable for this business, with the intention of engaging in it? It seems to me that it does.

I might go on and enumerate many instances of good success at the sheep business in western Texas, but since everybody is finding out its adaptation to the growing of wool, through the papers and different channels, 1 will not occupy time and space in this way.

A large portion and different sections of western Texas seem to be better adapted to raising sheep than to anything else. Much of this country is high, rolling, and dry, and to all appearances could not be bettered for the purpose in question. Experience is every day proving this part of the world to be everything that it seems to be for the sheep and wool-growing business; and there are thousands of men in the southern, northern, and western states, the Canadas, and the eastern world, who would do well to come to western Texas and engage in this business.

There has been a good deal said of late in regard to the depression of the wool markets throughout the world. This, no doubt, should be a caution to those who are inclined to embark in the wool-growing business in some countries, but not to those who would commence it in western Texas. The truth is, with the right kind of sheep, wool can be produced in these parts for twelve cents per pound, and good muttons for a half dollar per head, and money in the business at that. But does any one suppose that good French merino wool is coming down anywhere near this figure, or even as low as twenty-five cents per pound, to remain any length of time? And who doubts that good lambs and wethers will bring from one to three dollars per head, for years to come, in Texas? At this time wethers or good muttons are sold for ready cash here at three to five dollars per head.

There is this to be considered by those who would

make wool-growing their business. The sheep is a double producer in a compound sense of the word. 1st. In many flocks of this country a large number of the ewes have twin lambs, and many of them have two crops of lambs a year, (but experience has proven that it would be better for them to have but three crops of lambs in two years, or, in other words, it would be better to have the ewe recover somewhat from the effects of suckling before dropping another lamb). 2d. The flesh of the sheep being good to eat, if there should not be a demand for its fleece, there might be for its carcass or the surplus of carcasses. that the wool-grower might have on hand for sale. This being the case, by marketing his mutton he might be able to hold on to his wool for a better price, should he think proper, or, *vice versa*, sell his wool and hold on to his mutton. This, in a manner, gives the wool-grower two chances to one against the grower of other kinds of stock. But it is not every man's fortune to have a taste for the sheep business, or the patience to attend to sheep properly or in a way to make them very profitable. The hardier kinds of stock are much better for some men to raise, although there is not so much roughness and hardship attending the raising of sheep, and as an evidence of which I will here relate a circumstance. Having been in Australia, and when traveling in the interior of that beautiful island, upon which there are many millions of sheep, I frequently met with large flocks, and would often make inquiries of the shepherds pertaining to the business in that country. I, one day, when on a prospecting excursion for gold with a company of young men, accidentally came upon a flock of about three thousand sheep, with only a little girl and two shepherd dogs to look after them. After inquiring of the shy little girl, of twelve or thirteen

years, who seemed to be almost afraid to talk to a
stranger, where I could get some water, I went where
she directed me, and there found a little but and the
mother of the little shepherdess, a Scotch woman of
middle age, whom the cares of life seemed to have but
little worn. This woman told me that she had the
entire charge of this flock for weeks together, with
only the assistance of her little daughter and her true
shepherd-dogs. In the season of shearing, trimming
of lambs, etc., they were, to a certain extent, relieved
of their charge, but, generally speaking, the whole care
of the flock devolved upon the mother and daughter
the rest of the year; and during the day either one or
the other was always with the sheep, unless, at times
when they were brought within sight of home and
left with the dogs. At night the flock was inclosed
in a yard adjoining the little house of the shepherdess,
in which there were many cracks and openings, but
through which blustering snow never came to interfere with its comforts. I was curious to know why
the care of this large flock of sheep was left to a
woman, the like of which was unusual in the country,
and asked many questions. I learned that it was the
discovery of gold upon the island to which she owed her
situation, this discovery having created a rush to the
mines of nearly all the men in the country; the flock
she was watching having been left in a small inclosure
by its former shepherd where it was likely to starve, the
owners, who were merchants in Melbourne, being unable just then to get any one else, she volunteered her
services for a round price. "But," said she, the tears
trickling down her cheeks, "I had a little boy to help
me then, or I could never have thought of such a
thing. More than a year since it pleased God to take
him from us, and I had no one to help me then but
my little daughter, whom you saw with the sheep.

Surely," she said, "when my little Johnny left us I thought I should die with grief; but being cheered-up by those who were sent, for a while, to my relief and assistance, I continued on, as best I could, until another rush to the mines left me again with only my little daughter. We now manage the flock, most of the time, by ourselves, and, with the help of these faithful dogs, get along very well." Thanking her for her kindness, and wishing her all possible good luck, I bade her good day, and went on my way, thinking of the trials and strange fortunes of poor mankind, and of the courage and fortitude of this woman. What other kind of stock could she have got along with as she did with these sheep? Of course not any, which is pretty good evidence that wool-growing in these mild climates is not attended with the roughness and hardiness that is required at the raising of cattle and horses, or even sheep, in colder countries.

Now if a woman, with her little girl and shepherd-dogs, could do so much with a flock of three thousand sheep in Australia, what could not a man, having one or more little boys, do at this business in western Texas? or a couple of young men, for instance, who were determined to make a fortune at the business? It is the writer's intention to buy a flock of sheep, before long, and commence the growing of wool in western Texas. I shall go to some hilly or mountain range, and erect a comfortable shanty or two for the accommodation of my family, and then, with the assistance of my little boy, now in his ninth year, I will manage my flock, which I hope may number five hundred to begin with, but if it is not more than fifty, or even as few as twenty-five, I am determined to make a beginning, and the growing of wool in western Texas shall be my business in the future, unless

Providence otherwise decrees. Should I start off to-
morrow, as I am situated, I would not think of buying
a foot of land, unless I might meet with a chance of
buying a small tract, which should suit me for a home
and a sheep-range, and which I should buy (if at all)
mostly on time, and upon most favorable terms. If I
had plenty of money, my first lookout should be land,
a large tract of which I would secure as soon as I could
find one that should suit me. But as my means are
very limited, I should take up at some suitable place
for the raising of sheep, where I might feel myself
justifiable in stopping for a while, and where, with
the permission of the owner of the section, league, or
grant upon which I might be, I would bring my flock
and carry on my sheep business until I should be able
to negotiate for lands of my own. Would not such a
course as this be better for the beginner.of small means,
than for him to get a tract of land in a stock-raising
country without having any stock to bring on to it or
money left to purchase a beginning of some kind of
stock?

The time is coming when the beginner at the stock
business in western Texas will have to purchase his
lands at the start. Then, of course, his money will
not go as far as it now will. It will then be harder
for the man of quite limited means to get into the wool-
growing business in this delightful country. But it
will be a long time before this fine sheep region is so occupied that settlers will be obliged to buy much land
in order to carry on the business—perhaps fifty years.

Judging by the past, I should say that those who
engage in the wool-growing business in western Texas,
and have a taste for it, after learning a few important
facts in regard to the management of sheep, will, in
nine cases out of ten, succeed most admirably—such
facts, for instance, as these: that sheep should not be

let or driven out early in the morning before the dew
is off, particularly into tall grass—short grass is best
for sheep; they should not be suffered to run upon
fresh prairie burns in the winter season, etc., etc., all
of which facts can be readily learned from men of experience already in the country at the business. It
has been the opinion of some, that in consequence of
the great demand for sheep by those who have and
are now getting into the business here, there must soon
be a scarcity of sheep for sale everywhere in these
parts. But thus far this opinion has proved incorrect.
There has been for sale a plenty of sheep at the old
town of Goliad, all along this season, and it is believed by some that there will continue to be a plenty
of Mexican sheep offered at this place for years to
come. This is a point where Mexican stock of different kinds is brought by Mexicans and others, and as
long as there is a demand for sheep, speculators will
continue to bring them on. In fact I may safely say
to any one who wishes to come to western Texas and
engage in the business, he may come with a certainty
of getting sheep somewhere here, should he prefer not
to bring them with him. There are those here who
have and others who will commence the sheep business and soon abandon it, for the want of experience
and a taste for the pursuit. There will be some flocks
offered by such men. I know of men here who have
the wool haggled off their sheep, and thrown in the
dirt together like pulled wool. They can hardly distinguish coarse from the fine quality. Most of such
men will give up the business to those who are better
qualified to carry it on. A great many who have recently come on from Vermont, New York, Ohio, and
other states, have brought small flocks of good sheep
with them by railroad and water. This makes a
pretty costly beginning, but if it can be afforded, it

6

is no doubt the best thing that a person, coming on
to engage in the business, can do, that is, if he has
been acquainted with sheep-raising.

The importation of sheep and hogs into western
Texas is safer than the importation of horses and cattle. It is the impression of the writer and others that
the demand for sheep here will cause speculators
to bring them in across the country from Illinois,
Indiana, Ohio, Kentucky, and Tennessee. They are
already being brought from Missouri and Arkansas;
and that they will be brought from both old and new
Mexico and offered for sale in different parts of western Texas, is a certainty. Let me assure those who
would like to know it, that there are a plenty of wide-
awake fellows who know that this is bound to be a
wool-growing country, and that sheep are in great
demand here, and not a few of them will try to make
a little money by supplying this demand from wherever the sheep can be got. I should say to those who
are coming, come on with or without your sheep; you
can not well go amiss. It might be well for many of
you to bring a few bucks to improve the flocks you
may buy. I would say to Illinois, Ohio, and the
western states, you might as well surrender the sheep
and wool-growing business, and bring your stock
down here: we will give a good price for it. As for old
New England, Vermont, and those countries where
the grass grows out of the rocks, trudge along in your
own way at anything you please, only send us a few
more of your sheep, and some of those fellows who
know so well how to manage them. This, remember,
is the Australia of America, where we don't have
to cut and cure a hundred tuns of hay to winter
a thousand sheep,—no not a pound. This is the
place to live,—where now the Indian is no longer
dangerous to the white man; where now an unsteady

government and the roughness of society is no longer
an objection to the country; where things have changed
and have become not only endurable but pleasant and
attractive; where, from various causes, the importance
of the country has but recently been fully understood;
and where now thousands of respectable and intelligent people, from all parts, are coming to make their
fortunes and settle down for life.

IMPORTATION AND IMPROVEMENT OF STOCK.

The furnishing of improved and good blooded animals to the stock-growers of Texas, with which to improve their stock of different kinds, is to be an extensive business, in which many can and will eventually
operate; and I believe the men who are best calculated for this work are generally living in the north.
I do not allude to any particular section. The boys
of Kentucky could, no doubt, do a glorious share in
the improvement of the stock of Texas, particularly
her cattle and mules, and they are already here at it;
but as yet they have barely made an impression. The
great work is hardly begun.

I am not the fool to suppose that all I have to say
must be listened to or followed as infallibly correct: I
am aiming at the truth, and what better can any one
do? I have a favorite idea, that I will here suggest,
in regard to raising fine bulls in Texas. For several
years I have been engaged in the purchase and driving
of beef and veal-cattle for a shipper in western Texas.
I long since discovered that there are now and then
improved cows, scattered over our prairies, among the
common stock of the country, and sometimes there are
stocks of cattle that have quite a number of such animals among them. Their owners, as a general thing,
do not esteem them very highly, as they know not
their blood and value, and often do not distinguish

. them from their other cattle. Some of these cows are half breeds, from Durham sires and Texas dams, some quarter breeds, and others more or less mixed with improved blood. I have often thought that if one had a suitable pasture, which might be of the cheapest lands in Texas, and was able, he could purchase these cows when and where he might meet with them, and bring them into his pasture, and then place with them a thorough-bred animal, from which he could raise a very good quality of bulls, that would answer remarkably well to turn loose upon our prairies, and commence the general improvement of the common cattle of the country. The increase of females he could continue to improve, and finally bring his stock to a state of perfection. Meanwhile, he could be offering bulls of a better and better grade, until he would finally be able to offer No. 1 improved or thorough bred animals, that would answer to turn upon our prairies without fear of loss from exposure. As his cows, lands, and everything, but his thorough bred animal, would cost him but a moderate amount, it is plain to see he would be enabled to sell young bulls for much less than it would cost to import them, and still afford a profit. And although these animals would not, at first, be as good as full bloods, yet they would be what the stock-grower would not be afraid to buy, and much better for him to commence with than imported animals that might die from neglect, or which he might not feel inclined to attend to in a way to make it profitable. The partially-improved cows, of which I speak as being scattered over the country, are generally from animals that have now and then been brought here and turned loose, and have died from neglect or some other cause. Sometimes they are issues from some one's animal who is attempting to improve his stock. By selecting the choicest of unimproved Texas cows, even, and using them in the way above described, a person could make money at the business, and the stock-grower had better have half breeds, that are raised in the country, with which to commence the improvement of his stock, than to have many of the humbugs that are imported.

Not far from my place of writing there is a pasture of several leagues, recently inclosed, now containing between three and four thousand head of animals. The owner of this property, several years since, purchased a Durham bull, which he has kept most of the time in a pasture adjoining his door-yard; during the season he has run with the gentleman's milch cows, which are of the commonest Texas stock. This gentleman has several crops of half breeds from this animal, and is now raising three quarter breeds, and next year, I understand, will have enough animals, that are more or less improved, to serve all the stock in his large inclosure. If this gentleman can improve from the commonest cows of the country, how much better could a person do with the choicest of Texas cows, or the partially-improved ones to which I have alluded? The gentleman who has this large pasture is an exception in the business. I know of no other person in this part of the country who has made so extensive a pasture.

I have mentioned this case only to show that by bringing on a fine bull, jack, stallion, etc., a person can raise fine stock here in the country for sale, all things considered, to as good and possibly better advantage than he can import such stock for sale. I may be mistaken in this, for I am well aware that there are several gentlemen in the country who are making fortunes by bringing on improved stock from the north and elsewhere, which they dispose of at good prices.

I said that the gentleman having the large pasture purchased a fine bull several years since. He has since purchased several fine bulls of the enterprising Kentucky boys who are here, and is now in advance of any one in this part of the country in the way of improving his cattle. I presume that not one in a hundred of the stock-growers of western Texas have made a beginning at the improvement of their cattle as yet.

There are millions of useful animals in Texas that are not half as good as they should be, and the man who will come here with good improved stock and settle in the right kind of place, can raise from it and sell to good advantage all he can part with. I am acquainted with a young man, the brother of a noted and wealthy wool-grower in Vermont, who came to western Texas several years ago, bringing with hi 1 a fine flock of Spanish merino sheep, all the way from Vermont, and selling them out directly, returned to the same state and brought on not only a fine flock of the same kind of sheep, both ewes and bucks, but male and female calves, and a fine breed of pigs, from all of which he has since been raising and selling at most profitable rates. This gentleman finds it impossible to supply the demand for his improved animals from the increase of his stock, and consequently continues to bring them on from the north for sale and to keep up the excellency of his stock. He has exchanged more or less of his fine stock for mares, and is now raising mules in connection with his importing and fine stock business. Last winter he brought on from Vermont and other states his fourth flock of sheep; this making him an extensive importer of fine stock into the state of Texas from the northern states every year, but one, since his first arrival here with a flock of sheep. His last flock was partially made up of Ohio sheep; and he also brought on, from some-where in the north, a lot of fine stock for another gen-tleman. And right here, to shew the reader how the importer of improved stock into Texas may subject himself to the danger of shoals,—of which I have spoken,—I will tell him something of the management of the gentleman for whom this stock was brought on. The stock consisted of some three hundred heavy wooled sheep, ewes principally, and some ten or twelve young Durham bulls and heifers,—(they were calves, yearlings and two years old.) After the first-mentioned gentleman had landed this stock at Powder House, in Texas, from off the ship across the gulf, it was given over to a couple of young men who were sent to take charge of it and drive it up the country. These young men, or boys, knew nothing about nor-thern stock, and could not have known much about stock of any kind, for they started out over the prairie and so managed as to be caught out in the night, miles from any dwelling, on the open prairie, and, instead of watching their sheep, they laid down and went to sleep. The flock wandered away from their camp or wagon, and the wolves got after it and killed some twenty head of the sheep, which cost, delivered here, the snug little sum of nearly twenty dollars per head. They gathered up the balance of their scat-tered flock next day, and went on, now driving too fast, and then too slow, or sometimes laying up when they had no business to be, starving their stock around some house where the grass was all eaten out, (it being the dead of winter), and so managing that by the time they had driven four or five days, or before they reached their destination, nearly all their fine Durham stock died, from the effects of the voyage and the abuse of these young men, who were sent to drive them to their new home. Had there been some one sent for this stock who had considered that the voyage had injured it more or less, and that it should be driven and managed carefully, it no doubt would have reached its destination, and have done well. He paid double its value in the north, and the young men, or boys, should never have been sent for it, which proves a want of experience and attention as much as it does danger in the business. The gentleman who brought them on and delivered them to these youngsters, went on foot with his own flock, and arrived safely at home, in the interior, without loss or trouble; and he told me, when meeting him on the road with this very flock, that he could not wish for better success than he was having, or a better business than he was doing. I now hear that this fall he will go on to Vermont or Ohio and bring to Texas his fifth flock of improved sheep and other stock.

This gentleman's ranche is situated on a beautiful clear stream of water, where almost all the country in his vicinity is covered with scattering trees, the shade of which is just the thing for his imported and improved stock. The grass of his lands and range is the better quality of sedge, which is short and fine, and grows around the trees and upon the little open prairies, which are skirted with the scattering trees of these timbered prairies. The timber upon his land, in places, is sufficiently thick to enable him to take out enough to fence it up into fields and pastures, and leave enough standing for the purpose of shade, firewood, and other conveniences. Stock importers require more or less inclosures and pastures for their fine stock. This gentleman told me long ago that he had sold a large number of animals, getting for his bucks from twenty-five to a hundred dollars. Numbers of such men as this could come here and settle over the country, at different points, bringing with them their fine stock, the increase of which, together with prudent importation, would make them rich. They could sell to the stock-growers around them, often taking horses, mares, cattle, half breeds, or Mexican sheep, in exchange for their animals, and become Texas stock-growers, as well as improvers and importers. Men coming here for this purpose should not be particular about bringing the most expensive stock at first, unless they might be the owners of such. But they should bring well-bred if not thorough-bred stock. Bring no humbugs, as this would result badly for those who might bring and palm them off. There came to western Texas, a year or two since, some men from Missouri with a large drove of jacks. The jacks were all haltered, shod, corn-fed, and fat,—*valuable jacks of course.* They exchanged them for horses, mares, and mules, and the stock-growers of the country who purchased them thought they were getting great bargains by giving ten or a dozen mules and horses for one of these corn-fed jacks, with shoes and halter-muzzles on. But after the Missourians had got away with their horses and mules, some one whispered that these jacks were nothing but half breeds, or perhaps, El Paso Mexican jacks, which had been driven around into Missouri, when young, and after being pushed through on corn and fixed up for sale, were brought to western Texas to gull the stock-growers with, which did not flatter the purchasers so much, although they proved valuable jacks to them, they not having as good or better ones, and some of them none at all. They were probably half breed jacks, raised in Missouri from Mexican jennets and ordinary American jacks or something of the kind. Of course after selling these animals for Kentucky or American jacks, they could not, after practicing such an imposition, come into the same section of country and do well

7

with another lot of jacks, although there are many
men here who are glad to get half breed jacks, but
they do not like to pay for full bloods and get but
half breeds.

There are men in the country who have brought
numbers of improved Durham bulls here (*of course
they were Durham*) and sold them for from seventy-
five to a hundred dollars each at a year old. Many
a dozen calves have I killed or "deaconed" at three
or five days old, when the milk of the cow became
good, which would have made much better animals
than some I have seen that were brought here and
sold, at one or two years old, for a hundred dollars
cash. Persons bringing stallions, jacks, or bulls here,
should bring them when young, if possible. It does
not make so much difference about the age of sheep,
and not so much with the horse kind as with cattle.
I believe that from a year to two years old is a better
age than older for horned stock to bring to Texas, although they are brought here of all ages, and when
properly attended to, do very well. Swine, as a matter of course, should be brought when quite young.
The trouble and expense of bringing a half dozen little pigs, carefully boxed up, would not be equal to
that of bringing one grown hog, and nothing like as
disagreeable. Too much attention can not be given
to animals when on their way here. It matters not
what kind of stock it may be, it should have the very
best of attention on the way, whether brought by land
or water, and when arriving here from across the gulf,
it should be taken at once to a suitable place for keeping it—that is, it should be taken (hogs, perhaps, excepted,) far enough back from the coast to find for it
high, rolling, and dry lands, good clear water, and a
plenty of shade, where it will be sure to find a good
quality of grass. Imported stock generally requires

more or less feeding in the dead of winter, until it becomes well acclimated, and even then there-should
always be a supply of hay or fodder laid in, in case it
may be required, unless your stock should be upon a
musquete range or a plat of Bermuda. The fall or
winter season is the best time to bring such animals
here. By being brought in the fall or winter, the
warm weather of summer comes gradually upon them,
and with care they are very sure to live and acclimate
finely.

The spoiling of the cow's bag, from having more
milk than the calf can take, is made an objection to
improving the prairie cattle of Texas. But that objection amounts to nothing, if the importer has got the
beef Durham breed, which are not noted for superior
milking qualities; and whether they are or not, I know
they will answer first rate for this country. I have
traveled many hundred miles in the interior of Australia, and never in that country saw anything of the
kind but improved cattle; and I believe all the cattle
there are of improved English breeds, and many years
ago there were ten million head upon that great island.
Never did I hear any complaint of the spoiling of cows'
bags in that country in consequence of their giving
more milk than the calf required, and of course the
calf is raised there as in Texas—or, rather, generally
speaking, nothing but the calf takes any of the milk
from the mother. I know of several extensive stock-
growers here (and one is our ex-lieutenant governor)
who are improving from the Durham, and they make
no complaint of this kind; and if this is an objection,
the introduction of male animals and a gradual improvement, from the first to the second remove, and
so on, would obviate this difficulty. Let no one give
this objection to the general improvement of Texas
cattle the least weight, if he has the beef Durham breed

to bring here.   Everybody knows that the cow of this
breed is more inclined to fat than milk.

There are thousands of people in Texas who would
be glad to get animals with which to improve their
milch cows, or from which to raise good ones.   There
are different kinds that would pay well to bring here.
The milch Durham or the red milchers from Kentucky would do very well.   There are, no doubt, other
kinds, with which the writer is unacquainted, and
some that he knows of that he can not designate as of
any particular kind, that would be first rate to bring
here.   Let those who bring stock of this or any other
kind to Texas, to dispose of as good or thorough-bred,
bring with them vouchers from respectable men of
standing in their communities that their animals are
what they represent them to be and not humbugs.
They can then advertise their stock in the journals
of the country, and offer it at public sale or otherwise.
They can then, with propriety, point out to the stock-
growers of the country the many advantages that
would result from a general improvement of their animals, and induce them to engage in the work.   After
having established a reputation in the business, the
importer's word would be a sufficient voucher for the
good blood and excellency of his animals.   I believe
that nothing could be done, with the same trouble and
expense, that would add more to the wealth and prosperity of Texas than to turn loose, upon her prairies,
among her cattle throughout the state, ten or twenty
thousand beef Durham, or good improved bulls, that
is, if these animals were raised in the country, so that
they might not die from exposure.   But to raise them
in the country, of course there must first be extensive
importations and improvements.

It will be a glorious day for Texas when her stock
of different kinds is well improved, particularly when

her cattle and sheep are like the millions of these animals upon the island of Australia,—when she is not
outdone in the quality of her millions of useful animals. What is more beautiful for the husbandman
to look upon than a large drove of entirely thorough-
bred beef-cattle, or a yoke of the right kind of oxen;
a lot of excellent milch cows; a flock of superior mutton, or a flock of fine wool sheep, heavily coated down
to their toes and up to their eyes in wool; a drove of
mules, fifteen hands high and well put up; or beautiful and serviceable horses, and solid, heavy, and
profitable hogs? The day will come when the prairies, hills, and valleys of Texas, will be covered with
such animals, and then the LONE STAR state will be
the admired of all the great American constellations;
then it is that the United States can boast of an Australia that is not across the wide deep, but near at
hand, joined to her by the ties of sisterhood, in ready
communication both by land and water, and all the
relations that can make a great and free people a unit
in feeling and interest.

In conclusion, let no man think of coming to Texas
with valuable animals, unless he has a taste for the
business—unless he delights in the raising and taking
care of such animals. For no other kind of a man
can make money at the business; and such men, I
know, can do as well as any one would wish to do at
anything of the kind. Some men have no more business with this kind of work than has the "huge paw"
of the honest laboring man with Blackstone. It is a
business that requires constant attention, and no man
but one who loves to feed and nurse his animals,
whose knowledge of them is sufficient to enable him
to understand their natures and instincts, whose sensi-
bility is such that he can not bear to see them suffer,
who loves to linger around them and consider their

beauty and usefulness, watch their improvement or
decline, and readily render any attention they may
need, is fit to bring fine stock to Texas with the idea
of raising from it as a business, or making money
with it. Let those fellows who can lie down and
sleep by their fine stock, if need be, and watch over
and take care of them on their long journey, and when
here give the very best attention—I say let such men,
or those who are able to hire such men, bring fine
stock to Texas, and they are sure to make money with
it, and no other kind of men can make money by importing improved animals into Texas, either to sell or
raise from.

I have written this last and made many remarks
that may appear as discouraging to the importation
of northern or foreign animals into Texas, only from
fear that my remarks in favor of the business might
induce those to pitch into the thing who have no business with the like. Some one who, perhaps, without
this precaution, would start out for Texas with a lot
of valuable animals, whose knowledge of them might
be but slight, and who might trust to others equally
ignorant to take care of them, and after their dying or
doing badly for the want of attention and good management, would curse the writer of this book for getting him into such a scrape.

A year or two since I met a couple of Irishmen who
were driving a fine Durham bull. They had landed
in Texas just the day before. It was a warm day,
and the bull had his tongue out, and although the
men were on foot, they were driving the heavy fellow
too fast. I asked them whose animal he was, and
where they were taking him? which they told me,
and added that he was brought from Kentucky. I
then told them that they were not in the north where
that bull was raised, and unless they stopped pushing

him, they would never reach their destination with
him alive. I alarmed them considerably, and they
afterward moved him quietly along. Had they continued hurrying this animal as they were doing when
I met them, he would never have been worth anything
in this country, even had they got him to his owner
in the interior.

I might mention cases of caution in regard to imported horses, jacks, and other animals, but trust I
have said and shall say enough to the wise.

Now you that bring fine stock here, consider well
what you do. With the right management and attention there is nothing that would pay a person better;
with bad management and neglect there is nothing
that would more certainly be attended with loss.
Bring for a beginning, until experience shall have
taught you, the beef Durham or beef kinds of cattle
principally; the milk kind to a certain extent; not
overgrown horses, but something like the Morgan
species of the north; the improved coarse kinds of
sheep to a certain extent, but the finer kinds principally. I believe what passes in the north for French
merinos are the best fine wools for Texas, as they are
more hardy and better protected with an oily and
heavy fleece than the Saxon or extremely fine wools,
and can stand our climate without shelter of any kind.
As for hogs, let every one be his own judge. I believe the big Berkshire is considered a first rate hog
for Texas.

There is one thing about which, I trust, by this
time the reader will agree with me, and that is that
the man of limited means, had better come here and
purchase our common stock and improve it with animals that he may bring with him or afterward get,
than to invest all his means in foreign stock and run
the risk of getting it safely here and acclimating it

successfully, that is, if his intention is to become a Texas stock-grower and not the furnisher of imported and improved animals.

I will here repeat that sheep are brought to Texas and managed with better success in the hilly regions by strangers or those who are new in the country, understanding the business elsewhere, than any other kind of imported stock, unless it is goats, a kind of stock that I have as yet said nothing of, but which, if I mistake not, is to be highly esteemed and very useful in this country.

GOATS.

To present this subject in a light that seems to me most important, I will introduce an article from the Springfield Register upon the Cashmere goat:

"Some twenty years ago Dr. Davis, of South Carolina, at that time holding a government office in Turkey, actuated by a patriotism which was creditable to himself and likely to prove beneficial to his countrymen, thought of the possibility of introducing into the United States some specimens of the Cashmere goat—the celebrated animals from whose wool is manufactured the Cashmere shawls. These animals are justly prized by the people of Thibet, who reap a heavy revenue from the sale of the wool, and who had preserved the stock zealously from exportation. Dr. Davis, with an ardor equal to that attributed to Jason, in his expedition in search of the golden fleece, obtained the consent of the Sultan, and, organizing an expedition, entered the land of Cashmere, and obtained nine goats, two males and seven females. After great vicissitudes, and with a loss of several of his party, he succeeded in bringing these animals to Constantinople, whence he shipped them to Carolina. Six years ago the pure bloods had increase in number to thirty, besides having been extensively crossed with the native goat throughout South Carolina and the adjoining states. Some enterprising agriculturists of Tennessee recently organized a company, and having purchased some of the pure stock, entered into the business of raising the wool grown from the cross-breeds. We condense from a statement furnished us of this matter the following facts:

"The wool from a third cross and a common goat is exceedingly fine, and is now manufactured in Scotland, where it is worth eight dollars per pound; each animal yielding three fleeces, averaging three pounds each, during the year. These animals have already been successfully reared as far north as New York, and the quality of the mixed breed wool has been decided to be not inferior to that used in the Cashmere shawls, so extensively imported into this country. It is desirable to encourage these efforts to improve the blood and the product of the animals. The production of this wool ought to be universally adopted; it does not require full blood, but the product of pure blood and the ordinary goat of the country, is all that is required. It has been ascertained that the wool from goats three generations removed from the pure blood, each time crossed with the common goat, is of a most superior quality. B. F. Bristow, of Jacksonville, has some pure blood bucks, which he proposes shall be taken by the farmers of Illinois to cross with the common goats, and letters addressed to him will receive prompt attention, and be responded to with full information.

"We trust that our farmers will take this matter in hand, and reap, at a very small cost, all the benefits to be derived from the product of a superior wool."

Now in regard to the growing of this Cashmere wool in western Texas, I have to say that the com-moon goat of the country is already quite plentiful here, and that both old and new Mexico, I should judge from accounts, are half covered with them. Although I have had several hundred of these animals in charge in this country, and have seen a good deal of them in different parts of the world, I do not profess to know much about them. So far as sheep are concerned, I was raised with my nose at the grind-stone. But goats I always looked upon as an animal of little value, and for some reason or other never had an inclination to learn much of them. But converting them into wool-producers of a most valuable kind, and bringing them before the world in the light that the Register and others are doing, inclines me to think that they may yet become very useful animals, and that western Texas will be second to no place in the world for the production of this *cashmere* wool, from which is made the finest of fabrics.

The same remarks in regard to the raising of sheep will generally apply pretty well to the raising of goats; although the common goat will live and do well where the sheep will not, and to do very well I believe require a somewhat bushy range. If heretofore they have, in many countries, been comparatively useless, they have been most at home upon comparatively useless lands—lands of sterility, whose only growth was weeds and bushes, or possibly half naked hills with only here and there a spear of grass, a weed, and scrubby bush, or briar. But when they become improved so as to produce wool worth eight dollars per pound, if possible, or even one dollar, would it be prudent to let them run among bushes and briars where they would tare, rub, and pull out more or less of their valuable coat, every fiber of which, at the price per pound mentioned in the Register, would be an item. It seems to me that then they would require

about the same kind of range. and treatment as do
sheep, in which case, immense portions of western
Texas would, be just the country for them. Should
they retain, after their improvement, the nature and
habit, and require the treatment of the common goat,
then they certainly would nowhere do better than in
this country; for I have, time and again, for years,
seen thrifty and most productive flocks of goats in all
parts of western Texas; and again, I have frequently
seen large numbers of goats with flocks of sheep in
Texas, said to be kept with the sheep for the purpose
of keeping the sheep healthy, and these goats seemed
to be thrifty and productive, and appeared to be doing
as well as though they were away from the sheep in a
flock by themselves. If, then, the Cashmere goat can
be successfully and profitably crossed with the common goat of the Carolinas, Tennessee, and Illinois, it
most certainly can be more promisingly crossed with
the millions of common goats of Texas and Mexico,
where they require no food, winter nor summer, but
what they crop from the range.

There is in Texas a few, and in Mexico thousands,
of goats that are peculiar for their beauty and the
value of their skins for fancy and water-proof or storm-
proof pantaloons. They are called by Texans mountain goats, and they differ from the common goat of
the country in their coat, which is, along the back
and sides, from head to tail, down to their knees and
gambols, a long, flouncing fleece of hair which gives
them, if they are not beautiful in symmetry, that appearance at least. Having never seen one shorn or
made inquiry upon the point, I can only say that I
believe them not to be of the ugly form of the common
goat, but pretty in body and general appearance. It
appears to me that this goat would be far better to
cross with the Cashmere than the common, short-

haired, ugly-looking goat of the country. If length of staple in the fleece, and beauty in general appearance of body, is an object in the improvement, then I must be right. And again, their natural proclivity to a fleece must necessarily give a greater weight and better staple to the fleece of their progeny with the Cashmere, than can be given to the issue of the common, short-haired and Cashmere goat. If, then, I am right, we have two superior breeds of goats under consideration. Shall they be brought together in western Texas, and the fleece of their issue made an article of profitable export? Are there those coming to Texas who will consider this matter, and possibly bring on with them some of the full blood or cross breed Cashmeres, and go into this business? or, I might say, lead the way and experiment in the business, and demonstrate to the world that our inexhaustible range and millions of Texas and Mexican goats are to be useful in the production of Cashmere wool.

I see there is a recent importation of these animals from the old world. There is no doubt a prospect of converting the millions of cheap Texas and Mexican goats into superior wool-producing animals.

ALPACA SHEEP.

Many years ago, when the writer was in New England, there was an opinion prevalent among some of the wool-growers of western Massachusetts, that the South American Lima or Alpaca sheep could be successfully reared upon the Green Mountains; and a number of gentlemen had it in contemplation to purchase a large tract of that chain of mountains for the purpose of raising animals upon a pretty extensive scale from the Alpaca and the large English breeds of sheep. These gentlemen were of the opinion that the cross could be successfully made, and that the growing of the wool, of these cross breed animals would be a profitable business. That the Alpaca sheep could be raised upon the Green Mountains, they felt sufficiently assured from evidence near at hand, which was that a gentleman had a small flock of twelve or fifteen Alpacas, the most of which he had raised upon these mountains. But by careful inquiry and investigation it became doubtful with them about successfully crossing these Limas with our large English sheep, and they gave up the idea they had of sending to South America for a number of the animals with which to make a start. Since then I have heard but little of these Lima sheep, the wool of a certain kind of which I have always understood is valuable for the manufacture of shawls; and if there is any part of the United States where they can be profitably raised, I should suppose that the mountains of Texas would be admirably adapted to this purpose.

I saw, in a number of Harper's Weekly or Monthly, a year or two since, an account of a small drove of Alpacas that were driven from South America, through Mexico, to the United States, and shipped thence to England. This driving was described as a tedious and risky business. If these animals are worth all this trouble and expense to Englishmen, and can be profitably reared in eastern climates, do they not deserve the attention of Americans, and are not the mountains of Texas the place for them? I heard a gentleman say, who pretends to know, that they would do exceedingly well upon the mountains of western Texas.

CAMELS.

Camels are already here in western Texas, breeding and doing good service for the government. And who knows how many of these ancient and hitherto, to us,

valueless animals that have been so long in the hands
of the Arab and aborigines, or almost exclusively controlled by people of little cultivation and enterprise,
are to become a hundred fold more useful in the hands
of an enlightened and great people ?

JACKS AND JENNETS.

I believe I have said nothing about the raising of
jacks, as a business, in Texas. It is not long since I
heard the representative of the district in which I am
living telling about an old gentleman who has a jennet that supports his family. He says he is well
acquainted with the old gentleman, and knows him
to be a truthful man. This jennet has brought him a
colt every year for several years back, some of which
he has sold for five hundred dollars when quite young.
And from this animal the old man has raised a stock
of females, besides her jack colts, which he sells only,
that would produce jacks enough in a few years, if
well attended, to make a person rich.

I have frequently seen in this country half breeds
from Mexican jennets and fine Kentucky jacks, that
would compare well with many animals of their kind
that I have seen in different parts of the world, said
to be superior, well-bred animals; and I am prepared
to say that almost any person in the north who has a
fine jack, and a little money to spare, could bring him
here, and, by securing a number of good Mexican jennets at a low figure, he could get rich raising jacks—
provided his management was judicious. He would
have to take some pains to acclimate his jack, and
keep him in good order for the first year or two. His
use to some one, over and above what he would
require of him with his jennets, would pay for this and
more too. The keeping of his jennets would cost him
nothing but a little watching. Neither would the

keeping of his increase cost him anything, unless he preferred to grain his young jacks, which no doubt would pay in the end. If he were situated upon a good musquete range he would require no grain to raise half breed jacks, that would bring fine prices at from two to four years of age. I have heard of good Mexican jennets selling in Mexico for two dollars and a half per head. They can now be bought at a low figure in western Texas.

DOGS.

I believe I have considered the stock-raising business and the improvement of stock in Texas, with remarks upon all the different kinds of animals that are really useful and necessary in our country, unless it is some of a different species, the raising of which would not constitute a stock-grower of any country. There is of the canine species a great surplus in this country, but instead of shepherd-dogs, which would be useful here, this surplus is principally made up of prowling wolves, and the mischievousness of the one determines, to a certain extent, the value of the other. These shepherd-dogs are brought on from the north, to a certain extent, and I am told are in great demand by the many who have gone and are going into the sheep business. I suppose there are more of them brought by land, with droves of sheep, than in any other way,—which sheep, I hear, since the beginning of this work, as I anticipated would be the case, are being pretty extensively brought across the country from Illinois, Ohio, Tennessee, and other states, into northern and western Texas. It is almost useless, I suppose, to say to those who are coming here for the purpose of raising sheep, that they should bring with them, if possible, more or less of these shepherd-dogs.

As game is abundant, pointers, setters, and other hunting dogs, are valuable here.

FOWLS.

The raising of fowls in western Texas is the easiest of all imaginable employments. Not far from my place of writing a farmer, during the fowl-raising season, keeps his little negroes at the herding of turkeys, hundreds of which he raises annually, and which live upon insects and grasshoppers in the prairie and about his premises. Chickens and all other fowls that a person may see fit to keep, do remarkably well, and can be raised in the country at little or no expense. There are fowls in the north that would be an object to get in Texas; but of the awkward Shanghai enough are here, and can be easily obtained.

GENERAL REMARKS.

I believe I have not distinctly conveyed the idea that some stock-growers of Texas raise stock of all kinds, in preference to raising one kind exclusively. One I spoke of, who brands about three thousand calves, and one who raises about a thousand mules, and this is their almost exclusive business; but others I know who raise cattle, horses, mules, sheep, goats, hogs, and even jacks, in moderate numbers of each kind, and also cultivate a snug field of corn, a plenty of vegetables and fruits. By so doing they can better manage to keep their stock near home, neither kind particularly interfering with the other, as the cattle range in the valleys, the sheep and goats upon the hill-tops, and the hogs in the bottoms or timbers. The horses generally take their choice of the cattle-range, and at times mingle a good deal with them, and again the herds of horses and mules are entirely by themselves, and will have no other stock with them.

Our government has been in the habit of sending her agents to Mexico for mules. She now consumes a large amount of the mules, horses, and oxen raised in Texas. She does much toward establishing the price of these animals, and is apt to pay pretty well for them. Government contractors in the transportation business, also consume a great many of these animals, particularly oxen. But who are to be the great consumers of western Texas' surplus productions? Her exports will of course be mostly north and eastward; her beef, either fresh or salt, is to be consumed by the cities along the whole Atlantic coast of the United States; her mules and horses by the planters of the south and farmers of the west; and her wool, of whatever kind, which I believe will yet be the most extensive article of export, by the manufacturers of the north and east. Then who should feel an interest in western Texas? I answer, the north, south, east, and west. But if the north and east are awake to their interests, they will get and hold a controlling influence in the trade of Texas. The east should look with earnestness in this direction, for it is western Texas that will eventually be able to furnish the looms of New England with wool at about half its present cost, and leave a handsome margin for the grower.

If I am right about the ability of western Texas to raise wool at about half its present cost to eastern manufacturers, should not the east push forward and secure a steamship communication between Boston and Texas, and at the same time show to the wool-growing world the great importance of western Texas as a wool-producing region? Dot the hills and mountains and the immense sheep-ranges of western Texas with the wooly tribe, and American manufacturers

8

will supply the place of imported goods to a great
extent in the future. Why should not the east reap
some of the advantages of the large and growing
trade of Texas, for which so many of her articles of
manufacture and export are so well adapted?

The importance of Texas and her future resources
are getting to be so well understood, that she is now
watched with a jealous eye by different marts of the
world. Her eventual extensive communication with
New Orleans by railroad, will make her the principal
dependence of New Orleans for her fresh beef and
meat of all kinds. Who, in western Texas, would not
be delighted to see a train of cars rolling away from
the foot of her hills, over her plains, and through her
forests, on to New Orleans, occupied by happy pas-
sengers, and freight-trains loaded with beeves and
veal-cattle, hogs and mules, and piled several tiers or
stories high with sheep, to be laid down in good time
and order for the butcher or purchaser? Surely such
a road will some day, not far off, make the people of
western Texas glad, and will be the pride of and a
strong hold of the Crescent City upon our trade, par-
tiality and sympathies.

What a different country would our western Texas
be if it were within a few hours' pleasant ride of New
Orleans. How would the cooped-up citizens of that
place rush for the mountain air of western Texas, in
the dull season and heat of summer, if that road,
already commenced, was pushed on to completion.
And how are these roads, the life of time in these
days, to thread the rich mantle of western Texas and
carry life and joy to the hearts of her people in the
shortest possible time? Only by setting forth the excellency of our country, and showing to the world its
great advantages, which will call to our assistance
thousands of enterprising men in the way of perma-

nent settlers, whose interests and well-being would
prompt them to labor for the cause of railroads, and
whose patronage would be the needed support of such
roads.

THE GRASSES OF WESTERN TEXAS.

Having hurried over the different kinds of stock-
raising, as it is now carried on in Texas, and touched
upon the general improvement of the inferior stock
of the country, etc., I will now venture an opinion
that nowhere can the raising of stock of any kind be
made more pleasant and profitable, at present and
for ages to come, than in these regions of country,
and I will attempt to show the correctness of this
opinion.

In the first place, there are grasses in western Texas
that, in connection with the advantages of the climate,
for stock-raising purposes, I believe are not surpassed
in the known world. The names of the most superior
of these grasses are Musquete, Bermuda, and Buffalo.
The principal grass, however, of a large portion of this
country is the Sedge. This, mixed with Wire grass
and other spontaneous growth along much of the coast
of the country, does very well at present for the raising of the hardier kinds of stock, particularly cattle,
as the business is now carried on; and further in the
interior, upon the more hilly and mountainous portions of our country, this Sedge grass being shorter
and finer, does very well for sheep, and will continue
to do so until things become more crowded here.

The day is coming when this fair land, this most
favored of creation, must produce and contribute to
the wealth and happiness of millions. It can not be
that a country like this, which gives forth in its rough,
uncultivated state, a constant grazing livelihood to
millions of useful animals, is to be always overlooked

and forever left the mere play-grounds of a few idlers, who do not appreciate the lovely spot that God has given them; which country, if generally brought into a good state of cultivated grazing, would be, to say the least, the great ever-green pasture of America,— the richest grass-plat of the world. I do not say that there are no industrious men in western Texas. But that there is a want of industry and of different men here to make the country what it should be, or, in other words, to develop its capacities for production and usefulness, there is not a doubt.

O that I could see western Texas, its planting portion excepted, one broad sheet of cultivated Musquete and Bermuda, furnishing the consuming world more beef, wool, horses, mules, etc., than any other portion of the United States of the same extent. I wish those men of energy and taste, who are looking abroad for new countries with the intention of purchasing lands for stock-raising purposes, of any kind, might be induced to come here and travel over this country and satisfy themselves in regard to its excellency and wonderful adaptation to this business.

But to return to the work of showing the correctness of my opinion. This musquete grass, that I said was so fine, is of several kinds, but generally known as the curly and bearded. There are large portions of southern, western, and northwestern Texas, that are covered with these musquete grasses, and when I have said that they yield abundantly, and that in the months of November, December, January, February, and March, (of course our coldest months,) the cattle running upon a musquete range are as fat as stock ever gets to be by feeding upon grass only, in any country, and that one single man, with a half dozen Mexican horses, can, in the way things are now managed here, attend to a thousand head of cattle, and that horses, sheep, hogs, etc., can be managed comparatively easy and cheap, I have said enough, if true, to prove that the stock-business here, so far as profit and labor are concerned, is second to the same business in no part of the world. And there are plenty of good men who would vouch for the truth of what I say. But Texas will soon be much better than now for the raising of stock; as her different kinds of stock are improved, so will her superior grasses be cultivated, and the means of keeping stock bettered. And yet, although the country is to be, some day, settled up and completely occupied, and mostly, too, by stock-growers, its capacities for useful grazing will be many fold greater than now, and the profits of the stock-business here can not for ages decrease. At present, perhaps, nineteen twentieths of the grasses of the country go to decay, or are consumed by fire. This annual waste of grass will be gradually consumed by stock, and when too closely grazed, much of it will eventually give out and be succeeded by weeds. This seems to be the fate of the Sedge grass, which suggests the idea that native vegetation, like the native man, must be pushed away, or else it must be cultivated.

I have talked of the profits of the stock-business here in ages to come, and let me take a wide and far-off view of the case. The Bermuda grass, I believe, is not a native of this country, but nothing grows more luxuriantly than it grows anywhere in these latitudes. There is not a mud-hole or a sand-hill in western Texas where it would not grow with apparent exuberance, and when set upon the rich plains or deep-soiled prairies, over rolling, hilly or mountainous lands, of any soil, it loads the earth as though it were stacked by hand upon it. I wish it were in my power to describe it. Among all the vegetable productions of the earth, there is nothing more beautiful to look upon than this unequaled grass. When I think of its beauties and its many virtues, I throw down my pen to give it another scrutinizing examination and further consideration before attempting its description. When set out and unmolested, it puts forth a fine, solid stem; from this stem other branching stems come forth, and then come clusters or cunning nests of fine spears, covered with fine blades, which, in connection with a like offspring of other grand parent stems, make up a wonderful whole of thick, verdant, sweet, and nutritious foliage; so luxuriant and heavy, that, seemingly, the earth is burdened with its weight, or, in other words, having matured and given up its juicy greenness, it seems to lay in woolen warmth or shady coolness, as if to protect its mother earth from the effects of heat and cold; but really to fatten all healthy animals that may graze upon it. By taking several stems of this grass into the mouth and chewing it well, you will discover that it has the flavor of sheep-sorrel, though nothing like as tart. Its slightly tartish taste is undoubtedly the reason why animals are so fond of it. My description is of new settings of this grass that have grown to maturity. If grown from old or well-formed sod, it would require a somewhat different description, and should be described in its different stages—I mean its infancy, childhood, youth, and maturity. But it is useless for me to try to do it justice; and I believe that words were never given to man to adequately picture the beauties of nature.

Now let us suppose it possible that, in the older settled states, or still older countries of Europe, where the lands are all fenced into lots, fields, meadows, and pastures, there could be a pasture, inclosing stock, producing more grass than any land ever produced of Timothy, Clover, or any other northern grass, and adjoining this pasture there is another, which, having had no stock upon it during the fall months, has grown a fine crop of grass and cured itself into the best of hay upon the ground. Now in the midst or dead of winter, when the first-mentioned pasture is likely not to afford sufficient grass for this stock, we turn the stock every day, after the dew is off in the morning, on the pasture of self-cured hay, taking it off before the falling of dew in the evening, to prevent tramping and uncleanliness when wet, as well as to prevent gorging and disease. I say suppose it possible that such a course could be pursued, and that this much might be all the extra work required for the wintering of stock in those countries, would it not be a hundred fold preferable and much less expensive than the present indispensable course of hay-cutting and curing, putting up for winter, and feeding out several times a day, from four to six months of the year, besides building barns, stables, yards, racks or mangers, troughs for feeding grain, fixtures for watering, often shoveling through the deep snow to do your work, and having so many apartments for so many different small lots of sheep, cattle or what not, and scores of other conveniences that are required for the wintering or fattening of stock in these northern climates or frosty regions of any part of the world? Think of this, my cold country friends, and try to imagine the virtue and beauties of these Musquete and Bermuda grasses, and this delightful country, western Texas, where they grow so luxuriantly, and where stock live and do well, summer and winter even, upon the rough, wild, and inferior grasses of the country. The Buffalo grass is of short, fine growth, and is not found anywhere near the coast. It is excellent for stock, where it is found in the high regions of the interior. It is very nutritious, and that portion of west-

ern Texas producing this grass is excellent for sheep
and goats. ..

It is not upon the buffalo or the Buffalo grass that
the writer is inclined to dwell. This animal, with the
red man, is fast migrating from the country of Texas,
and surrendering the range to domesticated animals;
and although there are many of them in northern and
northwestern Texas, I believe they will, ere long, be
among the things that were, so far as this state is
concerned. I judge from the fact that, not many
years ago, they were known to occupy ranges here
where now not a buffalo is seen within hundreds of
miles. As for the Buffalo grass, it may be useful for
all time to come, for aught-I know. I am told by
those who have traveled over it a good deal, and who
have worked mules and horses upon it, that it is the
strongest grass in the world, that animals will endure
great hardship upon it, without grain, and that it is a
good winter grass. I will venture to say, that in those
latitudes where snow does not fall, the stock-business
can be made as easy and profitable upon Buffalo grass
as upon any other: at all events, I should not be afraid
to risk it.

There has been a great deal said about cultivating
northern grasses in Texas. This, I think, would be
perfect nonsense. In the first place, there is no northern grass that would be half so good for this country,
provided it would do well here, as our Musquete and
Bermuda; but the northern grasses, such as Timothy,
Clover, Blue-grass, etc., I believe would not do here,
and so far as I know, there has been no attempt made
to explain the reason why. I think I have myself
discovered something to this effect, and that is that no
grass can be hardy and durable in Texas but that
which has a fine, compact or solid stem; no grass that
puts forth a coarse hollow stalk like timothy or clover,

is fit for this country. Something like the Musquete or Bermuda, which is next thing to everlasting, or which is hard to kill out, will be the suitable grass for this climate when our inferior grasses give way.

The surplus and cheapness of lands in Texas inclines many of its inhabitants to believe that unless a farm is situated upon a fine stream with a superabundance of timber and water, and more than enough of every-thing, it is not worth having. But if people of the north and other countries understood the manage-ment of stock, or generally believed that they could successfully manage the stock of Texas, and knew the profits of the business as well as the virtue of these lands, it would not be long before every rod of unoc-cupied land in the state would be made use of. But here it lies, munificently covered with grass, the great and almost only dependence of the stock-grower, who rides over it day after day, and year after year, as though it was fit only for him to despise, and he calls it worthless hog-wallow, the grass of which he com-mits to the flames whenever it may please him—which grass accumulates for the want of stock to eat it down, the land not having more than two or three, or possibly a single head to the thousand acres upon it. This land were it in England or New York, would be considered the best in the world. I am now al-luding to lands near the coast, but there are thousands of acres in almost any county of western Texas, which are considered nearly worthless from the simple fact that people can let their tens of thousands of cat-tle live upon them for nothing. What an idea! Hundreds of thousands of acres of lands in the state of Texas, in the United States of America, away from all danger of Indians, in peaceable sections, the soil of which is inexhaustible, and yet almost valueless. Land that if once put in a good state of cultivation

9

will last forever, and, if well set to Musquete or Bermuda grass and, mowed twice a year, I believe would
produce four tuns of the finest hay in the world to the
acre, and equally good or better for pasturage. And
this, too, in the finest climate, where snow is seldom
or never seen, and where cattle, horses, sheep, etc.,
live the year through upon grasses that are no where
to be compared with those under consideration.

I would not have a better country than western
Texas, although to those who do not look forward
there are seeming objections to it now; but to the
man who looks out upon the future of this great country there is cause for wondering at the stupidity of
men and contemplating coming events with pleasure
and satisfaction. I said I would not have a better
country than this, nor would I, for the greatest objection to it is the easy support it affords to man, thereby
begetting habits of idleness. But energetic and intelligent men of the right stamp will yet fill it up. Now
that the real condition and importance of the country
is being understood by people of other parts of the
world, it will not be long before dwellings will be near
enough together upon these unoccupied lands in Texas
to enable a person to see from one to the other, or to
pass from one to the other in a few minutes.

GENERAL REMARKS.

I will here mention a few facts of a general character in relation to the Bermuda and Musquete grasses.
I have several dozen fowls, and having no dogs, they
are shut up every night to keep them from owls and
vermin that live in the timber near my house. When
let out in the morning, these fowls go directly to a
plot of Bermuda around the house, and crop the grass
as industriously for an hour's time as would a flock
of sheep on being turned out of a fold upon fine grass

of a morning. Fowls can nearly live upon it, if not quite. The Bermuda grass, when eaten down so close that there is not a spear, stem, blade, or any part of it more than an inch long, is so thick with short green blades that there can not be a sign of the soil seen beneath it. It is a solid sheet of short, green blades, and hides the earth as well as though it were platted or knit together. So far as this grass produces—and I believe it will, when cultivated and pastured, produce as much as any grass that grows—it is impossible for the mind to conceive anything of the kind more perfect and beautiful. The curly Musquete is something like it in appearance, and one might suppose it to be of the same family of the Bermuda; it is considered by those who are acquainted with both to be as good as the Bermuda. This much is certain: in the months of December, January, February and March, this grass is well known to be as good as it ever is, and I have repeatedly seen beef cattle off from Musquete ranges in these months that I believe were as good as No. 1 northern corn-fed beef. I do not say that they would weigh with northern stall-fed animals of the same age, but they were full fat, and their flesh firm and heavy, yet tender, juicy and sweet.

The bearded Musquete grass, besides producing a heavy bottom of fine blades, puts up a stem that heads something like barley, although in its native state nothing like as heavy as good barley—yet when compared with many other kinds of grass this bearded Musquete might justly be called grain; and if well cultivated or once set in well prepared ground, I believe it would produce of seed, besides its bottom growth, what would be equal to a pretty fair crop of barley or oats.

It is contended by some that these Musquete and Bermuda grasses, for fattening cattle, are equal to corn. Whether they are or not, if in the dead of winter they will keep stock fat, they are good enough, particularly the different kinds of Musquete, which cover hundreds of thousands of acres of unsettled lands in western Texas, upon which every one's cattle are at liberty to run. Now, you men of money, who are seeking new and fine countries, let me ask you, How would you like to own a league of this musquete land in the valley of the Nueces, which is as pretty valley land as there is in the world, and already covered with this wonderful grass, which lands will produce corn, potatoes, fruits, and I might say, almost every good thing abundantly, and where stock cattle can be bought at six dollars per head, brood mares for twelve and fifteen dollars per head, and where beef cattle are now worth from sixteen to eighteen dollars, and will soon bring twenty dollars per head, at three and four years old, right at home,—and where half-breed mules at three years of age will readily bring from seventy-five to one hundred dollars—the lands being worth from one half to three dollars per acre.

If the cry of gold was started across some broad ocean five times the width of the mad Atlantic, how many thousands are there who would sacrifice the little they possess, rake together every dollar they could, and blindly rush to those regions of gold—in nine cases out of ten to be disappointed, and either beg their way back or send home to get money to enable them to return, or possibly commit suicide, in despair, for the want of luck or pluck to dig through what they thought to be a fine enterprise, never dreaming that here in Texas there are openings to which most gold diggings are no more to be compared than the least star in the firmament is to the glorious sun. I mean what I say. There are thousands of men who went in times of excitement to California and Australia, who, had they come to Texas at the time and invested the little money that it took to get them to those countries, would now be rich and independent men; instead of being what they now are—many of them not only poor, but dissipated, gambling wretches, or, what is equally bad, spendthrifts of that which, by chance having made so quick and easy, they knew not its value, and casting it adrift, soon found themselves in the rapid current of despair, and too often in the whirlpool of destruction.

Why should not men of the north and European countries come to Texas? Beef cattle are already raised here and driven to the far north, and not only consumed there, but packed up and consumed perhaps by the ships' crews of every nation that may have a vessel afloat; and Texas is but just in her infancy at this business. She will yet astonish the world with her vast productions of different kinds of meat, horses, mules and wool, or anything that is raised upon grass. If a beef can be grown to three or four years of age, as some contend, for two dollars and a half, a good half-breed horse or mule of the same age for five dollars, fine yearling sheep for a bit per head, merino wool at an actual cost of not more than six and a fourth cents per pound, hogs and other animals, fowls, etc., proportionably cheap, why will not more of that great surplus population of other countries come here and produce with their labor, energy, enterprise and capital supplies for those whom they leave behind? If a person owning two farms—one upon which he might live, where from four to six months of the year the earth might be covered with snow, the other twenty miles away, where snow might never fall, the one at home good for the growing of grains, vegetables, etc., and where labor might be cheap and plentiful for the raising and storing up of this produce ; the other producing the best of grass in abundance the year through, where stock of all kinds could live without any preparation for winter, and where he (the farmer) could raise his stock for one half or fourth of what it would cost him to raise it at home—would he not be likely to send his stock, with a portion of his family to attend to it, to the farm twenty miles away and let it be used for the raising of stock, and use his home farm for the raising of grains, etc., since if he were to use his grass farm for the raising of grain, this grain would have to be gathered and put in order for sale or use just as much as though produced on the home farm, which we will suppose could not be done to advantage for the want of cheap and sufficient labor ; and if the grass farm were used for the growing of grain, etc., it would throw the stock back on the home farm, where there would have to be a useless and laborious storing up of hay, etc., for the wintering of this stock, and six months of the most valuable growth of the grass farm thrown away, and unnecessary labor and expense used in the wintering of the stock, when it could have lived without any preparation for winter, had the grass farm been unmolested and not put to the growing of grain, or had been left to produce its winter growth of grass and constant grazing for the stock. So in regard to Texas, when considered in connection with the older states of the Union and different parts of the world. As mankind are one great family, why should not that portion of this family at home which is yet too large, and where labor is yet too cheap, where there are many who are not needed, where the unfortunate ones of the family have too often to stint their bellies for the want of supplies or means to get them, where most of the soil could be used to advantage for the raising of grains, etc.—I ask why should not these over-grown branches of this great family send off more of their surplus labor, energy, enterprise and capital to this part of the world to produce certain supplies for those whom they leave behind, and take in exchange for them money or an equivalent thereto in such things as they might require from abroad. Yes, since the productions of this part of the earth are so cheaply and easily brought forth with so little labor and capital, where suffering from cold is comparatively unknown, where extremes of heat are less oppressive than in cold northern climates, where there are so many leagues after leagues of cheap, unsettled or unoccupied lands, as good as can be, where is the great productive and fragrant green of the world, and beauty all around, where beggars are unknown, and fortune smiles upon nearly all. Yes, I say, since all this is, let men pick up their things and come over here, and raise beef for New Orleans, Mobile, and soon for Cuba, for Chicago, New York, Philadelphia and Boston, for Canada and the Lord only knows where. Come here and raise mules; come here and grow mutton and wool; come here and produce pork and bacon; come here and get rich out of this immense surplus of grass which is now consumed by fire upon the great pasture of western Texas. Here is the place to live; here the glittering lone star, the beacon light to benighted Mexico, will be the great and unequaled producer for the consuming world, where millions of cattle trail the valleys and sheep are to range upon a hundred thousand hills.

MEXICO, ITS DESTINY, ETC.

I will here say that from the beginning it has not been my purpose to write anything like a thorough description of Texas or any portion of it, nor any other country or portion of country. My principal object was only, in a style of my own, to give the reader an idea of the present inviting condition of this part of the world to people of other parts of the world who may have it in contemplation to emigrate to other countries, or who, if possessed of information such as this book may possibly afford them, might be induced to look this way, and give western Texas a consideration at least, before surrendering themselves to the claims of other countries.

There is probably nothing concerning these parts at present that would be anything like as interesting to some men as the subject I am about to consider. This is Mexico, her government, people, territory, etc., and I regret that I am not possessed of information such as would enable me to handle the subject more to my own satisfaction at least. I can, however, follow these matters sufficiently for the purposes of this work.

In the first place, Mexico is what may be considered a "kingdom divided against itself," which, according to the sacred oracles, can not stand. Every body knows that all over this unfortunate country there is dissension and civil war. There is no stability to her government, consequently no security of peace or property to her citizens, real or transient. Every successive usurper or miscalled president, governor, or what not, every division of short-lived power, is there wringing the very hearts of a God-forsaken people, by unjust requisitions upon their property, and constant arbitrary calls to arms in causes that seem to prove themselves impregnated with nothing but weakness and shame—there being no central power commanding sufficient respect and support to enable it to conquer and maintain a permanent peace.

Who can say what are the causes of this deplorable state of things in Mexico, how long they are to exist, and what will be the result of her inevitable and irretrievable fall? Does her religion, whose votaries and leading promulgators are equally important personages in the pit of the cock and bull fight, or in the house of their God, have anything to do with her shame and inability to restore and maintain order? Is the religion of the country a mere mockery, and have the long-faced and ignorant priests of this religion become, in Mexico, to be born and raised at a trade, or in a manner that almost debars them from a knowledge of what virtue should be or really is? Is this the cause of the trouble and inextricable difficulties there; or has this country or government sunk so low and beyond all hope of permanent restoration from the dishonesty of its statesmen, politicians and military men; or is the whole country dishonest? Is it there no credit to a man to be honest? Is it the nature of the climate of Mexico, and the little exertion that is there required to live, that makes her people idle, and has the sin of idleness worked her destruction? Has her mines of gold and silver been her damning curse; or is it the tendency of the Spanish race to go down, and from mixing with and extending co-equal rights to the inferior race of aborigines of the country, is it meeting, in this instance, a speedier fall than is allotted to the mother, as well as other Spanish countries? Are these any or collectively the principal causes of existing circumstances in Mexico? Whether they are or not, if Matt. xii, 25, can be applied to her, then, according to the Bible, she or her present government is doomed to become extinct, and it may be her race of people, like the Indian, also. Is Mexico yet to be linked to the country that is characterized by the Yankee? Corruption ex-

ists more or less everywhere on the earth, but like
combustible matter it will in time ignite, and everywhere burn out. Man seems to be imbued with a
spirit of virtuous and intellectual elevation that at
present is beyond his comprehension, and strange are
the slow and tidal workings that are taking him to
his distant miraculous hight.

The great comprehensive truths, says President
Quincy, written in letters of living light on every
page of our history, are these: Human happiness has
no perfect security but freedom; freedom none but
virtue; virtue none but knowledge; and freedom nor
virtue has any vigor or immortal hope except in the
principles of the Christian religion.

Is there freedom in Mexico, where any man's property is liable at any time to be demanded or confiscated by its dictators or loose government officials, or
laid waste by unrestrained divisions of lawless power?
Is there freedom, where a man knows not when he or
his property is safe, and where he is so easily con-
demned to death or imprisonment upon charges of
crime, whether false or true; where he is arraigned
by assumed authority and barbarously treated in
the most rotten tribunals of justice, upon mere pretense, or for the most trifling misdemeanor? Is
there virtue where a majority of men can be bought,
and compelled to kill or participate in the killing
of their neighbors, and where, so far as the mar-
riage contract is concerned, or vows of connubial
love, affection and constancy are regarded, children
know not who are their fathers? Is there knowledge
where the populace superstitiously allot to their hypo-
critical priests the power of invoking at their will an
earthquake of destruction upon them; and is the Christian religion in Mexico? What kind of religion is
that whose church levies and extorts from its ignorant

suppoters a tax or duty upon their infant children as they are born into the world, and when the father is unable to pay this heavenly admittance into these paradisean surroundings, the child is confiscated, and eventually sold by this *one and only true* church into Christian bondage, or kept as the meek or most abject slave of this sweet institution, in default of payment for the right of birth or existence? What kind of religion is that whose priests are vile debauchees? What kind of a shepherd-dog is that which steals into the fold of his own flock, and with wolfish play throttles and sucks the life-blood of its pretty and innocent lambs? What kind of an angel was that beautiful little girl of twelve whom I saw decked with golden wings and sparkling diamonds, and in robes of satin richness, brilliantly bespangled, making her way through the streets, followed by those who kissed the earth whereon she walked, and she marching to the frightful ding-dong of bells, on her way to that church or cathedral, to stand as a living representative of celestial purity? And what kind of gods were they who were there to behold with lustful delight that purity and innocence, and with the unholy thought of some day robbing, with religious sanction, this beautiful creature of her most sacred boon? And, again, what kind of a god was he whom I saw in the circus of the cock-fight, dictating to his whelps, and deciding the most trifling questions of dispute in regard to the game; who himself staked and won six hundred dollars on a favorite cock, after bribing the gaff-setter, and whom I saw, a day or two after, sprinkling most holy waters upon the heads of those who paid him for the pardon of their sins, and this, too, in the presence of the image of Christ and the Virgin Mary! Can it be that anything bearing the name of religion is good and useful, and should the religion of a people, however degrading, be unmolested? "He is a bad citizen," said Napoleon, "who undermines the religious faith of his country. All may not perhaps be substantially good; but certain it is, that all come in aid of the government power, and are the essential basis of morality." Would he be a bad citizen who would undermine and scatter to the four winds the false faith of Mexico? One would suppose that the religious faith of this country might not be so good, but that it might come in aid of just such powers of government as there exist, and that it might be the basis of just such morality as characterizes her people.

Just how long Mexico will remain as she is, or how long it will be before she is regulated and protected externally as well as internally by the United States, would be difficult for any one to say. But from the appearance of things, the time is but a little way off when something must be done in the way of consummating her connection in some way with this government, but how she will be connected with or what her position will be at first under the United States, I suppose no one as yet pretends to know. But when the stars and stripes shall wave out and over her, in whatever spirit the eventful time may require, then Mr. Copperface will have to put up his knife and be still. He may jog a little at first, as does a watch after having long beat to irregular time, but when the work of regulation and protection (such as the United States would send there or extend over her) shall have commenced in good earnest, then there would be safety and security to the traveler and American resident in Mexico. Then, my countrymen, will be the time for somebody to make money as fast as by digging for gold and silver in the richest of unfailing, *surely productive* mines; and who are to be the lucky fellows?

Will it be those who are living in western Texas, New Mexico, and all along the frontier? or those who are living far away from the scene of action? Who are to get the best berths? who the loaves and fishes? who the rich claims in the mines of Mexico—those world-renowned mines that the indolent people of the country have left for ages half dormant and unworked, controlled as they have been by a fast sinking, mongrel government? Said William Wirt, in his remarks upon Aaron Burr: "To youthful ardor he presents danger and glory; to ambition, rank and titles and honors; to avarice, the mines of Mexico."

You stupid fellows, away yonder, do n't you see the bird fluttering?—if it flies, whither will it go? Are you of those who, having eyes, see not, and ears, hear not? Here are mines that are certain to yield, and will pay for working; here is a country full of gold and silver, full of an inferior race of people, who are to be furnished by somebody's merchants, and who are able and will have to work for some enlightened people,—the Lord only knows who; full of horses, mules, sheep, goats, cattle, etc., the lands of which are not only mostly rich and fine for the culture of various kinds of grains, vegetables, and fruits, "but," says a writer in De Bow's Review, "afford timbers for useful dyes, prized gums of commerce, and medicinal extracts. Besides gold and silver, there is scarcely a known metal which is not found in her mines." Her mineral wealth must be inexhaustible. The reader can form some idea of what the country might have been, in the possession of a different people and under a different government, when he considers the amount of her church-property, which "is between two hundred and fifty and three hundred millions of dollars; and that at the city of Mexico the clergy own more than half the buildings, and the whole are valued at eighty millions of dollars; and the income of the church is also annually eighty millions; the annual yield of her mines, twenty-four millions of dollars; her agricultural wealth, two hundred and sixty millions of dollars; the value of her domestic manufactories, ninety millions of dollars annually; her manufactories, in number, are forty-six cotton and eighty woolen, located in the central states of the so-called Republic; and about forty thousand pounds of silk is made annually at the different silkeries."

Can any one doubt that, if citizens of the United States could have known, years back, that they could be perfectly safe and could feel secure in person and property in Mexico, they would now be there in thousands, making money in some way or other? What great advantages would have arisen had such a state of things existed for the last half century or more! Why the Mexican people would have become, ere this, somewhat Americanized, and more or less fitted for citizens of the United States. They would have become, in a measure, reconciled and to a great extent favorable to our institutions: as an evidence of which, Texas has had a very favorable influence upon the bordering states of Mexico. But now nearly all remains to be done. To take her altogether into the United States, as she is, to exercise the rights of a separate state or states, would be a dangerous experiment, and is what the people of the Union would probably not submit to. To take her as we have been doing, by piece-meal or parts, would no doubt be much the safest way for the United States; at least in this way Mexico could be regulated and civilized by degrees, and by the time she should all be consumed or gradually taken up by our government, she might be pretty safely harnessed for pulling in our traces. But she has become so distressing to herself and trou-

blesome to other countries, that this mode of disposing
of her is out of the question. She is being urged
upon the United States, and if we would shape her
destiny and keep her out of the hands of some other
power, we must accept her in some way, and satisfy
other governments in regard to her future course, or
guarantee them against further injustice from her.
Then, since she is to be ours, in some shape, and
eventually no doubt to comprise different states of the
Union, why should not the eyes of all good men be
turned upon her, and every laudable means used to
meet and counteract the withering effects of her superstition, wickedness, and ignorance, and fit her as much
and as soon as possible for her coming place?

And how is this to be done? Why simply to turn
a tide of northern emigration this way, and European
emigration with it as much as possible. The western
territory of the Union is already blocked in with intelligence, and is safe, and would do for a while if not
settled so rapidly. The Canadas and all north of us
are doing well enough, for the present, at least,—for
British America is free and happy. There is no danger north, east, nor west; no dreadful monster in the
black garb of half civilized superstition and ignorance
to meet and overcome in those quarters; no walled-
in treasures, controlled by hypocrites with pretended
rights and powers from on high, who can call to their
support their hordes of semi-savage dupes. The danger is this way: This very Mexico, unless wisely managed, may yet explode the great magazine of human
rights. But what is to be done? The moral, social,
industrial, educational, political, pecuniary, and religious wealth of the United States is immense, and
could pay out largely to save and elevate immoral,
idle, ignorant, impolitic, bankrupt, and irreligious
Mexico. But the question arises, how are we to bring

this healing and regenerating of things to bear upon her, preparatory to her coming into the Union, or without first taking her into the Union and subjecting ourselves to the perils of overthrow before she is put to rights and rendered harmless? My answer is, that we should take her at first as a government, subject to the United States, with an express and unqualified provision that no state should ever be formed out of her territory and admitted into the Union, until it should count a foreign white population of a certain number,—a purely white foreign population from the United States and other countries, with their increase, (aside from its original population and its increase), that should number, perhaps, as many as a territory now requires for an admittance into the Union. With such and other precautions, I, as an American and citizen of the United States, should not be afraid to extend our power and protection over suffering and deluded Mexico. It may be that the constitution is in the way of such a course; but whatever becomes of Mexico — whether she become British, French, Spanish, American, or retains her independence— the engines of civilization should be set hard at work in this direction; and when the time or opportunity presents itself, strong settlements of the Anglo-American caste should be made in her territory among her people.

As western Texas is the center of my theme, I must not endeavor to sweep too broad a floor, and leave the whole but indifferently clean. The settling up and improvement of western Texas is itself a stepping-stone at one of the doors of Mexican alleviation. Texas was herself once a broad wilderness of her's, and had it not been for the colonization enterprise of the Austins, and the superior qualifications and untiring exertions of the younger Austin, details of which can be seen in the Texas Almanac), she might now be the victim of Mexican perfidy, and the theater of her blasting contentions. This is quite plain to Mexico and to Mexicans, many of whom are living in Texas, and constantly going from one country to the other. If, then, the force of example and bordering strength is effective and important, why not add as much as possible to the already wide-spread information in regard to this beautiful country? Show the profits of business, and the inviting condition of things in general in western Texas, and let the interests of men prompt them to its shores to participate in its many advantages.

While yet in sight of this Mexican question, there is one thing to which I would call the attention of all good and intelligent Americans. Missionaries are sent abroad over the earth to convert the heathen and ameliorate the condition of mankind. Is it not to our government that Americans owe their great advantages and capacities for doing so much good abroad? Is not our government the rock upon which stands the great light now shining forth to the world? To be sure, our moral and educational institutions impart to this government its vigor and the healthy blood that courses in its veins, and are its only hope in the future; and one would suppose that it might be adequate to the purpose. But suppose seven or eight millions of lost people—lost to everything or wanting everything that could create or sustain such a government as ours—were to become altogether, with their country, an extreme one side section, a part of our confederacy; might not this possibly destroy our missionary strength, and dim this our brilliant and promising light of the world, by lessening the vigor and purity of our government, unless our moral and educational strength should be proportionally increased

10

and applied in a way to rapidly impart this wholesome blood of our nation's system into the veins of this vast but shattered additional limb of the government? If so, had not missionaries and those Americans who feel an interest in the enlightenment and saving of the world, better first see that the most attractive light, and the one by which they get their strength, and by which their feet are guided, and to which mankind seem to turn with a gazing hope, is replenished and does not lose its lustrous beaconing, and secure to it, if possible, the means of shedding abroad for all time to come, before turning aside to strike their sparks in other lands, however dark and heathenish they may be?

When we consider the evils of party spirit, universal suffrage, gold discoveries, and many others with which our government has already to contend, the idea of adding thereto by taking, in a body, under our shelter, with the greatest precaution even, the millions of superstitious and ignorant beings of Mexico, to be led, without principle, in elections and government matters, by their false gods, and they too (their leaders) to be led by those who might stoop the lowest or bid the highest, well may we pause and consider—well might the freemen tremble. But, to make the thing safe, we must face the music in good time. If the thing is inevitable, " let it come," and let these shepherds, whose devotion is the conversion of sinners and salvation of souls, gather up strong flocks of intelligence and determination, and with a mild and Christian spirit make as soon as possible, powerful settlements among the half heathen of our own continent. Let some one follow in the footsteps of the immortal Austins, and colonize another Texas within the limits of Mexico. I do not mean that I would array sect against sect, for war and contention of any kind is repugnant to my feelings. I simply mean that I would bring the intelligent and true Christian in friendly contact with the deluded and ignorant; I would bring industry, enterprise and everything that is great and good in contact with idleness, degeneracy and everything that is detestable and wicked. In short, I would gentle and improve the savage and degenerate blood of Mexico by establishing colonies or strong settlements of the Anglo-American race among her people, in every advantageous quarter that should offer money-making inducements, or honest paying labor and available operations. Such as tilling the soil, digging for gold and silver, lead and minerals of any or all kinds; merchandising, raising horses and mules, growing wool, manufacturing, mechanism, school teaching, medical practice, etc. And how, I ask, could good and Christian men better serve the dearest of causes than lead the way in such enterprises, for the purpose of opening new channels and widening the fields of true Christianity and human happiness? And lastly, but by no means leastly, for the purpose of forging new chains with which to bind the north and the south forever together; and render, if possible, this an imperishable Union.

To be understood I must go a little further on before returning to my dear western Texas. I would not disguise the fact that I would have northern people go to Mexico, and so would I like to see southern people go there. This mingling and mixing up of the people of the different sections of our great country will, no doubt, prove a most excellent thing. But the advantages of populating Mexico with northern people particularly would be immeasurably great. Settling down in the south seems to create in the northern man a higher estimation of the Union, a renewed love of the Union, a deeper, stronger Union feeling and determination to 'stick to the Union.' It gives an attraction to the center. ' Northern people in the south, so far as I know, do not meddle with or disturb its institutions—I believe they generally become southerners, according to a correct definition of the term, so far as it should relate to sectionalism in these United States. But they have a desire to see the difficulties of the country peaceably settled, for the idea of being politically separated from the land of their birth, if I am correct, is perfectly distressing to them; therefore, here in Texas or Mexico, if it belonged to the United States, the northern man would impress upon the minds of his children that there is a great North for which he has a peculiar regard—a great and powerful people in the north, whose intelligence, energy and advancement are unsurpassed, and with whom we should strive to cultivate the best political feeling and relations; for, in connection with them, we are the greatest, the most powerful and happy people in the world; but separated from them, wherever the line might be drawn, we would be comparatively weak, and we know not what might be our destiny as a people—separated, we could not look forward with that certainty of a glorious future for our country.

Such and like sentiments instilled into the minds of their children, could not fail to impress them with a deep sense of the importance of the Union, and create in them a true attachment to it, and they would cling to the land of their fathers and strive in support of that which should promise the most—the undivided Union—which would counteract, to a great extent, the feelings imbibed by those who are raised to hate the Union on account of sectional agitation. It may be urged against this position that California would

willingly cut loose from the Union, but I don't believe
that she could be induced to do so, even though the
mountains should ever divide us and no railroad
should ever connect us. But, with a connecting railroad, nothing short of a Rocky Mountain earthquake
that should throw us all into the seas, would ever
separate the Pacific from the Atlantic states; and
should such a thing occur the separation of California
from the Union, and the South from the North or the
Union, are by no means analagous cases.

Whoever goes to Mexico should strive to elevate
the character of the Mexican people, that they may
reach the day, as soon as possible, when they will not
be liable to dangerous corruption in elections and
governmental matters—what an immense work of
ages, and how deserving the particular and even the
undivided attention of good and wise men!

Before returning more closely to the idea suggested
upon the title page, I will say that I do not pretend
that the introduction of a different religion into Mexico, could by itself work out the desired effect and
save the country. But it is industry, commerce, internal improvements, mechanical, educational and
useful operations of a thousand kinds, in connection
with good morals and truly religious operations that
would work the desired change. For a Protestant
minister to go to Mexico alone and divulge his doc-
trines would, I suppose, be equivalent to throwing
himself away. A physician, of Protestant faith, by
himself in Mexico, if he were so disposed, could be a
stronger champion in a religious way than could a
Protestant minister, provided he should perform miraculous cures or ingenious humbugs; Mexicans
would, of course, then consider him inspired, and
were he equally accomplished in religious matters he
could show to them the wonderful works of Protest-

antism. I mention this merely to show the character
of the people, not to encourage such low work. If a
man.to accomplish good and drive out corruption
must resort to the scurvy pretense of Catholicism, as
it exists in Mexico, as has a certain *distinguished
character*, there might be danger of his becoming
corrupted also, or it might not be an unnatural conclusion to suppose him possessed of but little good to
impart to others. For selfish ends such a course frequently works admirably.

Settlements in Mexico by people from the states,
of a reasonable religious faith, should they be successful in their business operations and rapidly improve
the country that they might possess, would naturally
suggest to the mind of the Mexican, that a better religious faith than his might be requisite to prosperity
and advancement with him or his countrymen. I
mean to be understood that to show the Mexican the
effects of a good religion, is better than to undertake
to force a different religion from that of his own upon
him ; for when urged, in a religious way, he would
hug all the closer the one he now professes, though it
might curse him ten times as much as it does.

To make successful settlements in Mexico the direction of the work in its beginning and for some time,
aside from religious matters, should be entrusted to
the right kind of men who are already acquainted
with the language, the people and the ways of the
country. The simplest, unpretending, yet wide-awake
means will accomplish the greatest good in this business. To get together a company of outcasts, whose
only idea is gain either by fair or foul means, without
a shadow of a creditable aim in life, without a claim
to respectability, and lost even to self-respect, and
make a great cry and empty show and pretensions,
without work, good regulation and behavior, is all

nonsense. 'No enterprise ever so promising could amount to anything in the hands of such men. If a settlement for mining purposes is to be undertaken in Mexico or any of these half-savage frontier territories, the managers of the enterprise should know what they are about—they should not only be men of great determination and skilled in the business, but they should know beforehand that they are to be very sure of successful digging in some well-known locality, where they are equally certain in regard to the durability of water around these diggings, or that their preparations during a dry season are where they will be followed by a sufficiently wet one for their purposes. They should know about the means of getting their supplies, and what would be their probable cost up to the time that they could probably realize from their operations, and prepare for the same, otherwise they would be liable to discouraging disasters that might break up the company and possibly the enterprise altogether.

The men who direct such enterprises in Mexico, or upon the frontier, should encourage the emigration of stock growers and farmers to settle around them if possible. There are sections in the vicinity of gold and silver regions in the frontier territories that are well adapted to the raising of sheep and goats in particular.

New mining companies should determine from the start to have no cut-throat, gambling, dissipated, disturbing wretches among them; and I believe every such company, that is sometimes from necessity shut out from society and away from the gentle influence of woman, would be much more successful if they would not only interest moral and Christian men in their enterprise, but a minister of the Gospel, who should hold forth in a religious way occasionally, and use his influence to keep up as good a state of morals as possible. Good industrious men who are willing to work for a fortune, if rightly organized, in companies and directed by the right kind of experienced managers, could certainly do remarkably well at mining and stock raising in various quarters along the frontier of Mexico, and the day is most certainly not far away when Mexico itself will be the place for many an American to fill his pockets in a thousand different ways.

I am credibly informed that at this time good brood mares can be bought in the interior of Mexico at five dollars per head, but men who have recently been there for the purpose of bringing out horses, have returned without them, considering it unsafe to purchase even at these low rates; for, as they say, could we have got them for nothing there was no certainty of our getting them out of the country at this time, and there would have been a risk of losing our lives with our horses had we bought and started with a drove. The troubles of the county endanger a person's life as well as property, and he knows not on whom to depend; but, when it is safe to go there again, which time is not far off, then, my boys, whom it may concern, think of buying good brood mares for five dollars per head, and horses, mules and sheep in proportion. Think of this country (western Texas), where, if you please, you can bring them and so profitably raise mules, horses, produce mutton, wool, etc. Of course, in times past, there has been more safety in going to Mexico, and thousands of men have been there and made their piles at buying stock for a mere nothing; and, when there is safety in going there again for this purpose, there will be a plenty of men at the business, some of whom are now standing ready and will pitch in as soon as a good time offers. Some

will buy for the purpose of driving to Texas and
further north to dispose of at wonderful profits, but
many will buy for the purpose of raising stock in
Texas; and I know of men and am credibly informed
that there are plenty of such who are anxiously wait-
ing the day when a large portion of Mexico, at least,
will be ours, or when they can go with the protection
of our government in some way, and purchase and
peaceably occupy the most beautiful spots in Mexico
that they ever saw; as fine cultivating lands and
stock ranges of entire musquete, in as delightful a
country and climate as there is anywhere upon the
face of the earth. That will be a glorious day for this
part of the world! Many a Yankee will find his way
into Mexico, and buy out the indolent and ignorant
Copperface for one-fourth the value of his stock and
lands, or I might say for mere nothing, *i. e.* one-
fourth the value or mere nothing to the Yankee; but,
perhaps, the full value to the Mexican. Yes, that
will be a glorious day when the Yankee boys shall
plant an influence in fallen Mexico that will live and
grow into such importance as could originate with no
other people.

The people of Mexico are a mixture of Indian, Negro and Spanish, and not a few full-blood Indians and
Negroes are her lawful citizens and participate in the
affairs of her government, religion, etc. Should not
this be a caution to abolitionists? The people of poor
benighted Mexico are inextricable in their connection
with the red and black man, and is not their destiny
Indian like? Then if Mexico, from her connection
with the wild man and other causes, must go down,
why not the Yankee boys occupy her lands and
country, whose resources and importance she has been
unable to develop? I would not be understood that
the present inhabitants or population of Mexico should

11

be murdered or driven out of their country, but I
would be understood that the present peculiar race of
Mexican people are doomed to become extinct, and
that sooner or later their country is to be characterized by a different people, although fragments of its
present race may remain there for many centuries to
come, but will all eventually be absorbed in another
race, or lose its identity in some way and the country
take an entirely different character, and why should
not that character be given by the Yankees? Why
not let this country or this part of North America be
characterized as is the whole United States? Cross
the ocean and drop your anchor in any distant port of
the world and go ashore, and when the stars and
stripes are seen waving out upon the penant of your
ship, if every stranger in your presence, when speaking of that ship don't call her a Yankee, " I'll pay the
drinks." I care not from what port of the United
States she hails, or where first launched, whether
California, Norfolk or Portland, if she hoists the flag
of stars and stripes, when the skipper of any vessel
of any nation levels his glass upon her, the chances
are his words will be, " She's a Yankee."

Go abroad, my friends, born and raised wherever
you may have been in these United States, and you'll
be called or considered a Yankee. And why should
not the people of the United States be termed
Yankees? Is that word only an empty sound? Does
the word Yankee associate with it nothing but the
idea of Indian jargon or wooden nutmegs and the like?
Who settled the Yankee states, and how have these
states progressed? What are their institutions of
learning, and what have they been for many years?
What their common school system? Who the statesmen and learned men they have produced? and what
the talent, the capital and kind of men they have sent

abroad and settled all over the United States? What their manufacturing and mechanical skill and productions? What their inventive genius? What the part they act in the commercial world, and what their religious influence? Who and of what are the commercial cities of the United States composed? Who built the canvas city upon America's ocean?. Who built the puffing city upon the inland waters of the United States? Trace, if you please, the great men and the great works of the whole United States to their origin and see what the Yankee states have done—see if they have been behind. Why the very father of the country, upon my title page, first saw the light in old Connecticut.

One would suppose that the writer might himself be a Yankee, but he is not, nor is he so bigoted as to suppose that there is no people or doings of consequence in the United States but the Yankees and their doings. He is, however, somewhat acquainted with the Yankee character, and although a little partial to them, he would like to see coming to western Texas with them people from all the states and all parts of the civilized world. The mines and wealth of Mexico, her vast extent of rich musquete and cultivating lands, and her millions of stock are near to our borders, and will be easy of access to the western Texian, and the man who is on hand in time will be the lucky fellow. So come from everywhere; this mixing and crossing of the white civilized races of mankind is, no doubt, developing great advantages in the Yankee nation, but with the Indian and negro a dangerous experiment if Mexico is an example. Yet it might not be so dangerous for the descendants of Great Britain and their adopted kin, or mixed offspring of the United States to live and intermingle with the inhabitants of Mexico, since the Anglo-

American's destiny seems to be ever upward and onward. Yes, it matters not what the obstacles in the way, what the difficulties to overcome, what seeming impossibilities to do away and lights of trouble to surmount, wherever you may find him he is ever moving steadily but surely on and upward—mid sunshine or tempest he is alike the same, immovable in his lofty course, and it seems that his is to be the universal language of the north western world at least. The English tongue seems not to know the word fail, it carries with it universal success.

LANDS, VEGETABLES, FRUITS, VINES, TIMBERS, FLOURS, FENCING, MIRAGES, GRAINS, DWELLINGS, AND BUILDING MATERIAL; CISTERNS, CLIMATE, AND HEALTH; YELLOW FEVER, NORTHERS, SEA BREEZE, ETC.

Although I have talked of most of these matters in connection with stock-raising and other subjects, yet I have considered them with only here and there a word, and will therefore take them up separately, with a few remarks.

There are millions of acres along the coast of western Texas, and some distance back from the gulf or bay shores, that are known as "hog-wallow lands." Why they are called by this uncouth name I do not know, unless it is from the peculiar unevenness of their surface, which some one may have supposed to look like the work of hogs. This unevenness resembles, in appearance, land in the north or timbered countries, which are sometimes left, after chopping them off, for the stumps to rot out and take to grass, with their natural, unmoved surface, which is often very knolly, or, in other words, a surface of little hillocks, all covered with grass. The soil of these hog-wallow lands is generally black, and when moist, of a sticky nature. Its depth is from two to six feet, underlaid with a kind of clay. A person might travel a lifetime over these lands and never see a stone of any kind. It is heavy, at first, to break up, but after being well turned over to the depth of three or four inches, the grass and roots of all kinds in it readily die out, after which one or two good plowings make it pleasant land to work, if worked at the right time. It should never be tramped by stock, of any kind, when cultivated. It is very productive, and it is said will never wear out or become less productive from use. These lands are disagreeable to work when wet, but if, after a crop of corn or anything else is taken from them, they are soon well turned over, in a dry time, they require no further preparation for the next year's crop: and they are generally very pleasant to plow up directly after taking off a crop, before the soil gets too much settled or too closely packed together. I have known men fail to make a crop by putting off the plowing of their hog-wallow field until late, when it would break up in lumps, and having no rain in time to pulverize and settle the soil together, the seed could not take root for want of moisture. There is an unusual amount of lime in this soil, and when plowed, in a dry time, it turns up more or less in lumps, and becomes dryer, and not until a soaking rain will it settle and prepare itself for a crop. Water slackens it nicely together as it does lumps of lime. With the right kind of management, a person is very sure of a crop upon these lands. For, although when stirred up, it admits the air and loses its moisture, when pulverized and settled with a soaking rain, it excludes the air and retains its moisture better, perhaps, than almost any other soil. The farmer who is ready for the spring season, is almost sure of a crop upon these or almost any other lands in western Texas. Corn can be planted as early as January, and as late

as April, for a summer crop, which gives ample time
for replanting, should the first planting fail from any
cause. In fact, men have been known here to raise
two crops of corn upon the same land in one season.
The hog-wallow generally speaking, are among the
cheapest lands in the state.   This is owing, to a great
extent, to their being heavy to work, and their want
of timber; but, as I have said, one great reason of
their being so cheap, is that men can pasture their
tens of thousands of cattle upon them for nothing, and
this is the case with much of the land throughout the
state,—the principal owners possessing each so much
that they are unable to fence it, and· many of them
having no stock to inclose, would have no use for their
lands were they able and disposed to fence them, as,
if fenced, they could only be available to them as pasturage; and furthermore, it would not add enough to
their value and quicken their sale sufficiently to pay
the land-holder for fencing, unless a similar course
should be generally adopted throughout the state,
which would, under the present state of things, be an
impossibility.   Could land-holders prevent the stock
of the country from running upon their lands without fencing it up, they might sell much more than
they do, and at paying rates. But there is no remedy,
and consequently the bulk of the range of western
Texas is to be open to the world, as mere commons,
for many years to come.

Although the lands along the rivers and principal
water-courses in western Texas will be generally taken
up and occupied at no very distant period, the great
body of prairie-range, out from and between these
water-courses, will be open perhaps for ages to come;
and to this, as much as to almost any other one thing
contained in these pages, would the writer call the
particular attention of the reader. These lands, out

from the streams and timber, in the center of our
broad prairies, many of which are first-rate, can generally be had at a much lower figure than can those
bordering on the streams and having more or less
timber upon them; though, the Lord knows that well-
watered and good timbered lands are for sale here
without end, and cheap enough as yet. But if 1 were
this day a new-comer in western Texas, and here for
the purpose of raising cattle, horses, mules, and the
like, knowing what I do about these open prairies, 1
would by no means give up my undertaking should
I find every rod of the land having water and timber
upon it taken up or occupied. I would, in this case,
go into the center of these prairies without water or
timber, either upon hog-wallow or rolling up-lands,
and establish a ranche. If in the hog-wallow prairie,
my ranche should be upon the highest, sandy piece of
ground I could find,—a plenty of which sandy places,
a little above the common level, are always to be
found. Here I would have one advantage, at least,
over my neighbors upon the water-courses, and that
would be a fresh start of grass in the greatest abundance, which could not be as abundant where cattle had been grazing for years along the streams of
water. I would go to work and supply my cheap
place with its deficiencies—water, shade, and wood
—and then I would haunt my cattle or stock to
it, which of course would necessarily be Texas
stock at the beginning. I would supply my want
of water for stock purposes with ponds, made of
natural basins, to hold water as long as possible, and
with wells, whose depth, in hog-wallow lands, need be
only from fifteen to thirty feet. For the use of the
house I would have cistern water, the best in the
world. To supply my want of shade, I would inclose
a small piece and plant China trees, the rapid growth

of which would not only soon supply an abundance of
shade, but plenty of fire-wood and posts for fencing,
which latter would be equal to the best of cedar; and,
as I should work all the time with the satisfaction of
knowing that my lands, which cost me a mere trifle
at the start, could not be beat for the growing of the
better grasses, should I ever see fit or have occasion
to cultivate them; that they could not be beat for the
growing of sugar cane; as good as any in the world
for the culture of the grape; second to none for different kinds of fruits, such as peaches, figs, pomegranates, etc.; second to none for nearly every garden
vegetable that grows; good as need .be for corn, the
great feeding staple of the country. I say. as I should
work all the time with the satisfaction of knowing all
this, and that the breeze from every quarter would
ever generously cool and relieve my healthy home,
and that railroads would surely some day add much
to the value of my property and to the cheerfulness
and happiness of society and the country around me,
and that people would, after a while, wonder that they
had not seen and appreciated the value of these open
prairies, I could work with good cheer and always be
pleased with my location, and never envy my neighbors upon the water-courses, whose lands may have
been, from the first, supplied with timber.

These remarks I design as a hint in regard to the
future of these broad hog-wollow prairies, some of
which, in places, are twenty and thirty miles from
river to river, with but little timber or water-courses
of any account to be seen. There is, now and then,
a scattering cluster of trees to be seen, when crossing
almost any of these open prairies, and plentiful ponds
of good stock-water, unless it is in a dry season.

Considering the cheapness and virtue of much of
the land in these prairies, the great abundance of grass

around many fine localities that could be selected, they are deserving the attention of stock-growers who would secure a cheap home and an extensive range. Such lands can be had for a half dollar per acre, in considerable quantities, which sooner or later are sure to be very valuable. But at present, as I remarked, there is no end to the fine land for sale in western Texas, that is well-watered and timbered, and upon durable streams. Should I select a ranche or permanent home for the stock-business in an open, rolling conntry, deficient in wood and water, I should pursue pretty much the same course as in the open hog-wallow prairies.

When I talk of these open, central points in the broad prairies of western Texas as places of residence, I am looking some ways into the future. But it is a subject that is every day gaining importance, and attracting attention in this country, particularly the purity of the air and the healthfulness of these dry localities. Although we can, in certain places and directions, travel twenty or thirty miles, in open prairies, from one durable river to another, without seeing much of any timber or water, a person can not, as a general thing, travel these prairies, in any direction, that distance, or half that distance, without crossing rivers, creeks, lakes, and bayous, the banks of which are more or less heavily timbered; some enough only to furnish fire-wood and partial conveniences to those who may settle upon them; others affording the greatest abundance for fencing and all conveniences of the kind to the settler, except a good quality of lumber; a plenty of Florida pine, however, and sometimes northern pine and spruce is to be found in our bay-towns suitable for building purposes.

The sweet potatoe is the most natural for the climate and soil of western Texas, although Irish potatoes grow well, yet they do not seem to keep from one planting to another, which is a great objection to them here.   But the sweet potato, which I believe is relished by all, after eating them a while, produces abundantly, and there is no difficulty in storing them in a way to keep.   Irish potatoes are raised a good deal in the spring, and serve until sweet potatoes come on in August, sooner or later.   With a little pains the Texan can have fresh Irish potatoes the year through; and this pains is only to raise a spring and fall crop, and, if it is necessary, to lay them by or store them awhile for planting purposes, they need only to be carefully spread in a dry loft, or packed in perfectly dry sand.   I believe they are sometimes left in the ground from one planting to another, when two crops a year are raised.

Nearly all the garden vegetables of the north grow finely here.   Spring and fall gardens are always made, and many persons contend that the fall is the best season for gardening.   Any time in the winter, unless it is an unusual one, a person can go into our well-managed gardens and take from the ground, just as they grow, beautiful vegetables of almost any kind. Finer melons never grew than can be raised in any part of western Texas, and two crops a year at that; also, pumpkins, or any thing of the kind, produce finely.

The most natural fruits for this country are peaches, figs, grapes, plums, pomegranates, strawberries, raspberries, tomatoes, etc.   Apples, pears, quinces, currants, and the like, are produced in the interior, upon the hilly and mountainous portions of western Texas. Oranges, dates, bananas, etc., are raised, but not generally, and with what success I am unable to say. The following are some of the wild fruits that are common in parts of western Texas: wild plum, wild

grapes, haws, persimmons, mulberry, dewberry, blackberry, etc.   Nearly all the bottom forests and much
of the upland timbers of the country are more or less
burdened with wild grapevines, which are loaded with
grapes, and they are the most thrifty and juicy grape
that ever grew.   Europeans are here manufacturing
wine and brandy from the grapes of these broad vineyards—not of forbidden fruit, but fruit to which the
whole world is welcome.   These grapes are too tart
for pleasant eating, though some people take them
down with a wonderful relish, as though they were
half sugar.   When fully ripe the black, luscious looking fellows are very tempting.   They are excellent for
jelly, jam, and preserves, but · require a little more
sugar than the cultivated grape,—I should suppose
about the amount that is required for currants.   Any
amount of vineger, of the best quality, can be cheaply
and easily made from this immense forest production.
I have drank excellent wine from this abundant fruit.
The cultivated grape, of any kind, can be and is, to a
certain extent, successfully engrafted into the wild
vine.   The fruit of the wild vine is called mustang.
To make up the one hundredth part of this spontaneous production of western Texas into wines, etc.,
would give employment to hundreds of people; and
when the labor and expense, attending the establishing
and cultivation of vineyards, is taken into consideration, one would suppose that the making up of these
free grapes into wines, brandies, and the different
relishes, for which they are good, might be made a
profitable and extensive business.

When at Cape Town, Africa, the writer saw the
free use of wine, which was largely produced, but was
not comparable, in quality, to an article made here in
western Texas from the wild or mustang grape.   Of
course I do not allude to the Constantia wine of Cape

Good Hope, but to a common article called Cape Town wine. Is it not reasonable to suppose that a country producing the wild grape so vigorously and abundantly, would be supassing fine for the cultivation of the choice kinds? The truth is, this heavy, black, hog-wallow land is as good as the best in the world for the raising of grapes, thousands of acres of which, all around where I am now writing, are to be had for the small sum of from fifty cents to two dollars per acre.

The haw, such as is found in western Texas, is delicious eating. . I have eaten haws from trees in this country that I would prefer to the raisin. I have often wondered what they would amount to if cultivated. I have found them in the winter, in thickets of brush, plump and sweet—not as rich as the raisin, but better by far for anything like sumptuous eating. They hang on the trees nearly all winter, and ripen by degrees. The frost sweetens them, unless, after freezing, they are too much exposed to the sun and wind—and I believe too much exposure to frost injures them. The best that I have found were protected in thickets of brush from the effects of the frost, and from the sun and wind, which, after freezing, dries them up and makes them tasteless. From the fact that very thrifty trees grow the choicest fruit, I am inclined to think that the fruit would be much better if the tree was cultivated. The color of the haw that I allude to, is blue, but I believe it is generally called the black haw.

The dewberry is very much like the blackberry of the north. The vine, however, is different, being low and scrubby. There is generally a plenty of this fruit almost anywhere in western Texas. It ripens in the spring, and lasts but a short time.

The mulberry affords beautiful fruit, in abundance,

either wild or cultivated. There are several kinds found in our forests.

The river bottoms or valley lands of western Texas are generally of a deep, dark soil, and are very productive. They are occupied extensively by cotton and sugar planters. The forest growth of these bottoms is live oak, pecan, elm, prickly-ash, hackberry, mulberry, white-oak, pin-oak, wild peach, etc., etc. Of these the live oak, wild peach, and others, are ever green. The wild peach, mulberry, magnolia, China, etc., are fancy trees, and are growing about many of our dwellings, ornamenting and shading our door-yards. Our most lasting forest timbers are live oak and mulberry. Timbers for mill-wright, wheel-wright, and other mechanical purposes, are plentiful here.

The crop of the pecan-tree puts many an easy and honest dollar into the pockets of many Texans. The annual export of pecans from western Texas is very large. Early in the fall hundreds and thousands of Texans resort to the river-bottoms and timbers to gather pecans.

As for flowers, this, of all others, is nature's favored spot. From the remotest mountain-top to the sea-shore some gardens are richly robed with all the mingled colors and beauties of the rainbow, and so pleasant to the smell and refreshing to the eye that words fail to convey an adequate idea of their loveliness. After leaving the black hog-wallow lands, which are mostly covered with the sedge grass, we generally find a good deal of dark sandy soil and a rolling country, and besides the timbers upon the rivers and creeks there are immense forests of open timber or timbered prairies, well supplied with the sedge grass and watered with beautiful streams. The principal timber of these forest prairies are the post oak and black jack, interspersed with a variety of other kinds.

Here and there among these post oak lands are rich
valleys, particularly along the rivers and creeks.
There is now and then a piece of hog-wallow, but
long stretches of entirely post oak or timbered prairie
lands, of a sandy soil are found, which are not as rich
and productive as the hog-wallow or bottom lands—
but let the reader bear in mind that these are all good
grazing lands, and that when it is required they will
all produce the musquete and Bermuda grasses most
plentifully. Nothing will grow more luxuriantly and
produce more abundantly upon any land, in any part
of the world, than will these grasses upon almost any
of the lands of western Texas. These leagues upon
leagues of sandy post oak lands, although now ap-
parently idle, are to be the pride of the country as
vast sheep walks and general stock growing regions.

The musquete lands or those lands producing the
musquete tree and grasses have a dark rich soil, of
good depth, and are generally of a smooth surface.
They produce fine corn, potatoes and vegetables generally, and in the interior or mountainous regions
fruits in abundance, and I am told the different kinds
of grain of northern growth. The principal native
tree upon these lands is the musquete, and I should
say it is almost the only tree found upon ranges of entirely musquete grass. This tree produces a bean
which Mexicans feed to their horses, for which I am
told they are excellent. The musquete is generally a
scrubby tree, but grows sufficiently tall and straight to
make fine posts, which are said to be as lasting as the
cedar of the north. The roots of this tree afford an
excellent article of dye, and I believe are an article
of export from Brazos Santiago. The root is said to
comprise much the larger portion of the tree.

The Mexicans and many Americans build from
this timber picket fences. These are made by dig-

ging a narrow ditch the width and depth of the blade of a spade, in which the bodies and limbs of trees, after being chopped the right length, are set on end as close as possible to each other, around which the dirt from the ditch is closely packed, there being no frost to heave a fence or foundation in this country. When built of musquete this makes a lasting and profitable fence, and such fence when in order is very safe, as nothing will attempt to jump it when of ordinary hight, say from four to five feet. I have seen a fence of this kind made of live oak trunks and limbs, which I believe may last fifty years and more by sometimes resetting.

The Texians have another way of building a good fence with this scrubby timber, with which the settler would soon become acquainted. It is made by throwing the dirt from a ditch all on to one side, in the line of a fence, and planting the short pickets on the embankment, the ditch and the elevated foundation serve as a good share of the fence, as pickets of three or three and a half feet in length will do in this case. Post and board fence is made to great extent in this country, half the hight being frequently made up as above, of a ditch from which the dirt is thrown along one side, around a row of posts that have been slightly set and which are deeply and firmly secured in their place by the embankment thrown up from the ditch, which may be two and a half feet in width and depth more or less. Two and sometimes three six inch fence boards nailed on to this row of posts, upon the bank of the ditch, is all sufficient for the purposes of the country. Sometimes when lumber is hard to get a ditch answers the purpose of a fence; again, large fields and pastures near the coast, where lumber is nearer at hand, are fenced with posts and boards altogether. A little back from the coast stone fence is sometimes made, though seldom. Concrete fences are being made pretty extensively about the towns, for dooryards, gardens, etc. Rail fence of various descriptions is made, but I do not see any here that will compare with the capped and ridered fence of the north, I mean such as are capped with inch and a half stuff, bored with three and four inch auger, this too with horse, steam or water power. Hedging is being pretty extensively commenced, of which I shall speak further on.

The musquete timber is excellent for firewood, and besides affording posts, pickets and the like for fencing, it is used for other conveniences by those who are settled near to it.

The man of intelligence and of refinement, who has cultivated a taste for agricultural pursuit, and can appreciate things in general pertaining to the business, and who is capable of the least sublimity of thought, will, when traveling over fine musquete ranges, after considering their beauty and many virtues, together with the excellent climate in which they are, turn his thoughts upon the Creator with a bursting soul of purest thanks for the feelings of delight and enjoyment that here possess him. In fact, anywhere in western Texas, such a man, with a knowledge of what is around him, would feel that the Founder of the universe had been partial to and had wonderfully favored this beautiful nook of creation.

The highlands of western Texas are more or less gravelly and rocky; and, as I have before said, produce a finer quality of native grass than do the low or coast lands. But the reader will not forget that each and every section of our country has its peculiar natural advantages over other sections. Large ranges of these high, rolling and hilly lands, with hardly a tree upon them for miles around, except now and then a single tree or cluster, are well supplied with clear running streams, having branches which find their way between the hills down to that stream whose bed may be sand, pebble-stone or rock.

When upon these high but gentle hills, which slope in every direction, valleys, more or less extensive, are all below and around you, and you are seldom out of sight of timber. Again, these beautiful hilly prairies are nicely studded with live oaks and thinly scattered with a variety of trees, single and in groups, which gives great relief to the eye—there are also splendid water-holes, found in sections, which are beautifully overhung with live oak, or shaded in their loveliness by a collection of trees and bushes of some kind. It is upon these countless hills the soul may expand, the thought take wing and fly away into ceaseless space, to return laden with gems of beauty. Here it is that man feels that the *Creator*, in every star and figure of beauty, has pointed to happiness; yet, poor man, he forgets it and goes again to grovel in the dust! O that I might forever remain in those transports of purity and happiness experienced upon these fixed billows of earth! O that I might forever forget every sinful thought and always contemplate the beauties of nature in this our lovely land!

Kind reader, is there anything about your present abode that is distasteful or offensive? Does the sun of your life seem checkered, darkened or obscured? If you would cut loose from every bondage of mind and be contented and free, come and dwell upon the highlands of western Texas. Plant upon the mount of your choice a seed, root or something for every hair of your head, and rear around you golden trees and nature's beauties of our own fair clime. Remember that the turf of your lands, if not at first, may be made of Bermuda and musquete; and that if your

12

cattle do not range upon a hundred hills, the cupola
of your dwelling with the aid of your glass may
o'erlook the herds of useful animals scattered upon
ten times a hundred hills. This is no delusion, no
foolish absurdity, but the simple truth. It would be
very difficult to give the reader anything like a correct idea of all the variety of appearance in the vast
surface of rolling country in western Texas.

The seasons here as in other countries bring their
peculiar appearances. The mirages alone of winter
and spring in the level regions of our country would be
a fit subject for the poet. You are situated, for instance,
upon a small stream, slightly skirted upon either side
with small forest timbers, and as if guarded from every
danger, overhung with massive live oaks reaching
out their giant arms, dangling in their evergreen
fingers their robes of moss, in defiance of the whirl-
wind as it sweeps o'er the plain. The majestic tree
waves its plumage and bids the storm howl on. Here,
in your peaceful hog-walled retreat, the days of summer and autumn pass away with their peculiar routine
of events ; and, ere long, the snows of the north send
their chilly winds of winter—the shades of an evening
are coming on, and all around is as usual—a frosty
night comes and goes—you rise at early morn, go out
and look around, and what do you behold? Where
but yesterday the vision dwindled away to nothingness in the distance, now everything sits gloriously
aloft—the ocean, the lake and the distant plain are
looming up distinctly in view—the far-off city cheer-
fully speaks in little volumes of uprising smoke, that
mingle in one and lay in a cloud upon the air. Little
objects upon the plain assume illusive lights—yonder
groups of trees are looming, up, happy dots upon the
scene. All nature is unmasked and seems pervaded
with change. Refreshing sleep and the cool air of

the morn has braced the system up, the spirits are buoyant, the eyes eagerly gaze on the new and strange scene. Yonder forest must be again examined, distances must be calculated, and every item of the absorbing scene far and near noted down. But, alas, that, that was a moment ago, now is not. The long dense connection of timber upon that river is divided and now in parts is only obscurely seen. The lake that really was is gone, and one that really is not has appeared. Dwellings, far away, that stood distinctly out have disappeared. The city and its grandest hights, are no longer to be seen. The ocean, with its ships of swelling sails and masts of towering hight, have beat a retreat. The distant plain and hights of far-off land o'er yonder forest-top are buried in sunlight's peculiar dusk. The mists of day, far off, in snow-bank clouds arise; the forest is now but here and there a shapeless tree, and now entirely gone. The din of a hundred ox-bells, the bellow of the cow and roar of the bull, the neigh of the horse and bray of the ass; the howl of the wolf and the merry laugh and talk of yonder crowd of mounted stock boys, with the crack of their whips; the rattling and deep roar of the train, the puff and shrill whistle of the engine as it rolls away, all combined with other sounds come o'er the plain, and beat a singular contrast upon the ear. The cattle and playful deer upon a hundred leagues have vanished. The sun is up, and shining forth bids the morn draw its vail, the strange and beautiful scene vanishes and nature is herself again.

To return again to the rolling, open prairies: we find many of them well skirted with timber, in every direction, where there are most lovely sites for dwellings and general improvements, with excellent lands for cultivation. The world of timbered prairie lands

of western Texas is generally rolling and hilly, but
often level. Fine streams make their way through
these timbers upon which there are settlers and a
plenty of room for more. Stock is generally found
in such ranges by hunting up and down the water-
courses and in the little open prairies. Here men
raise their fields of corn, and have their hundreds of
hogs about them which feed and fatten upon the mast
of the timbers. Wheat, oats and the like are here
produced, but so far as I know northern Texas and the
more mountainous portions of western Texas are better for northern grains than are the rolling lands
midway between the mountain ranges and the coast
of our country, yet I have seen good wheat grown
within forty miles of the gulf coast.

People are settled here in these timbered prairies
from Pennsylvania and different northern states, and
are doing well with their few cattle well haunted—a
bunch of mares kept together by a herder and generally having a bell-mare among them, to which every
horse of the herd becomes attached—and besides a fine
lot of hogs many of them have a flock of sheep. One
acre in fifty of these lands, however, are not occupied, and they are generally selling very low. There
are small rich prairies, free from timber, scattered all
through these prairie forests, varying in size from a
hundred to a thousand acres each, and more. Of
course towns or trading posts are convenient throughout the settled portions of western Texas. Of the extreme back and entirely mountainous portions of western Texas the writer is unable to say much From
accounts one would suppose them to be the finest of
country, producing a great variety of fruits, vegetables of every kind, wheat and all northern grains next
to perfection, and unequaled for the raising of sheep,
and surpassing fine for all kinds of stock. Almost

anywhere in the interior of western Texas there can be found timber convenient to any place upon which a person would be likely to settle, and but a few miles from any place he could possibly pitch upon, which timber would answer the purpose of building, unless a person might be pretty independent and could afford to buy lumber.

This is a country where, I believe, aristocracy does not, as yet, kill people—although there are those here who feel their importance; yet there are men of wealth and respectability, in the country, who are living in comfortable log and picket houses, and who have their frame dwellings yet to build, when they feel that they are well prepared so to do. A person can do more as he pleases here, freer from the ridicule and gossip of others than he can in some countries. He can put his money into stock, and build a picket or log house, living in which he can be comfortable and respected. After getting well under way in the stock business, of any kind, he can do almost anything he wishes. There is nothing like having a lot of beeves, mules, wool, mutton, fat hogs, or the like, to turn off when money is needed, especially when it costs but little or nothing to raise them. And again, it does not require an air-tight or closely-built house here to make a person comfortable. I have known new-comers to bring stock from northern and eastern Texas into our western prairies, and live with their families for a year or two in strong cloth tents, until they could inclose a field and make it convenient to build a house, which might then be of pickets, logs, or lumber, according to circumstances. The stock-business in this country, if well looked to, will soon enable the stock-grower to erect a dwelling and make such improvements as will suit him, and have at his command such luxuries as the country affords.

The material for dwellings and all kinds of buildings, aside from the bottom or upland timbers, some
of which split well and make good shingles, is by no
means very limited or inferior, besides the extensive
lumber-yards in our coast-towns, the owners of which
are always prepared to furnish the most extensive
builder with lumber, sash, blinds, and everything of
the kind complete, we have in sections inexhaustible quarries of stone, some of which is soft and easy
to work into a wall, and, after years of exposure, becomes extremely hard, and, I suppose, everlasting.
Most of the building rock of the country is easy to
work, and is considered first rate for the purpose.
An abundance of lime rock is found in sections, and
much more lime would be consumed in the country if
the men were here who would construct kilns and supply the demand, which would certainly be money-
making, as the stone and wood in places would be, if
not quite, almost free. A vast deal of building is now
going on in different parts of the country, the principal material of which is concrete, and I discover that
almost any one of any ingenuity can build up a wall
with this material. The wall is carried up with a box
or boards, between which layers of the concrete, in
the shape of morter, is packed and left until sufficiently dry, when the boards are elevated for another
tier of morter, and so on until the wall is completed.
There are various ways in which this material is
made. In the interior I have seen good fence and
buildings constructed simply of lime and pebble stone,
or gravel. If the wall made of this material is fin-
ished with a coat of cement upon the outside, I am
told it makes a durable and I can say a very pretty
fence. There are fine concrete dwellings in the country made from shell, the lime of shell, and cement,
mixed into a morter and laid up, as above, with boards,

and afterward plastered with cement. Buildings are also made of concrete brick, which are brick of shell and cement, and laid into a wall with cement morter, and afterward plastered with cement. Chimneys are also built in this way for frame houses, and with common brick, stone, and other material.

I should have said, when speaking of building rock, or stone quarries, that in places stone houses are much in use, and continue to be built. Clay bricks are, in places made, and some of our finest buildings are of this material.

Rain water is used to a great extent in this country, and consequently cisterns are required. In the coast-towns there is actual necessity for rain water, but the interior is abundantly supplied with cool springs and clear, running water; yet, from a belief that has become quite prevalent here that rain water is the best in any country, many will have cisterns, although they may have good wells and fine running water just before their doors. These cisterns are, to a certain extent, made of wood in the usual or old fashioned way, and set outside upon the ground, or sometimes under shelter of some kind, or in a room designed for the purpose; but by the permanent settler they are mostly constructed under ground, of cement and shell, pebble stone, or gravel and cement, or else of brick and cement. It requires some experience to build a cistern, of this kind, in a way not to crack. There are many striking proofs of the healthfulness of cistern water in other countries than this, and after drinking it a while, most persons prefer it, and will use no other, if cistern water is to be had.

It is superfluous to add that the climate of western Texas is delightful. I think in Martin's history of Australia, it is said that to go from Europe and live upon that island, is to renew one's youth. This, I think, may be as justly said of western Texas. I believe this climate has as beneficial effects upon the system of the foreigner or new-comer as the climate of Australia or any other country has upon its emigrants. Certain it is that this climate has a tendency to work out all the impurities of the settler's system; and if he is a little careful, during his acclimation, to assist nature a trifle, by taking simple alteratives occasionally, he can lay a new foundation for fine health and a good old age without any difficulty. Of course a stranger seldom thinks of doing anything to cleanse his blood and give a healthy action to his liver or system, whose pores, secretions, or general internal action, gets clogged in throwing off the over-charge of thick blood, animal heat, etc., that he brings here, and must be got rid of, to prepare the system for uniform good order and healthy action in this climate; and, consequently, his acclimation is more severe and of longer duration. What I mean by this is, that men who come here from cold countries, whose systems, of course, are to undergo a change, unless they take some simple alterative in the spring of the year or before the heat of summer to assist nature in effecting this change, they may be troubled with boils, prickly-heat, or something of the kind, upon the skin, which sometimes annoy the foreigner a short time, in the heat of summer, for two or three seasons, particularly those who go back from the coast and work for a living. But as acclimating never kills or injures, and as it is but a wholesome renewal of the system, and drives all corruption, aches, and pains away, what objection is there to it, since, after its experience, one is in a way to enjoy uninterrupted good health, with buoyant spirits, or as much so, probably, as he would in any other part of the world? Some people never experience any difficulty from acclimation, and it may be that a majority of foreigners never feel the least inconvenience from it; but as I am not writing a one-sided thing, I have thought it best to consider this as an objection to the country, though it is really not an objection, but an evil, that good may come. It is no doubt the impression of many that yellow fever is a common thing in western Texas, but this is not the case. It is only here when brought by vessels from New Orleans or some other seat of the disease; and when here, it is confined to the bay or coast-towns to which it is brought, unless those who have been exposed to it go into the interior before attacked, and then the healthy air of the country will not suffer it to spread or take the form of an epidemic. A person living five miles, or even half that distance, away from these towns, apprehends no danger from it. It has been taken a short distance into an interior town of eastern Texas, but it is so seldom an epidemic here, and then only when brought by ships, that I do not know why this should be a place for its consideration, any further than to say that if those who come to western Texas by the way of New Orleans will come when this fever is not an epidemic there, they will meet with no danger from it, and never have any fear of it here, unless they should see fit to remain in one of two or three particular towns of the coast where it might be brought. Of course much of the emigration to western Texas is by land through northern Texas. Such emigrants would never hear of yellow fever any more than where they now are. When we are relieved of the vast amount of vegetable decay in western Texas, no part of the world will surpass it as a healthy region.

The changes of weather in winter in this country, or the sudden appearance of *northers*, when the weather is extremely warm, would be a little surprising to the

13

foreigner, and one would suppose that these northers might be very injurious to health, but I am not aware that they are particularly so. I have no doubt, though, that people from neglect or carelessness, or from accidentally being out without a blanket or warm clothes to put on when these northers come up, sometimes engender disease from the effects of the sudden change. Although they are frequently pretty severely felt here, they would, in the northern states, be nothing more than snug, bracing, fall weather. A person, sometimes, has due notice of the coming of northers, and again they will take him by surprise. If in the winter, snow-caps or huge white clouds are seen in the heavens, dark, towering clouds in the north, with vivid flashes of lightning, and you are in a perspiration from the still, sultry warmth of the weather, and other various indications are visible, you may conclude that a norther is brewing, and ere long a distant roar and rumbling as if all the mad things of earth were let loose together, tells you that hot and cold elements have met and that *mucho-frio* is the hero of the battle. The chilly warrior has o'erwhelmed his foe and comes down upon him with all his fury and devilish howling. To experience one of these very sharp fellows on a broad prairie, in the night, is indeed a grand but dismal event. The howl and fury of the winds as they meet you, the dark dungeon gloom that suddenly envelopes the whole heavens and earth, surprise and bewilder you. But he that has braved the terrific and smothering snow-sweeps of New England or the Canadas, would laugh at norther's frolics and liken him to a roaring but harmless bull without horns. The beauty of the scene follows the dark and frightful beginning as the dark clouds subside and leave the heavens in clear, starry light, except the frown upon its northern brow, coupled with its dreary, icy face. As you travel along and look out upon that chain of prairie fire, with its swelling and receding links, and think of yonder comfortable home, the whistling winds and grizzly north lose their terror, and you are inclined to think it is not so bad after all.

These northers contrast wonderfully with the hot *siroccos* of Australia. When traveling with a party of miners in that country, we were once overtaken by one of these hot winds. We at once put out our cart-horse, which seemed to care nothing about the heat, when we made for trees and places of protection before the winds attained their greatest heat and severity. To try the effects of the hot air, which we had been assured would not injure a person, we would occasionally jump out into a full blast of the wind, and could hardly help thinking that our whiskers were snapping with fire, and that we would roast to a crisp in a few minutes, and back to our shelter we would go. But what astonished us most, was seeing those who were acclimated to those winds traveling along in them as though they were a luxury or nothing to be dreaded. It was supposed at the time that these hot winds were from some unknown desert, somewhere in the unexplored regions of the interior.

All the coast country of western Texas is usually favored with a delightful sea-breeze, penetrating from thirty to forty miles into the interior, and there is generally a fine breeze to relieve the settler or traveler in the open prairies of the interior. The heat upon these prairies is seldom as oppressive as one might suppose it to be. As for cold weather in western Texas, many of these pages were written in a groop or cluster of live oaks, in the open air, in the dead of winter; and so far as cold is concerned, a person could write most of the year, exposed to the elements, with only a shelter over head to keep off occasional rains and the sun. Wagoners and thousands of people sleep out the year through in western Texas. With two good soldier-blankets a person can lay out the coldest and wetest nights that we have in these regions.

RIVERS, DROUGHTY SECTION, SEAPORT AND INTERIOR TOWNS, GRASSHOPPERS, AND GENERAL REMARKS.

The largest river in western Texas is the Rio Grande, the boundary between Texas and Mexico, its length being some eighteen hundred miles. It is navigable by steamboats several hundred miles from its mouth. Much of the land upon this river is beautiful for cultivation, but it is generally cultivated by irrigation. A majority of the inhabitants along this river are Mexicans, and except Brownsville and the towns near the mouth of the river, there are none but Mexican towns upon it. There are American merchants and trading characters among these people along the river, and also American stock growers. There are many forts on the river which makes the country safe for American settlers. By irrigation they raise almost anything upon these valleys—corn, wheat and various grains, a great variety of fruits and vegetables, sugar-cane, etc., are here grown to the greatest perfection, in the peculiar way of farming in droughty countries, and that portion of western Texas along the Rio Grande and some distance east of it, may be considered as a droughty region. But even with this objection it is considered an excellent stock country. It is generally of musquete grass, and its want of water for stock purposes can be easily supplied in the way pastures are sometimes supplied with water in Kentucky, which is by plowing and scraping out basins, in which the stock grower feeds his hogs awhile for the purpose of packing and filling the pores of the earth to prevent the basin from leaking, after which, when once filled, it affords a permanent drinking place for cattle. A similar course could be most successfully adopted in this droughty section of western Texas, where durable rivers, creeks or lasting water are wanting, and many advantages would arise from this natural want of water, upon the principle that "there is no great loss without some small gain." In the first place, any amount of these lands can be bought for a mere nothing, which are as good as can be, only wanting water in dry times ; and, by supplying this want as above described, the stock grower could control his cattle with but little trouble and hardly any expense, as they could not leave their only place of drinking unless in a wet time, when they would not go far away on account of being so thoroughly haunted in the range of these artificial reservoirs. Natural basins can be found all over this country, which, with a little shaping and fixing, after having hogs or stock of any kind fed, penned or yarded, as the northern man would say, in or upon them, for a while, would make durable watering places for stock of all kinds.

The droughty country to which I allude is principally between the rivers Rio Grande and Nueces—a vast musquete section, a majority of which is yet to be occupied, and where beautiful tracts of land can be had for a trifling expense—where as fat beeves and stock as ever grew upon grass can be found in the dead of winter, and where charming homes and fine stock farms can be made and improved in a way to be forever valuable and profitable. All of this particular section of country is near to Mexico, and he who settles in it will have but a short trip to make over into the mongrel nation and pick up an honest dollar in the way of trade.

The outlets to this section of country are Brazos
Santiago and Corpus Christi.   There is steamship
communication between Brazos Santiago, Brownsville
or the mouth of the Rio Grande and New Orleans,
and vessels from different parts of the world visit
Brazos Santiago with cargoes of merchandise for the
Mexican trade, and the trade of the country generally
in the vicinity of the Rio Grande.   These vessels are
here loaded with such articles of export as the interior
of Mexico and the Rio Grande country afford ; some
of which are hides, lead, wool, bullion, etc.   The
steamships, besides taking merchandise, bullion and
usual articles of export, carry away to New Orleans
sheep, cattle, goats and horses.

Certain gentlemen have imported into the Rio
Grande section of western Texas, improved animals,
by steamship, from New Orleans to Brazos Santiago.
Such animals being for the improvement of their
Texas or Mexican stock, it might pay to look into this
matter and see if more of such animals are not
needed in this quarter.   I have seen large flocks of
sheep that were raised on the Texas side of the Rio
Grande, and it is no doubt a fine sheep country and a
good stock country generally.   There has been a
profitable and extensive trade carried on with the
Mexicans at Brownsville, and other points on the
Rio Grande, since the Mexican war, and fine fortunes
have been made and are being made in this trade by
merchants and tradesmen in those ports.   There have
been several attempts made to carry trade into Mexico by unlawful means, (fillibustering), which is a
proof of its being profitable.

I will state that as this matter is about going to
the press, I hear of the disturbance of Cortenas and
his followers, on the Rio Grande, but I can confidently say that this disturbance will be of short dura-

tion, and all will soon be quiet. The state of Texas has taken measures to protect its own frontier, and it will hereafter be perfectly safe.

Corpus Christi, the other outlet to this droughty country, is near the mouth of the Nueces river on Corpus Christi bay. It is a place of no very great importance as yet, and it may never be large; but a town of no little importance must eventually grow up somewhere not far from it, where vessels of good size will make a safe and convenient landing. The trade of the whole Nueces valley and country for some distance in the interior will support this town (Corpus Christi), or some other town that may grow up near the mouth of the Nueces river, which valley and country I have already said is a beautiful musquete region and is unsurpassed for the stock business. To travel up the Nueces river in the valley, upon either side, is what the husbandman or farmer of any country would love to do, and by so doing he could judge something of the capacity of western Texas for the raising of stock, and also of the necessity of a good outlet seaward for this and adjoining country midway between Port Cavallo and Brazos Santiago.

There are several little coast towns between these two points that claim to be good seaports, and some one of them will no doubt be a place of importance, as the country around and the interior that would support it is at this time considered the tiptop cattle range of western Texas. A good seaport and an attractive point of trade somewhere as near the mouth of the Nueces as possible, is deserving the attention of merchants and men of commerce. Corpus Christi and the small towns along the coast between it and Powder Horn have a small craft communication with Powder Horn. But the people of these towns look

forward to the day when they will have a direct communication with New Orleans and other important
places of trade.

In regard to this droughty section or droughty seasons and grasshoppers, I would not be understood that
the Nueces river country is an unusnally dry section.
It is along the Rio Grande and the country east of it
toward the Nueces that is considered droughty; but
it is to this same section of country where I hear that
men have taken their small stocks of cattle for the
purpose of being better able to control them than they
were in ranges where water is more plentiful.

That we have dry seasons in western Texas no one
can deny, and this is the case in Australia and parts
of California, and I believe in all extensive stock
countries where snow does not fall. If western Texas
were a wet country I do not believe it would be a
good stock country, and it, no doubt, would not be as
healthy a country as it now is. I have noticed particularly that stock of all kinds get fatter and do better in dry seasons than in wet ones, although they
have to walk much further for their water. I have
also noticed that stock of all kinds are freer from disease in dry seasons. In wet seasons sheep, unless
rightly managed, contract the liver rot and other diseases, that in dry seasons there is not the least danger of their being troubled with. In wet seasons
horses are troubled with Spanish fever and other diseases that are hardly known in dry seasons; and a
winter following a very wet summer and fall is sometimes very hard upon stock, particularly if they get
thin and weak, when they frequently bog down in
their places of drinking; but wet seasons are not frequent and the death of an animal in Texas is no
calamity to speak of—it costs so little to raise them
that a stock-grower hardly notices or speaks of the

loss of a few animals. Cattle and horses die here upon a prairie and their owners hardly ever take the pains to know the cause of their death. It is but recently that people have been at all particular about skinning and saving the hides of animals. Diseases, however, among stock of any kind are very few in this country, and the loss of stock from diseases in western Texas, is small compared with such losses in the northern states and other countries.

In regard to the effects of drought upon crops, the writer can say that western Texas truly and strictly speaking is a natural stock-raising or grass country, and not generally a superior farming country, although corn and other grains by being early planted and well attended, do very well in all parts of western Texas, and I believe that almost everything that grows can be produced here ; yet, owing to the somewhat uncertainty of the seasons and other causes, western Texas is considered a better stock than a general farming country, although some men say there is no better farming country.

Portions of western Texas have been troubled with grasshoppers ; and, to my certain knowledge, small sections of country have been stripped of their last spear of vegetation by these insects ; such has been the case in Australia, and still wool, beef, wheat, and everything as usual was produced in the country, except in certain small sections. Grasshoppers are liable to visit any country, but, I suppose, are more likely to trouble open prairie countries than those generally occupied, fenced up and cultivated. I have noticed that tramping and cultivating wild lands drives away musquitos, and I have no doubt it has a tendency to keep away grasshoppers. It is a well-known fact that there is a peculiar insect destroyer for almost everything that grows out of the earth, and that these insects trouble different parts of a country at different times, and why grasshoppers should visit western Texas again more than any other country I can not see. Their flight when last here was northerly, and where they will take up, lay their eggs, hatch and destroy again, nobody knows.

This talk about dry weather and grasshoppers in western Texas may cause the emigrant to pause for a moment, but if stock-raising of any kind is his object, let him come on, for drougtht or no drought, hoppers or no hoppers, no where upon the face of the earth can this country be beat at the stock business; and I sometimes think that those sections of western Texas, where dry weather prevails most, were designed purposely for sheep—sheep seem to do so remarkably well in our high and dry regions. Some of the finest sheep ranges of Australia are equally as dry as the droughty sections of western Texas. In conclusion upon this subject, the weather in this country, as a general thing, is about as the stock-grower is glad to be favored with, on account of ticks, branding their increase, diseases of stock and other reasons that I will not use space to dwell upon. For my part I prefer pleasant dry to drizzling disagreeable wet weather.

The Colorado, which I shall consider as the eastern boundary of western Texas, running somewhat centrally through the state, is the next river east in size to the Rio Grande, and is about seven hundred miles in length. Were it not for contemplated railroads this, no doubt, would eventually be made a navigable river for some distance into the interior. The Colorado bottoms are of a rich, reddish soil, and are generally pretty heavily timbered as far up the river as the rich bottom and planting lands extend. The width of the Colorado valley is from four to ten miles. Sometimes upon one side the naked prairie bluffs on

the river, and upon the opposite side the valley, may
be six miles, more or less, in width and heavily timbered. Again it is heavily timbered and is a wide
valley upon either side of the river.

This river is settled by cotton and sugar planters,
and most excellent crops do they raise. Much of
these bottom lands are yet unoccupied, and are for
sale, but at higher prices than are the prairie lands
adjoining them, or the lands generally from that on to
the Rio Grande, excepting now and then rich bottom
lands upon smaller rivers. Large stock-growers are
also settled upon the Colorado, and their cattle range
over the vast prairies upon whichever side of the river
the stock-grower may be.

This river empties into Matagorda bay, not far from
the town of Matagorda. Small craft ply between this
town and the main landing of steamships (Lower Indianola) in the bay. Persons wishing to settle west
of the Colorado river generally land at Powder Horn
or Lower Indianola, which are one and the same.
The reason for confining myself to this particular
scope of country is because the most of it is never
troubled with snow, and a vast amount of it is covered
with the musquete grasses, and is otherwise so favored
that I believe no extent of country of its dimensions
upon the face of the earth can excel it for stock-raising purposes. Of course I do not include the desolate plain above and between the head-waters of the
Colorado and the Rio Pecos.

The next river of any note west of the Colorado is
the Navidad, which connects with the Lavacca river a
short distance above its mouth or entrance into Lavacca bay. Texana, a town of considerable trade
and importance, is situated on the west bank of the
Navidad, several miles above its junction with the
Lavacca river. It is the trading point for stock-

growers and planters for many miles around. Small
vessels ply between this town and Lavacca, an extensive port of Matagorda bay, about ten miles from the
principal landing of steamships in this bay.

Austin, the capital of the state, is on the Colorado,
about two hundred miles from its mouth. The rich
bottom lands of the Colorado continue on above Austin, and the rolling prairie lands about this city corre-
spond with much of the beautiful country, and would
give the traveler a pretty good idea of large regions
of western Texas.

I am sorry to say that I am able to take the reader
above the city of Austin with only hear-say and what
I have read. From the many representations that I
have seen and heard in regard to the country west
and north-west of Austin, I can safely say that it is a
charming sheep country. But when you say north
of Austin, you are getting into regions where the
winters are more severe, and where I suppose it is
necessary to store up hay, etc., for the wintering of
stock. It may be, and I am inclined to think is the
case, that with the cultivated musquete and bermuda
grasses, rightly managed, northern Texas could winter stock generally without storing up hay or food to
any great extent. That northern Texas is a beautiful
stock country, all who are acquainted with it agree.
But I wish to confine myself, principally, to a section
of country where stock can live upon grass the year
through, without having hay or anything else laid up
to feed it in winter, and this section comprises most
of the immense country between the Colorado and
Rio Grande rivers, over much of which the writer has
repeatedly traveled.

The largest rivers between the Nueces and Navidad, are the Guadaloupe and San Antonio. These
rivers connect some distance above their entrance into

Espirite Santo bay, which bay has a navigable connection with Matagorda bay. The navigation of the Guadaloupe has been several times attempted, and steamboats are now, irregularly, running as high as Victoria upon this river, from the landing of steamships at lower Indianola, but without much hope of successfully continuing.

The San Antonio, and several of the rivers of western Texas, are frequently spoken of as affording good water privileges for mills and manufacturing establishments requiring any amount of power.

Cotton is extensively produced along the Guadaloupe, and its valley, for some distance, is wide and heavily timbered. There are also several very pretty towns situated on this stream. Cotton is produced to a small extent on the San Antonio, but I believe this river is considered the terminus of cotton lands westward and southward in Texas. I am, however, so little acquainted with the culture of this great staple of the south, that I should be out of place in attempting to say much of it. But I can say that cotton-growers in Texas seem to be a wealthy and prosperous people, and, so far as I know, a democratic people, of whom a country should be proud.

The timbered valley lands of the San Antonio are principally below Goliad. Above this town the river is not so heavily timbered. But its valleys are, to a great extent, of beautiful musquete lands on to the head of the river; and the country through which the upper San Antonio runs may be considered a pretty good musquete section, though its grass is considerably mixed with the sedge.

There are several pretty towns on the San Antonio river. Goliad and San Antonio are the two largest, and the last mentioned is the second largest city in the state. This city is about a hundred and sixty miles

from Matagorda bay, and a railroad from Lavacca
and lower Indianola—several miles of which are already completed, and thirty or forty graded—will
soon, no doubt, give San Antonio and intermediate
stations, and the surrounding country, a quick communication with the gulf-towns and New Orleans.
Besides the rivers already mentioned which empty
into the bays along the gulf-coast, between the Rio
Grande and Colorado, there are numerous others, the
most of which should, perhaps, be denominated creeks.
There are also bayous, of various sizes, between these
rivers, making out from the bays, which reach, as a
general thing, but a short distance inland.   The outer
coast of this section of country is almost a continuous
narrow strip of land, with only here and there a pass
or an entrance from the gulf of Mexico into the different bays, which are a continuous body or connection
of waters along the whole coast of western Texas.
These narrow divisions of land or islands between
the gulf and bays are generally stocked with cattle.

The rivers which I have mentioned and many others
of less size, are of course never-failing, and when the
usual places of watering sometimes give out, cattle
and horses resort to these rivers for water.   There are
also many streams, scores of which are of good size,
making into these various rivers, and this portion of
the state, except the droughty section alluded to, is
well supplied with running water.

The hilly and mountainous portions of this section
of country are more or less favored with beautiful
springs of fine cool water.   There are also many small
lakes and ponds, of various sizes, which are fine for
the watering of stock.   Also, many lagoons or places
of water in the beds of creeks that cease to run in dry
times,—such as half the island of Australia depends
upon to a great extent.

Now it is to these many rivers, bayous, lakes, ponds, creeks, lagoons, etc., from the Colorado to the Rio Grande, and from the gulf-coast of this country to the headwaters of the Nueces, San Antonio, Guadaloupe, and Colorado rivers, that I would call the attention of settlers. I have already spoken of droughty sections; of wide prairies wanting in wood and water; where good lands, in any quantity, in the finest of ranges for stock, can be had at present for a mere nothing; and have shown how easily and advantageously these wants can be supplied. But now it is to the tens and hundreds of thousands of acres of unoccupied lands along and about these many streams of water, that I would call the attention of those who come to western Texas to engage in the stock-business. This large tract of country, of several hundred miles square, embracing a great variety of soil, surface, general appearance, and climate, will every foot of it produce, in abundance, the fine grasses of which I have said so much. And unless its climate materially changes—unless the sun withhold its present warmth, or some unforeseen evil befall it—this particular section of country, when clothed in rich, cultivated grasses, will be a second Eden, producing as much for the support and good of mankind as any section of country, of its dimensions, in the wide world; and he that gets a home here will be a fortunate person. For here he or his children, with the least exertion, could never want. To point out the thousands of desirable, unoccupied localities, and fine tracts of land, fronting upon rivers and durable streams, or those that are plentifully watered and timbered, or in the midst of good ranges, that would do for stock-farms, small and large, in this section of country, would be the work of years upon a thousand pages. But before concluding this work, I will give the reader some directions about finding desirable localities and cheap lands for stock-raising purposes in western Texas.

FISH, OYSTERS, SHRIMPS, TURTLE, ETC.

The rivers, creeks, and lakes of the country are full of fish, and its bays, bayous, and coast afford the finest of oysters, shrimps, turtle, and fish. The principal fresh-water fish of western Texas are the cat, buffalo, sucker, trout, pike, perch, and carp. The jew, red, mullet, flounder, sheephead, trout, and bass, are some of our great variety of coast or salt-water fish. The various ways of taking fish, oysters, etc., in this country are the same, I suppose, as in all countries. The turtle to which I allude, are as heavy, when alive, as our beef-cattle ordinarily dress. They are caught in different ways, but the easiest way of getting them is to surprise them when out of water, or when benumbed with cold on the beach, and whap them over on their backs, where they will lay powerless. Alligators are plentiful in the bayous, lakes, and large ponds of the country, and they are in all our rivers that empty into the gulf, but principally low down in or near the mouths of these rivers. Their oil and skins are said to be valuable.

GAME OR ANIMALS

Hunted in western Texas, are deer, antelope, mountain sheep, wild goat, buffalo, wild cattle, wild hogs, javelena, or Mexican hog, bear, wolf, prairie dog, panther, leopard, wild cat, tiger, coon, opossum, jack, and common rabbit, squirrel, otter, beaver, muskrat, etc.

DEER.—He is no huntsman at all who can't go out and get a fine buck or doe, in a short time, in any prairie of western Texas.. A slide or stone boat, drawn by a yoke of oxen, is a good thing upon which to secrete one's self for the purpose of approaching deer. The usual way of hunting these animals is on horseback. The huntsman, to get near to a deer, or herd of deer, gets down and walks by the side of his horse, which is frequently trained to the work. Deer are easily approached by fixing the horns of these animals upon the head, with a dress and action in imitation of their own. When traveling through our prairies in the spring of the year, young fawn are often started from their hiding-places, and are easily run down with a good horse. The venison of this country is most excellent eating, and there is hardly a family in the country who does not use it to some extent, and many families are seldom without it. Deer are here seen in droves of all sizes; bunches of ten, twenty, and thirty, are very common, and a hundred are frequently seen together; and I have been in plain sight of a thousand and more at once, not far from the Nueces river, but in different droves.

ANTELOPE.—The antelope is much the same, at a distance, as a deer. They out-run the deer, and are noted for their beautiful appearance when running. Their horns are short, and nothing to be compared with those of the deer. I believe they are seldom seen along the coast, but are as plentiful back among the hills and fine sheep ranges, as are deer upon or near to the coast. The meat of the antelope is most excellent, and they are as easily taken in the interior as are deer upon our coast prairies. I am told, that by swinging over the head a piece of red cloth, attached to the end of a ramrod, antelope will circle around and come within shooting distance of you. I was recently told by a wagon-master that the men of his train shot not less than thirty of these animals while coming through upper western Texas, and that he saw thousands of them. Their size is about the same as that

14

of the deer, but I believe they are somewhat more compact and heavy.

MOUNTAIN SHEEP.—The mountain sheep I have never seen, but have repeatedly talked with those who have seen them. Some contend that what is called the Rocky Mountain sheep is really the antelope. Whatever they may be they are really a curiosity. That they will throw themselves from a great hight and light upon their skulls and wonderful horns, I have been assured is a fact by those who have taken pains to know. That the concussion from the fall or leap, in the way that they strike, does not kill them, is not so remarkable as is the fact of their ability to throw themselves such a frightful distance and control their position in the air, in a manner to strike upon their horns in the peculiar way that they do.

WILD GOAT.—The wild goat I know nothing of except by hearsay, unless they are the same as the mountain goat to which I alluded someway back; and, judging from descriptions that I have heard of them, I should suppose them to be the same, which leaves the supposition that they may be domesticated.

BUFFALO OR BISON.—The buffalo or bison I have already spoken of as migrating back from the settled portions of western Texas. They are to be found in upper western Texas, and are hunted by gangs of Mexicans, Indians and white men, who jerk and save their meat to some extent, and preserve their hides for robes, etc,

WILD CATTLE.—Wild cattle, besides those to which I have alluded, are found in places where there are no other cattle. They are hunted in places principally for their hides, but their meat, tallow and horns are saved to a great extent. The Rio Grande country affords a vast amount of beautiful hides. Wild cattle will soon be killed off or driven beyond the limits of good ranges for stock in western Texas.

WILD HOGS.—Wild hogs are plentiful in this country, and many a happy day is there spent in the bottoms and timbers of western Texas in pursuit of these animals. Dogs are trained expressly for tracking and baying hogs, which enables the rifleman to approach and send his bullets among them. Some families in western Texas have but little hog meat except what is secured in this way. But hogs are frequently caught in this way which are not considered wild hogs. They may be those having the ear mark of the owner, which from long use in the bottoms and timbers have become so shy that baying them with dogs and shooting them is the most expeditious way of getting hold of them just when they are wanted, which is during cold snaps of weather when their meat can be safely cured.

JAVELENA OR MEXICAN HOG.—The javelena or Mexican hog is an animal that I have heard much of but have never happened to see, although I have been in and around those musquete thickets, the Brazados of western Texas, where they are said to be plentiful. These animals are a singular species of the hog. They are small, but when molested very fierce, and it is a dangerous business for man or dog to meddle with them without using great precaution in the attack. They are said to have a kind of musk-bag upon their body, which makes them offensive to the smell, and unless it is taken away as soon as killed they are considered by some as not fit to eat. Others say that they have eaten them regardless of this and doubt their having any such offensive part about them. They are sometimes caught and sent abroad and sell for a good price as a curiosity.

BEARS.—I suppose there are several kinds of bears

in this country, but I have seen only the black bear, which is quite plentiful in parts of western Texas. There are many men here who delight in hunting the bear and who have good dogs for the purpose. Bear meat in this country is fine eating when fat. They are somewhat destructive to hogs in the bottoms.

WOLVES.—There is no wild animal in the country so destructive as the wolf. They are of two kinds, prairie and mountain or cayote and lovo. The howl of these devilish things is yet to be heard upon almost any prairie in western Texas. They are, however, easily killed by scattering pieces of meat around the prairie, or wherever they come, with a little strychnine carefully secreted within them. Stock-growers sometimes drag a dead animal or a large piece of meat some distance through the prairie, and occasionally leave a piece of meat properly dosed with poison in its trail, and wolves, if there are any about, will follow up this trail and eat this poisoned meat, and are generally found dead not far from where they find these effective doses. Stock-boys when cattle hunting frequently start up these rogues and give them chase. A number of us once came upon a wolf in the act of eating a calf that it had just killed. We took after it but it was so full of blood and fresh meat that it would occasionally stop and try to throw up to relieve itself and make better headway, but we were so close upon its heels he could find time only to gag and be off. The boys were soon throwing their ropes, at which he would snap and dodge; but a rope was finally fastened upon him, and the horse dashing away with one end of it at the horn of the saddle and the other snugly around a forefoot of the wolf, he dangled and dragged along until he seemed quite willing to lie down and die from the blow of a quoit that was dealt upon his pate. These animals do not destroy as many calves upon our prairies as one would suppose they might. Whenever a young calf is caught by one of them it gives the bawl of alarm and all the cattle within hearing rally around, make a great fuss and drive the wolf away. I have seen the prairie wolf take hold of a young calf when there was no other cattle but the mother of the calf about, and she alone would compel the wolf to let loose his hold. I once saw an affray of this kind where, after the cow had driven the wolf away from her calf, the whelp jumped at the cow and for a whole hour, at intervals, would cut up his antics around the mother for the purpose of getting the calf a little away from her in order that he might take another hold, but the calf instinctively kept close to the mother while she was desperately thrusting her horns at the cunning wolf. Sheep and goats, unless in an old settled place, require constant guarding in some way against these animals in western Texas. Many wool-growers in the upper country have proof folds for their sheep, and others have their shepherds lie down of a night near their flocks with their dogs about them.

PRAIRIE DOGS.—Prairie dogs are sometimes brought in from the interior of Texas and domesticated. They are a curiosity, and being small many people are glad to get hold of them as pets. Since the discovery of the Pike's Peak mines I see much is said of them by the papers throughout the country; but I have seen no account of their flesh being good to eat which I hear is the case.

PANTHER, ETC.—The panther, leopard, wild cat and tiger are found in different parts of western Texas, and are more or less destructible to all kinds of stock. They are frequently killed by our citizens and huntsmen.

COON, OPOSSUM, ETC.—The coon, opossum, jack

and common rabbit are as plentiful in western Texas and probably more easily secured than in almost any other country.

SQUIRRELS.—Of the squirrel I have seen but two kinds: one, a ground squirrel much like the northern *chipmunk*, the other in size and color between the common red and gray squirrel of the north, which last are very plentiful in western Texas.

MINK, OTTER, ETC.—Mink, otter, beaver, muskrat and weasel I have never seen here, but am told that they are found in the upper country.

FOX.—The fox is in the upper country and of different colors—silver gray and red I am told.

POLECAT.—The polecat is here all over any of our prairies; as I have heard it asserted the fur of these ill-smelling animals is found to be valuable, a person could pay himself to travel our prairies and kill them for their fur.

How many of the animals that I have mentioned, and what other animals in western Texas, are valuable for their fur, I do not know; but I should suppose that the huntsman and trapper might do well here in pursuit of animals for their skins and fur.

GAME, OR BIRDS—Hunted in western Texas are the turkey, sand-hill crane, prairie chicken, quail, plover, snipe, pigeon, swan, geese, ducks, etc. Our fancy and song birds are the mocking-bird, red bird, whip-poor-will, bird of paradise, turtle dove, etc.

The wild turkey is excellent for the table, and there are any quantity of them in western Texas. I have often been with crowds of stock-boys when coming upon droves or scattering turkeys in open prairies. Here and there would go a man or boy for his turkey, but not as hard as he could run at first. If he understands the work, he will try and keep the bird on foot as far as possible, for the purpose of getting it wearied before it takes the wing. But when he flies, the rider increases his speed, and if the turkey's wings give out any considerable distance from the timber for which he is making, the horseman is almost sure to overtake and capture him; but if the turkey can gain the timber, he is safe, unless the rider has a revolver or gun, with which he can sometimes ride near to the tree where the turkey is and shoot him down.

In the spring of the year, when the males gobble, there are thousands of turkeys shot in this country by the hunter camping out or going early in the morning into the bottoms or timbers where they are, and, on hearing them gobble, carefully approach and shoot them down from their place of roosting. They are sometimes made to gobble by imitating the hen, which is often done with the help of a peculiar bone taken from the turkey, and so fixed that by placing it to the mouth a very accurate imitation of the hen turkey is made; and many a strutting gobbler, in responding to the call of this bone, brings upon himself the unerring level of the hunter's rifle. Most people, with a little practice, can imitate the hen without the aid of the bone. Turkeys are here frequently hunted with dogs, trained for the purpose of flying them into trees, when the hunter shoots them down. They are found high and low wherever there is timber.

SAND-HILL CRANE.—The sand-hill crane is a bird somewhat larger than the turkey, with much longer legs and neck, and no tail. They are of two colors — white and light gray—the former being a little the largest. During the winter and spring they are very numerous upon our prairies. Where they go to hatch, I do not know. They are rather shy, although plenty of them are shot; and when properly cooked they are fine for the table.

PRAIRIE CHICKEN.—Prairie chickens are nowhere

more numerous than here, and they are easily shot by
any one who knows how to handle a gun. I have,
repeatedly, seen a gentleman and his' wife riding in
their buggy along the road or through the prairie, and
every now and then stop their horse for the purpose
of shooting a prairie chicken which their pointer had
set, and which the gentleman would shoot while standing in his buggy. After picking up the bird and re-
loading the discharged barrel, the gentleman would
get in and drive along until soon the fixed position of
the dog would bring them to a stand, and bang goes
the charge for another chicken. A dozen of these
birds are soon obtained in this way, upon our prairies.
Their nests are frequently found with a dozen or more
eggs, which sometimes afford the stock-boy a hearty
meal.

The New England quail are plentiful here, and are
a pretty mark for the hunter; and there is no more
tempting dish than their plump little bodies make. A
prettier sight there never was than a couple of quails
with their dozen little ones, just off the nest, tripping
along upon a sandy level. I have never seen them
driven into nets, as in Illinois. I believe they are a
little more shy here than in the North. Like the
prairie chicken, they are found all over western Texas.

PLOVER, SNIPES AND PIGEONS.—Plover are here in
abundance, but near the coast, principally, I believe.
They are a plump bird, and pretty game. Snipes are
everywhere, fat and fine, in western Texas. Wild
pigeons are seldom seen near the coast, but are more
or less plentiful in the upper country. I suppose the
more general production of the cereal grains nearer
the coast would bring them there.

SWAN.—Swan, geese and ducks are here during the
fall, winter and spring, in such numbers as were never
seen in any country but this. It is not unusual in

spring to see our bays and lakes for miles out, and along the beach as far as one can see, covered with millions of these water-birds. The beautiful swan is more shy than geese or ducks; but a good marksman may kill thousands of them. Their downy skins are very valuable when well preserved; and why a good marksman could not make money here at the saving of these beautiful, downy skins, I do not know. Their skins are worth several dollars each. It is said that when coming upon a flock of swan on a windy day, when out upon our prairies, if they are suddenly rushed upon, on horseback, and driven with the wind, they can not fly up, or rise from the ground, and they are easily shot among in this way.

GEESE.—Geese frequent, in flocks of hundreds, our short-grass prairies, and fatten upon tender grass and herbage. They can be seen by thousands at a time, in different flocks, upon our prairies. They light near dwellings, where the grass is short and sweet, and where they can nearly always be found for weeks together. They are a little shy, and know pretty well the distance to keep from an armed man. But any one can shoot them, and a good marksman can take down as many as he wishes. They are of two kinds, and are here called brant and geese. The brant are of a dull blue color, and their noise is more like the noise of the domesticated goose of our country. The geese are of a brown color, with black about their wings, breast and head. They are not considered first-rate eating, though, when well cooked and with the right kind of dressing, they are very good. It is not long since I saw a person who had a hat lantern constructed, with which to bewilder geese in the night. With this "torch-hat," as he called it, he said he could go among them and kill them with a club. He said he could get to them in ponds of water better than any

15

where else—the reflection of the rays of light upon the water having a peculiar effect upon their eyes, I suppose, is the reason of this. Should they fly up before getting near to them, he said they would come all about the light, which would enable him to occasionally strike one down. I have no doubt that the hat-lantern, torch-light, or whatever it might be called, would prove successful in approaching geese in very dark and foggy · nights, as I have myself made fires in thick clusters of trees near to ponds of water in which there were geese, and after frightening them up they would fly about the motts, and frequently come so low that they would strike the trees, and come flopping and tumbling down through the branches to the ground. Of course, when striking and tangling in the trees, the flopping of their wings could be heard, which would enable one to get nearly or quite under their place of falling, and ready to pick them up or strike them with a stick. Sometimes, when striking the trees with their wings spread, they would lie where first lodged, upon the dense foliage, for a half hour or more, dazzled by the light of the fire through the branches; and when tired of their position, would commence flopping, and down they would come. It takes a dark, misty night to do this, and in such a night a number of persons could soon procure feathers enough to make a fine bed, and as many geese as they would wish. I have several times, when cattle hunting, camped near ponds of water in which there were thousands of geese; and during the night, wolves, coons, or animals of some kind, would, every little while, slyly rush in upon the geese and keep them flying and squalling, and often succeed in catching them.

Let the reader imagine himself, of a dark, misty and stormy night, out upon a prairie in a cluster of trees, in which there is a large fire. It being a wet time, the ponds all about these trees are full of· water, in which there are thousands of geese and ducks, and loud-voiced cranes are about. Now, suddenly, rush into these ponds, upon your horse, among these geese and ducks, and start them up; soon they are flying in every direction, and the air is alive with these squeaking birds. The strong winds hurl them here and there in their efforts to rise and contend with the furious gale. The bewildering blaze brings them to and fro about and above the cluster of trees. Now, being lost and allured by the glimmering of the fire, they come too low, strike the trees, and fall an easy prey to those underneath, provided they are keeping a sharp lookout and get ready for the fall. Upon such occasions I have known sand-hill cranes to join in the dark and noisy confusion, and come flopping down through the trees, and run directly into the fire. This, no doubt, would be new to many Texans; but any one who will take the trouble to try the thing, in a dark and stormy night, and in a suitable place, will find my statements correct.

DUCKS.—Wild ducks are of many kinds and colors in western Texas, and their size is from that of a bantam hen up to that of the smaller brant. Many of them are not only beautiful in color, but excellent for the table. When returning, in the fall of the year, from their periodical northern flight, they go every day to the mast producing timbers and fill their crops with acorns. When the acorns, etc., are gone, they live upon tender herbage and grass. The little boys of the towns or country go out upon their gentle ponies, from whose backs they can safely fire their guns, and soon return with fine lots of ducks, geese, etc., etc., hanging to the horns of their saddles. For many months of the year they are very plentiful in and about all the fresh waters of the country. They

are also along the coast in bayous, salt water ponds,
and, as I have said, line the beach of the bays. I am
told that they lay along the shores or shallow waters
of our bays and live upon the little fish and what they
can find in the muddy bottom.

SONG-BIRDS.—Of our song-birds I will mention only
the mocking-bird, which is indeed the most interesting
of the feathered tribe in all the land. If the western
Texan's dwelling is well-surrounded with shade-trees,
he is not only blessed with the music of these birds
by day, but can hear their wonderful mimicry the live-
long night.

FANCY BIRDS.—Of beauties I will mention the red-
bird, whose song is sweet, but without many variations. They have become so tame, when about the
door-yard, that they will come to the door of the house
and pick up crumbs of bread within an arm's length
of you. My little boy has had them so tame that they
would come every day from the timber to the door of
the house for their feed of crumbs.

UGLY BIRDS.—Of our ugly birds I will mention the
buzzard, which is valuable as a scavenger. If an animal dies upon our prairies, these birds are the first to
discover it; and many a dead animal is found and a
valuable hide saved by the stock-grower, who observes
these birds as they collect and fly over the dying or
dead animal. It is said that these birds fly to a tremendous hight every day of their lives. They have
a singular habit of standing upon branches of trees,
fences, etc., and holding out their ample wings, perhaps for an hour at a time. Does not this, and their
high flights, indicate that they need considerable air-
ing in order to be agreeable to their not very sweet
smelling selves? The egg of the buzzard is much
like that of the turkey; and although the color of the

grown bird is dark or quite black, the young buzzard is white, and a comical looking thing it is.

THE EAGLE.—The king of birds, both the gray and bald eagle are here; and in the motts and lone trees out upon our broad prairies, their nests of sticks and coarse material are found. Here their shrill notes are heard in defiance of everything but man, and when he approaches to disturb their nest or young, they hover around as if to say, "Thou art my only dreaded foe."

THE CHRISTIAN MAN.

Who doubts that this is the place to live? Although the luxuries and refinements of older countries are not so much to be found; although some of us who are here might be better than we are, and a better state of morals and more decency might exist in some places; yet education, religion, society, morals, etc., are fast brightening up, and are certain to do as much for western Texas as these great elevators of man can do for any part of the world. And it is a good country for the good and Christian man. And why? Because there is a plenty of room here, and the good man can be unmolested in the enjoyment of his religion and property, and his example would exert a good influence upon those around him; because the good man's character would here, as in other places, stand transcendently out, and he would be looked up to and respected for his virtues. There are a plenty of men who, if not very good, have a reverence for the moral man, and would act uprightly and conduct themselves properly in his presence and within his knowledge, when otherwise they might not. I suppose no one would deny that a greater moral restraint would make a happier country of this, and that more truly moral men would benefit our communities, which should make it an inducement for the Christian to come, and a satisfaction for him to live here, since he could do it so profitably to himself and others.

RICH MAN.—This is a good country for a rich man, because he can here invest his money with more certainty of a fine income, with less attention, and feeling less anxiety for its safety, than he could in almost any other country. He can here purchase property, not with fear or apprehension of a depreciation, but with a certainty of its advance in value. He could here, if I may be allowed the expression, be a king among men, and not a man among kings. Gentlemen, or moneyed men, are living in nearly all the towns of western Texas, who own large stocks of cattle, horses, etc., upon our prairies, and· who sometimes own a ranche, ·riding-horses, etc., for the management of their stock, and again they pay by the head, or give a share of the increase for branding and the little attention their stock requires.

MERCHANT AND PLANTER.

This is a good country for the merchant, because the profits of trade and traffic are large, and the mercantile business, well managed here, is sure to make a person rich in a short time—at least, so it seems to me. I do not exactly understand the reason why, but certain it is that merchants, as a general thing, do better in western Texas than I have ever known them, as a class, do in any other country. I have frequently heard it remarked by merchants here, that stock-growers are their most ready cash customers. It is not unusual for the cotton crop of western Texas to fail, consequently cotton-growers frequently run long accounts. But the stock-man, always on hand with the money or a crop of beeves, mules, or something that will readily bring the cash, keeps the merchant on his "taps" until the planter makes a crop, which enables him to settle his long running account. Cotton, for the last season or two, has done better, and has raised the drooping hopes of many who had almost given up western Texas as a planting country. How much of the country west of the Colorado river bottoms will prove itself as reliable for cotton, I suppose is not yet determined. I have always considered western Texas as a great southern stock country, and I have yet to change my opinion. But if the seasons were generally different, I suppose there would be no better cotton lands than the river-bottoms of western Texas. I am acquainted with a large slave-holder, who, years ago, abandoned the raising of cotton in one of the best localities of western Texas; as too uncertain a business for him, *as he said*. He turned his force to the raising of mules, cattle, and the extensive production of pork, bacon, etc. I have talked with other large and reliable planters of western Texas, who say they would not exchange their localities for any that they know of in the older cotton-growing states, and probably not for any in the world.

It may seem a contradiction to say that the merchant of our country does remarkably well when the cotton-grower, who should be, to a great extent, his support, does not so well. But the truth is, cotton-growers are also, to some extent, stock-growers, and of late better crops of cotton have been produced; and it is to be hoped that the seasons of western Texas may continue favorable for the production of this "king" of crops, and call to the country planters to occupy all its good cotton lands. Should the seasons of western Texas continue favorable for cotton, planters could not do better than come here and secure the rich bottom lands of the country.

A good share of our merchants, in addition to their stores, have stock-ranches, and not unfrequently ex-

change goods for stock; and by employing a stock-
man to attend to their ranches, or their stock, if they
have no ranches, they carry on the two branches
greatly to the advantage of each other. The merchant frequently concerns some sharp-eyed fellow
with him, and sends him off, with a little money, to
Mexico for a drove of horses and mules. He sometimes sends on, in charge of an experienced, trusty
fellow, a drove of horses, mules, or beeves, to the
north; and, in purchasing such drove, he frequently
collects outstanding accounts, or exchanges goods for
animals, to some extent, and often making up a drove,
by hook and crook, and getting it well on the way, he
goes on by water and rail in time to meet his drove,
at some designated place, and, turning it into cash or
good short paper, to the best advantage he can at
Chicago or some other point, goes on to New York
and pays up, makes a fresh purchase of goods for his
store, and comes home.

Merchants also purchase and exchange goods for
various products of the country, such as hides and
peltry, wool, pecans, moss, etc. They also engage,
more or less, in shipping beef and veal-cattle, mules,
horses, etc., to New Orleans, Mobile, Cuba, and other
places.

Previous to the last two seasons, I noticed that it
was not an unusual thing for a merchant to get a
mortgage upon a plantation and negroes in western
Texas. But I have never yet known a stock-man
under the necessity of mortgaging his property in
order to make ends meet. This is not because the
stock-grower does not go in debt, but because when,
from any imprudence, or from going in debt for cattle,
lands, or to his merchant, finds himself troubled to
meet his payments, he can do as I have repeatedly
told him. But the planter, when he gets "pinched,"

can not sell his cotton and sugar until it is in the bale or hogshead, unless he pledges his crop before it is grown, and then, from drought or some other cause, it might fail, leaving him in the merchant's debt, his expenses are heavy and his debts increasing, which too often results in a mortgage upon his plantation and negroes.

There are other reasons for the ill success of the planter in western Texas. In coming to the country with his force and family, he incurs a large expense, and in the purchase and improvement of new lands, building, etc., another large outlay follows. His account, upon arrival here, commences with his merchant, depending, as he generally does, upon his first year's crop to meet his engagements, which crop is to be raised in a new climate, where the seasons are different, and upon new land, the like of which he is unaccustomed to tilling, and the correct management of which he does not exactly understand; and having relied too much upon his ability as a cotton-grower in the old state from whence he came, and consequently being a little extravagant and regardless of expense, he too often finds himself in debt, with perhaps but a fourth of a crop of cotton, which barely pays the expense of raising. Now comes the land-holder for the balance due upon the plantation, and the merchant for a mortgage upon his negroes and other property, which staggers the planter and leaves him but a short and unsuccessful career.

Now, although I am out of my place, I will venture to give the planter who comes to western Texas a little advice, that may not be to his disadvantage. When he arrives let him be moderate in the purchase of lands, which sould be of the rich river bottoms, with perhaps a strip of prairie. Let him invest, say one half or a portion of his means in cattle and horses, and of course he would get a stock of hogs, and if in the right kind of range, he might get a flock of sheep; but he should be careful how he meddles with sheep, unless he.has a great taste and inclination for the business. Now we will suppose, that with this kind of a start, his first and possibly his second crop of cotton fails. How is the planter to get along? Is he to be broken up? If he has been prudent and economical, it seems to me, not. Although his cattle, horses, and sheep, might not, at first, afford him as much of an income as would abundant crops of cotton, yet, in case of failure of his cotton crop, his stock would be his salvation. And again, should the country or his particular locality eventually prove too uncertain for the growth of cotton, could he not plant his rich bottom lands in musquete and bermuda, and still be " king" in the way of stock-grower?

I have known several planters to come here and go in debt, as I have stated, and from the failure of crops become largely involved, when, if they had invested a portion of their means, or parted with a share of their force, and put the proceeds thereof in stock, they would have undoubtedly got along until they could have been favored with a good season for cotton, the large proceeds of which would have swept their debts away.

I do not say this for those planters who are here and know ten times as much about the thing as myself; but for those who may come to the country in circumstances that could be easily embarrassed in this peculiar climate.

To the planter who has started as I have suggested, I say as I have said to the stock-grower: If he finds himself cramped to meet his payments, let him turn to his stock and dispose, if need be, of all the male animals or beef-cattle, young and old, from his stock, to the best advantage he can; part with his yearling males, wether sheep and lambs, wool, or anything that will not injure the increasing capacity of his stock. At the same time, let him watch old and successful planters, and make all necessary inquiries in regard to the proper management of the cotton crop in western Texas; let him work early and late, breaking up and preparing his lands for a good crop, which, by perseverance, will surely, sooner or later, bless him and enable him to "square his yards."

Would my remarks discourage the emigration of cotton-growers to western Texas?

Let us see how this really is. In the year 1860 we will bring A. from Alabama to western Texas, with a force of negroes, and settle him upon a certain river, where he shall improve a place with the expectation of getting a crop from the first planting. He contracts debts with the idea of paying them with his first crop of cotton; and, feeling sure of a crop, he has perhaps made some debts that he could possibly have avoided. His crop, from some cause, fails. He gets the payment, now due upon his plantation, put over to next year, and his merchant is also put off until the next crop. The next year he gets no crop, or but a slim one, and he begins to feel the weight of his debts, which are presented for payment, and he has nothing with which to meet them, except his negroes and the plantation with its appurtenances. The result is bad: A. and his family, overseer and all, write home to their friends in Alabama not to come to western Texas, and tell them their troubles, the whys and wherefores. Their correspondents, and all who hear from them, spread the gloomy tidings from western Texas, and people stay at home.

But let us, in a few words, bring B. the same year (1860) to western Texas, and settle him upon the same

river.   B. also goes in debt, and improves a planta
tion.   But he does not buy as much land as did A.,
instead of which he buys a stock of cattle, mares,
or sheep, and possibly brings with him a jack and a
few bucks, for the purpose of raising mules and improving the flock of sheep he may buy.   His first and
second crops of cotton turn out as did those of A. He
now depends upon his stock, which he sells off, as I
have directed, as close as it will do without injuring
its increasing capacity.   B. makes another effort for a
crop, which results most favorably.   The consequence
is, that he and those about him write home to their
friends and say, "Although our cotton, etc., did not
do so well for a year or two, our stock kept us along,
and this year we have made a tremendous crop, which
has set us away ahead.   We have learned the country, and a glorious country it is.   Come to western
Texas, my friends, and do as we have done, and you
will never be sorry."   The result is, the friends of
B. and family circulate the glad tidings from western
Texas, and more or less of the recipients of these good
accounts make their way to the country.

Is this discouraging the emigration of planters? or
is it putting a *flea* in the ear of the planter who might
come to western Texas and run through his property,
for the want of just such a hint as this, and thereby
retard the settlement of our cotton lands?

And again, you southern boys, please read my book,
which may seem to have been written more for the
Yankees, but only for the reason that I happen to
know more of them than of you, and know them to
be the people to make a great wool-growing country
of this, and develop its resources and importance in
other respects; but in many of my remarks I have used
the term northern to designate people north of Texas.

I would not apply my remarks in regard to the failure of the cotton crop to eastern Texas, nor even central Texas; for, if I am not mistaken, the Colorado bottoms are equal to any lands in the state for the growth of cotton, and the seasons along this river, I believe, are uniformly good for cotton.

To return to the merchant, whom I have purposely mixed in with the planter and stock-grower, as he is so peculiarly interested in the whole country. I said that the profits of trade in this country are large. This may seem to conflict with much that I have before said, unless it should appear that the profits of all kinds of business are correspondingly large, which is generally the case. It is a fact, that the merchant's profits upon his goods in western Texas, compared with the northern merchant's profits, are as a half dime is to a penny, or thereabouts; and this may be said of mechanical business and trade generally. What is bought in the north at wholesale for a penny and retailed for two pennies, is here retailed for half a dime at least. Were such a ferry as the New York and Brooklyn established anywhere between two cities in the south, however large they might be, the cost of a ride from one to the other would probably be five cents, at least, instead of a penny, as in the north. The blacksmith, for shoeing a horse in western Texas, will have more than double the amount the smith gets for the same job in the north. This is a true scale of prices upon which business is done in this country, and why should not merchants and tradesmen do well here? If a trinket of a penny's value, in a mercantile or shop establishment of the north, would here sell for a half dime, and often a dime, and if the foregoing is illustrative of business in general, what say you, merchants and tradesmen, of all kinds, to this being a good country for you? It may justly be said that it would cost more to run a ferryboat, to get articles of trade, and the blacksmith's iron, etc., in the south than in the north, but this difference of cost of raw material in the two sections, is nothing to compare with the difference in profits.

The penny or cent is rarely seen here. I do not mention this as a credit to the country, nor as a discredit to those states or countries where they are used. It is only to show the profits of trade in western Texas that I speak of this coin. I believe that a coin of this small value is a good indication. It is a proof of enterprise and industry. We will suppose that the penny coin of New York city might be done away with, and that nothing less than the five cent piece were there used, what would be the profits of the Brooklyn and New York city ferries, when getting five cents for what they now have but one cent, and with which they make money? The great necessity of the penny or small coin in the north is a striking proof of economy, and, more than all, of ingenuity. Were it not for the invention of machinery, and the ingenuity and economy of the machinist and ship-wright, how could such crowds of people go in the convenient and quick way that they do, for a single penny, from New York to Brooklyn?

I would not make people small, but if ever the time is when the penny will be indispensable in the south, it will be when there is more productive skill and ingenuity among her people, and when the profits upon articles of trade are not as large as they now are, or when more business is done to realize the same profits.

SPECULATION vs. DROVERS.

Western Texas is a good country for the speculator, so far as articles of speculation are produced. Because, by buying here, the speculator has not only the chances of a rise in the price of his property, but the advan-

tages of buying in a country where things are easily
and cheaply produced, and such things, too, as can
be cheaply exported to those countries where they are
more laboriously and expensively produced. For instance, a beef can here be grown to a weight of six hundred pounds at a cost of two dollars and a half, and
driven for two dollars and a half to a country where it
costs, perhaps, twenty-five dollars to raise a beef of the
same weight, and from that, with the twenty-five dollar beef, on to the same market at the same expense;
which, no doubt, (although the twenty-five dollar beef
is worth the most money), would result in a big advantage to the purchaser of the Texas beef over the
purchaser of the twenty-five dollar beef—provided, the
Texas beef is driven by the right kind of experienced
drivers. And when the cattle of Texas are improved,
there will be a still greater advantage in favor of the
purchaser of Texas beef-cattle, if speculation or driving
north be the object of the purchaser; and in fact, if
those northern men who now come here and take
beeves to Chicago and northern markets, would manage differently, they would make much more money
than they now do. If, in the place of taking wild,
rough, light-quartered animals, they would take choice
cattle only, and employ experienced managers and
drivers, they would, at anything like the present
prices in Texas, always be very sure to make, and
with good luck, their profits would be large. And by
always demanding choice cattle, the stock-growers
would see the necessity of improving their cattle,
which improvement would make a demand for blooded
stock, which the drover might take on to Texas with
him when he goes for a drove of beeves. Should a
northern drover think of doing this, he should go on
to Texas with his fine stock in the fall, and sell out

during the winter, and get ready to start in early
spring with his .Texas beeves for the north.

A drove of about seven hundred beeves was driven
from middle Texas to Chicago, about two years since,
which, it is said, cleared about ten thousand dollars.
This drove was no doubt very well managed; but
there was a large · number of inferior cattle in it, and
had they happened to have gone into a bad market,
these inferior ones might have caused a loss of money
upon the drove; whereas, if the whole drove had been
choice cattle of our country, they might have gone into the same supposed bad market and still have made
money. To my knowledge, there have been many men
here, within the last six years, who have bought large
droves of Texas beeves for northern markets. Some
of these men have not done well, simply because they
did not know how to buy, select, and drive Texas
beef-cattle.

When a northern man comes here for a drove of
beef-cattle, let him come in time to look around and
see where he can buy to advantage. He need not
make any noise, or let people know what he is about,
until he finds a large prairie or extent of country where
the beeves, for the year or two previous, have not been
much culled or sold out. When found, he should secure such cattle, unless they are known to be generally
wild and bad to manage. There are certain prairies in
Texas where northern men should be very careful
about buying: and wherever, or of whoever, he may
buy, his contract should call for all his or their beef-
cattle; that is to say, all such beef-cattle as he, the
purchaser or his assigns, shall consider good and mer-
chantable; and then, in his selection he should not
take a light, rough, washy and ugly beef, nor those
that are at all staggy. But he should select those that
are uniformly smooth, with as clean necks and horns

as possible; and, if the judge or selector is capable, those that would be most likely to drive and feed kindly, and, above all, those that are well quartered, or put up in a way to take flesh with fat, and be sure to weigh well. Of course, the drover or manager would have his men ready, and most of them with him, and his contract should call for the delivery of the cattle across one large river, or stream, at least, at some point where the balance of his men should be in readiness to help count and receive them, and where the wagon, camping material, extra horses, and the whole complement of drovers, cook and all, should be in readiness to move the cattle on, or hold and herd them here as head-quarters, until, perhaps, the drove is made up with cattle coming from other points. At this stage of the enterprise, if the manager and drivers understand their business, they will use the utmost caution, and give all possible care and attention, to avoid a fright or stampede; and for a week or fortnight, if the men study their own good even, they will use the greatest caution and do all they can to help the sleepless, wearied and care-worn manager prevent a fright or stampede, and watch closely that none may get away—after which time, if all has gone right, there is not much danger. Yet, unless a man is all attention, and is proud to do his duty, he should not be allowed a place among the faithful, hardy and trusty drivers of a Texas drove of beeves.

Whoever starts a drove of our cattle north, should, by all means, employ an experienced Texas manager, and consult him in regard to the kind of drivers to employ, and possibly in regard to the purchase of the cattle. The place for receiving a drove of Texas beeves, or for holding them, or a share of them, until the drove may be completed and ready to start, should be where wagons or men on foot do not frequent, and,

16

if possible, where nothing might occur to frighten
them. The writer has driven these Texas beeves for
several years, and for the two last years, in driving
many droves, he had but one stampede to speak of,
and this he would have avoided had he not, necessarily, at the time, been away from the drove. A northern or western drover should always receive and start
his cattle from Texas during moonlight nights, if he
possibly can, and as early in the spring as the grass
will do, when the weather is almost sure to be fine.
By moonlight the drivers can see what they are about
when around the herd, and by the time they have to
do without the light of the moon, the cattle should be
well broke in, so as to drive and manage without difficulty. A drover should be as sure as possible and secure the right kind of men, and, besides paying them
the wages agreed upon, he should treat them as liberally as he consistently could, and then he should expect them to do their duty. If he is inclined to be penu-
rious, let it be with some one beside his drivers; for
a lot of drivers will do any amount of mischief to the
employer they do not like, and *vice versa*, they will
watch over and almost die, if need be, with the cattle
of any drover with whom they are well pleased.

I mention these facts simply because I have known
northern men to come here and not do as well, by several thousand dollars, as they might have done in the
purchase of their droves, and then, to save money,
would employ inexperienced hands, and undertake to
carry the thing through on the cheap or stingy principle, and, consequently, get into trouble and make
nothing. The true way is to purchase the cattle as
shrewdly, closely and judiciously as possible, and then
compensate the drivers liberally. Save money out of
any one but the drivers, and if you are the man for
the business, you are sure to make money in the end,

and that largely, too. By treating the drivers liberally and well, I do not mean that you must give them
their own way, or let them impose on you. Use them
right, and they will suffer you, as it were, to see that
they do their duty. The purchaser should remember
that he is not going to market every week or month;
but that he has a long way to drive, and that it costs
no more to drive a choice Texas animal than it does
an inferior one, and the chances are ten to one in favor of the choice animal. For five long years I have
bought and driven Texas beef-cattle, and I have made
a good deal of money for those for whom I worked;
and I know that the right kind of men can make
money, with as much certainty as their is in human
affairs, by driving Texas beef-cattle to northern markets; but they must be " up and dressed " for the business. I have recently heard of one of five or six part-
ners, who were each more or less interested in three
droves of beeves that were driven from western Texas
to Chicago, last spring; and the partner of whom I
speak wrote home from Chicago that his share of the
profits on the two thousand cattle they drove, would
be over $9,000, and I believe there were at least two
other shares in the company whose interest was as
large or larger than his. In this large lot of cattle
were the eight hundred head of which I spoke, near
the beginning of this work, as being the sale of one
stock grown at $16 per head.

CATTLE SHIPPING.

The shipping of beef and veal cattle from western
Texas, to New Orleans, Mobile and Cuba, is an extensive and, to those who are calculated for it, profitable business. The writer is largely experienced in
this trade, to which he owes principally his knowledge
of western Texas. It is the buying, driving and ship-

ping of beef and veal cattle from different parts of
Texas to New Orleans, for a wealthy company,
that has, more than any other one thing, given
the writer such an extensive acquaintance with the
pursuits and inviting condition of the country to
foreigners. There is room here for competition in this
business, and it is to be a large and growing trade in
western Texas for, I might say, all time to come. The
writer could enlarge to almost any extent upon this
subject; but as no great good could arise from such
enlargement here, he will simply say that not a few
have made and are making money at this business,
and that "Yankees" and Germans are among those
who are doing as well as any in the trade. I will further say that, without any experience in Texas, I commenced this business for $60 per month, and soon got
$75, and then $100 per month, which situation I gave
up to write this book. Had I continued, I could, probably, have commanded any reasonable price for my
services. I mention this merely to show what a verdant man or plow-boy from the north can do with the
wild stock of Texas—*i. e.*, if he is of the right stripe,
and not afraid to work.

BEEF-PACKING.

Packing beef has been often attempted, but without
success; but recently it has been successfully carried on,
to some extent, in western Texas. It is a well-known
fact that if a process were generally understood
whereby beef could be packed in Texas so as to keep,
and pass inspection in our large markets, it would soon
be an extensive and, no doubt, profitable business.

There has been, to the writer's knowledge, within
the last three years, several hundred barrels of beef
packed in western Texas, for the New York market,
which bore inspection, and did very well for the packer,

although he labored under great disadvantages in the operation of packing. The beef-packing business in western Texas, deserves the attention of enterprising men. That it pays to drive beef from Texas to Chicago, thousands of miles, and pack it, has been well demonstrated; and why should it not pay to pack it in Texas, if the thing could be extensively done, and ship it instead of driving so far to the great markets of the country. The writer has recently learned that a gentleman has just come on from the north to Texas to invest a large amount of money in this business. He knows a process of packing that will no doubt insure success in the business. We have several months of cool weather in winter that certainly ought to admit of profitable beef-packing.

SPECULATION VS. HORSES, MULES, ETC.

Horses and mules have been, and are yet to a great extent, driven north, east and west from Texas. They are so cheaply produced here, and the work of improving them will be so rapidly carried on, that soon the speculator will be able to get fine horses and mules in western Texas for one half the amount that it would cost to raise such animals in some of the northern state.

These animals are more easily managed and driven than cattle. Our horse drovers, after getting the animals accustomed to each other and well broke in, frequently, when driving through our open countries, turn them loose without a herder when night overtakes them, and generally find them all together, not far off, in the morning. But great care and watchfulness should be exercised until the animals are reconciled to each other, and are inclined to stay together or follow the bell-man of the drove. Sometimes mules will unavoidably stampede from the scent of wolves or other animals, and various other causes. But an experienced manager is at home with them, and seldom meets with any loss. Such a manager should always be employed with a drove of our Texas horses or mules.

.The immense amount of this kind of stock in Texas and Mexico, its rapid increase and the cheapness of its production, should certainly call the attention of speculators this way. I know of a Missourian who has, for the last eight years, taken a lot of yearling mules from Texas to his farm in Missouri, and after feeding them on corn for a season, has taken them among the planters of the south, and sold them, generally, at large profits. He told me that he raised a hundred acres of corn annually, and that he disposed of it in this way—some seasons at several dollars per bushel. The bringing of those cheap Texas jennies to an abundant corn country, and raising half-breed jacks on corn for the Texas market, would not be a bad business. Fine jacks and stallions can be exchanged for Texas mules and horses at a profitable rate, provided the thing is properly managed. It would pay well for a speculator or Texas stock-grower to buy up old, foundered and used-up mares, anywhere along the Mississippi states, where they could be bought cheap, and driven carefully on to Texas, with a little expense, and kept there for the purpose of raising mules, or sold to the stock-grower in exchange for mules, beeves, or something of the kind. It would pay the speculator, who is watching for rare chances, to peruse well this book.

LAND SPECULATION.

From the appearance of things the land speculator could nowhere do better at present and for many years to come, than in Texas; but this business is too much on the " shark " order to admit of much encouragement from a friend of the poor man. I think I could write many interesting pages upon this subject, but it would conflict too much with the spirit of my work.

WOOL AND SHEEP SPECULATION.

In the opinion of the writer there will be in twenty years not less than ten millions of sheep in Texas, and possibly twice that number. In the meantime would not the speculator be justified in looking that way for wool, mutton, etc.? There are those who could probably come here at this time, and do well at the purchase of the common qualities of wool in small quantities. Those, raising fine wool, I believe, generally know pretty well where to send it to get good prices or realize the most out of it. But many of those who have small lots of coarse-wool sheep frequently sell their wool by the fleece, at much less than its value. I will close this subject by suggesting that the wool speculator read this work through, and perhaps he will be better able to judge of the good chances and wide field for his operations in this country than myself; certainly it would seem that the wool speculator might do well in a country where this article is so easily and cheaply produced. I will say that the speculator can hardly go amiss by taking sheep from the northern and western states, across the country, to northern and western Texas, provided he understands the business of buying, driving, and managing sheep, about which I will here drop a few remarks: All who are acquainted with the sheep business know the danger of overdriving them. When starting a flock for a long journey the greatest care should be used not to overdrive them for the first few days, if you do the very next day the chances are that some of your flock will begin to lag and go behind,

and áre to be carried in the wagon, and eventually to
be sold for a trifle, given away or to die. In regard
to age, condition, soundness of feet, etc., any person
of the least experience should know. Sheep in a four-
rod road will nibble their way along as fast as they
should go without being driven ; in fact, there should
always be a man ahead to keep them back when inclined to go too fast. When going through forests,
marshes or places where there may be poisonous vegetation, sheep should be well watched, and if possible
they should be well filled with grass and not hungry
when starting into such places, and they should be
put through as soon as it will do. There should
always be an antidote for poison in the provision
wagon or near at hand.

When driving a large flock in an open country, in
warm weather, they should be strung out and not suffered to huddle together too much, which heats them
and often results in many wind-broken sheep, and is
injurious to them in other ways. They should not be
suffered to gorge themselves or drink excessively and
then driven fast. When driving through an open
country the flock should always be guarded in the
night by one man at least, and the shepherds' dogs
should be in their places. If droves of sheep are not
closely watched in our prairie countries they are liable, in the night particularly, to divide up and stroll
off in gangs, and too often wolves get among them
before they are found, and frequently it is impossible
to trail or find them without troublesome and expensive search. Lastly, but by no means leastly, when
coming to deep creeks or rivers, the greatest caution
should be used that your sheep are not drowned or injured by swimming. A healthy, strong sheep will
safely swim a river of good width, provided it can have
a good landing place and the current of the river is

not too strong. A flock of sheep should never be put into a rapid stream, unless there is a broad, easy landing upon the opposite side, and then a few should be tried first, to see how they make the landing. There should always be a person at the coming-out place to squeeze the water from the wool of any sheep that is too much exhausted to get out without assistance. A large flock of sheep should be divided and swam in parts, or else it should be strung out, and but few allowed to go in abreast; and there should always be two men, at least, at the starting-in point, and should anything go wrong in the water, or at the landing, that would be likely to huddle them together or interrupt their swimming in the least, the flock should be instantly stopped and driven back, and great care taken that the balance of the flock does not take a run and get the advantage of you in their determination to follow those that, perhaps, are yet in the water and not out of danger.

A safe and excellent way to swim sheep is to have the flock, or a portion of it, upon the waters' edge, where there should be a skiff, with two men in it— one to sit aft and row the boat, without throwing out the oar in a way to frighten the sheep; the other to sit still aft of him, if possible, and to draw with a rope one or two strong sheep from the flock gradually into the water, as others are inclined to follow, calling them in a low voice with the sound to which they are accustomed. The moment they begin to follow, start the boat and head it so as to strike the opposite landing pretty well up. Without some awkwardness, this way of swimming sheep can not but succeed. In fact, it is a good way to swim horses, and cattle also, if you have an ox or an animal that will lead well into the water.

I could say much more upon this subject, as my ex-
17

perience in the business has been quite extensive; but I have said enough to caution any inexperienced or careless person who may start out for Texas with a drove of sheep. I do not think that in driving from Illinois to Texas, through Missouri and the Indian territory, there would be much swimming to do, unless it should be an unusually wet season; and before risking much by putting sheep into rivers, I should pay for crossing them on ferries, or in some safe way, particularly if the flock is not generally in good condition and strong. In conclusion I will say, what I have in substance often repeated, that a drove of sheep, or animals of any kind, should always have a good, experienced and prudent manager, when driven such a journey as the one in question. Such a trip would naturally be eventful, and emergencies might arise; consequently, whether going from the north to Texas, or from Texas to the north, with stock of any kind, a trusty, experienced and prudent manager should be employed.

I once knew a Pennsylvania drover, who came to Texas and purchased a large drove, consisting of six hundred beeves, for the Philadelphia market. The stock-growers all got the start of him in the sale and delivery of their cattle, and then, to cap his bad management, he hired shop-boys, town-loafers, and inexperienced men to drive this large drove of beeves, simply because he could hire them cheap. The consequence was, that his drove wandered off several times, and many of his beeves were never found. A lot of green hands, without the right kind of a Texas stock-driving manager, will frighten a drove of Texas beeves, horses or mules, in a way to bring disaster upon the drover.

Had this Pennsylvanian employed a number-one Texas beef-buyer, driver and manager, and had consulted and advised with him in regard to the selection, purchase and delivery of the cattle, and in regard to the employment of drivers, etc., his speculation would have proved a paying and pleasant one; whereas; the result of his bad management, of course, brought down his curses upon Texas and everything in it.

MECHANICS,

. Of various kinds, will find Texas, and particularly western Texas, an excellent field of operation. The country is prosperous, and building is going on very extensively. Besides dwellings, stores, warehouses, wharves, and the like, there are cotton-gins, grist-mills, saw-mills, various factories, bridges, etc., being constructed. • Manufacturing of various kinds is quite extensively carried on, and its material extension in many branches is confidently anticipated. Why should Texas send her vast amount of hides abroad to be tanned, while she is so well supplied with the finest of tanning bark? There are a thousand and one suggestions of this kind that I might make in regard to this country, were it not that I have other matters under consideration with which I wish to conclude this work.

I will say, in conclusion to mechanics, that the country is fast filling up. Emigration is continually pouring in, and an increasing demand for your capital and services is to be the result. And furthermore, that I know a plenty of mechanics and mechanical laborers, who have invested their profits and savings of their business and labor in stock of some kind, and giving it in charge of stock-growers to brand and look after, have become important and wealthy men.

THE POOR MAN.

Western Texas, of all others, is the country for the

poor man; and also for the man who would retrench, or who is unable to keep pace with the prodigality of the times in the country where it may be his fortune to live. I have somewhere spoken of a cluster of trees as the place of my writing. Many of these pages were written in the open air, 'neath this group of live oaks, in the fall and winter season. During winter, much of the time a person may set comfortably in the shade of a tree for the purpose of writing or anything else. Of course we have cold snaps or northers, of short duration, and short spells of cool, chilly weather, but no snow in western Texas. Consequently it is a country where the poor man can get along without expending all he has for the purpose of building a house to make his family comfortable. He needs not a dime to build, in our timbered sections, a house in which his family could be comfortable and respected, and where he could live until his business and prospects would justify the erection of a better and more expensive one; and, aside from the very few and cheap house-keeping material that would be required to get along for the time, he could put all he might have into stock of some kind, and then buy a home to the best advantage. If it is not more than five acres to begin with, it will do until the increase of his stock, and what he can pick up in other ways, will enable him to buy more. Small stock-growers resort to various means of money-making, outside of the stock business, the object of which, very often, is not to draw from the increase or proceeds of the stock for the support of the family, or for any purpose, except some solid investment that will add to their wealth. Almost any land-holder will suffer a poor man to settle upon lands suitable for stock-raising purposes, with the understanding that the settler shall buy as soon as he is able, or at some stated time.

I will say, that in western Texas the titles of lands
have been much in dispute, and are somewhat so now.
It therefore behooves a person to consider the title he
is to get, before paying his money for land. This is
often an advantage to the settler, from the fact that
the contending parties will allow him to improve a
place, with an understanding that he shall pay to the
party whom the law shall decide as being the rightful
owner, and from whom a good title can be perfected,
which often gives the settler ample time to get ready
to pay for his place by the time the successful party,
in law, is qualified to convey to him an indisputable
title. There is, however, an endless amount of good
lands for sale in western Texas, the titles of which are
perfectly clear and undisputed. In fact, the courts of
the country, within the last few years, have settled
questions of law and firmly fixed the titles to a vast
amount of the heretofore disputed territory of Texas.
Now it is to the poor man, who arrives in western
Texas with but little or nothing, except his head and
hands to get along with, that I would address myself
for a while. I will hereafter mention some of the different kinds of labor for which there is a demand in
western Texas. But besides these, there are many
things to which the poor man, particularly the apt and
hardy northern man, can turn his attention with but
little or no money to start with. Where I was raised,
I know of men who were in the habit of going into
the deep forests of the country to hunt deer for their
peltry and venison during the whole winter season.
They would travel upon their snow-shoes from one
month's end to another, separated from all human
habitations by scores of miles, and were well satisfied
if they could get the hides and saddles of one or two
deer per day, which they would lug upon their backs
for miles into camp, and perform more hard work in

a tedious, snowy country, to secure ten pelts, with their
two quarters each, than it would require to secure a
hundred in this delightful country. If a person will
use the right means in this country, he can make more
money at this business than he could in any country
I have ever seen, and I have been in many parts where
deer were considered plentiful. And the beauty of
the thing is, that here it is not cold, tedious, and disagreeable. The hunter could here settle in some secluded place, where he could go on foot and do well,
but with his gentle Mexican pony, trained for the purpose, do much better; and where he could go with a
slide or stone-boat, drawn by a gentle yoke of oxen,
and secure ten or twelve deer per day, the hides of,
which he could tan and get fifteen dollars per dozen
for, in a northern market, if *well* tanned: the process
of which tanning is easily learned. Deer-skins are
dried and packed away untanned, for the merchant, to
a great extent, in this country. The carcass of deer,
when so plentifully secured, unless the huntsman were
living near some town, would not sell, but his family
could be well and constantly supplied, and a drove of
hogs could be fed or kept about home with this surplus of wild meat.

These remarks, I am well aware, would seem to
conflict with remarks that I have and may yet make:
but there are, in all countries, men who will seclude
themselves for the purpose of hunting, and why should
they not be in Texas as well as anywhere else?

Would the hunter doubt his ability to make money
in a country where there are millions of deer, and
where, upon many of our prairies, there can be seen
droves of hundreds every day, and where, on horseback, by looking in different directions, a person can
sometimes see five hundred or a thousand at a time?
How often have I thought, when traveling over this

country, that hundreds and thousands of huntsmen, in different countries, would be delighted to know what they could do here, and would come, if they knew, and convert these wild animals more to the use of mankind. It certainly seems a pity that they should live in such numbers upon our prairies, without the least expense to a mortal man, and left so uselessly to die with old age, or fall a prey to wolves, panthers, tigers, and other useless animals, when they might be so easily secured and made to answer a better end. Huntsman, why not come here and send a bullet to the hearts of these old bucks, and make soft and beautiful leather of their skins, and send it to your cold countrymen to clothe their hands, in the shape of mittens and gloves; with which to make soft shoes for the old and feeble, and whip-lashes for the drover, or note-layers for musical instruments, and a thousand other purposes? Why not come here and secure millions of these geese and ducks, and send their feathers to your cold countrymen, to make warm nests for their shivering maidens, in which they may sleep comfortably, when the cold frosty winds whistle around their chambers? Come and send home the snow-white, downy skins of the swan, to comfort the cheery cheeked daughters of icy lands: come and decoy our animals of fur, and make use of this great waste of everything.

The different towns of the whole country require more or less hay and wood, and the grass upon the prairies is free to any one who has a mind to cut and make hay of it,—and who knows how to swing the scythe and manage the mowing machine? Many a little load of prairie hay have I seen sold for ten and fifteen dollars; and many a tun of northern hay have I known to sell here, in our sea-port towns, for forty dollars; while the interior of the country is covered with musquete grass, which makes the best of hay, and all around these coast-towns there is heavy sedge grass that will do very well, and is now taking the place of northern hay. Mowing machines are being brought on, and quite extensively used. Farmers and stock-growers save more or less hay for the working stock that they wish to keep up and handy by. They give employment to these machines. Although a pasture of musquete or bermuda grass, near at hand, would obviate this necessity, yet men are slow to cultivate grasses in a country that has always yielded abundantly and does now, except immediately around extensive ranches and farms that have been occupied for a long time, where the grass is eat out.

There is an immense amount of freighting done in the country by ox, mule, and horse teams. Many a rugged man gets his start at the stock business by freighting goods into the interior. It is not unusual here to see as many as twenty heavy-loaded wagons, in a string, drawn by from four to six yoke of oxen each. Mexican horse and mule teams are considerably used, but more by the Germans than other people. The government freight business is very large in western Texas. Heretofore the government has done its own freighting from the coast into the interior, but recently this business, in the lower country, is contracted out, and the contractors employ Mexicans or re-let their contracts, in parts, to those who own a large number of Mexican carts and oxen, which are driven by Mexicans. It is not unusual to see a string of thirty or forty Mexican carts, all loaded for the interior, with government stores and supplies. The oxen are yoked by the horns. These Mexican ox yokes are nearly a straight stick, grooved a little to fit the head, just back of the horns, and snugly lashed to them with raw-hide straps. It seems rather cruel to men of the older states to see these animals work in this way; but the weight they pull, the distance they travel, and the amount they will endure in this peculiar yoke, is astonishing to all. It is nevertheless a wicked way to use oxen, as holding the head in one position for many hours at a time, is evidently very painful, and the appearance of the ox is always that of great suffering. Mexicans are becoming a little Americanized in this respect, and are adopting, more or less, the American way of working oxen.

It takes some little capital to get at the freighting business; but a man of good character can generally get together a few oxen and a wagon on time, and get at the business with but very little money. There is always more or less job work, of many kinds, to be done in the towns of the country, such as street-making and repairing, garden-making, building fences, and getting material out of the timbers for fencing, breaking up prairie lands, furnishing the towns with vegetables, butter and milk, poultry and eggs, game, oysters, fish, etc. The gathering of moss, with which the forests of portions of western Texas are loaded, and which is used to a vast extent as a substitute for hair by the upholsterer and manufacturers of innumerable useful articles of furniture, etc., can be done by any one. This moss is prepared for sale and use by rotting and washing of the covering of its fiber, which resembles much in appearance and answers to a great extent the same purpose as the hair from the tails and manes of horses, etc. The rotting is done by burying it in the ground for a length of time. It is then taken up and washed, picked, pulled, and cleaned, until fit for use. Thousands of people buy moss, in the shape of mattresses, lounges, etc., who do not know what they are buying, as it answers the purpose very well, and is often sold for hair.

The gathering of pecans in western Texas, during the fall and winter seasons, often pays the poor man handsomely. , Men with their families, children and all, turn out and gather hundreds of bushels, for which they get from two to four dollars per bushel. Many a poor man and family have got their start in this way in Texas, and become wealthy stock-growers and farmers.

I have before stated that the forests of this country are tangled with grape-vines, which yield abundantly of juicy fruit. There are those here who are turning these grapes into money, in the way of wine and brandies, any amount of which can be made, and the grapes are free to all.

There is to be any amount of hedging done in western Texas. Unsuccessful attempts have been made at hedging, or, rather, those who have contracted for the growing of hedges have abandoned their work and left it for others to complete. The reason of this, I suppose, has principally been the want of a knowledge of our climate and the soil, which would undoubtedly have enabled the contractors to complete their contracts, as those who have continued the work, I hear, have made out first rate for themselves and have succeeded to the satisfaction of the planters and stock-growers for whom the hedging is done. Of course, the Osage orange is principally used, and is no doubt the best plant in America for this purpose. There are land-holders, stock-growers and planters in western Texas who would, no doubt, rather build their own hedges than contract for the rearing of them, provided they could save anything by so doing—which, probably, they could by employing men who understand the business. There are men in the northern and western states who could find employment here at this business, and I presume there are those who could

make money at the setting and rearing of hedges until a year or two old, or until a complete stand is in-
sured and sufficiently grown to be given over to less-
experienced hands to work and manage. Scores of
men in this country have attempted to make fences
of this kind, and have failed for the want of experienced help and management. That fine hedges can
be made here, is a certainty; for I have seen here and
there through the country, short pieces of fence of this
kind that was as good as need be for any purpose. In
fact, I have seen short pieces of hedge-row that grew
up and came to a good fence in the open prairie, without any attention after being set, and poorly cultivated
and trimmed only two seasons, and then left for thousands of cattle to tramp and interfere with, if they
were so disposed, every day. And, again, I have seen
good, well-grown hedge-fence from other kinds of
plants in this country; but I am sure the Osage, with
good management, is much superior to anything that
can be used in the country for the purpose of hedging.
Young men who understand the setting, pruning, and
correct management of hedges, could go to Texas and
soon accumulate enough to start the stock business.

The producing of honey can nowhere be made more
profitable than in western Texas, from the fact that
bees can work almost the whole year, and that the
prairies and forests are covered in such profusion with
flowers and blossoms, and the different material from
which they extract their honey. They are not liable
to freeze here, and are perfectly secure from all the
dangers and difficulties of winter in colder countries.
It is said that bees do not do so well here when kept
in the open prairies as when kept near the bottoms
along the rivers, or in the prairie forests, where the
winds do not interfere with their flight to and from
their honey flowers, or the material from which they

extract the sweet. If those men whom I have known at this business in other parts, were here, taking one half their accustomed pains at the business, they could soon make money enough to enter largely into the stock business. The poor man, without a dollar, can secure bees from the forests and fill as many hives as he pleases; and a person with a little spare means could build those shelved bee-houses which have long since proved so fine and profitable, and which prevent the trouble and losses from swarming.

The writer is himself a poor man, and, as few as his virtues may be, he can say that he has been good to the poor man; and when I tell him that I have been in all the grand divisions of the globe but one, and have seen much of the world, and that western Texas is the finest and most promising country of any I have seen for the poor man, I am not trying to deceive him. When I tell him of a country where a few square yards of strong cloth will make him a house that will do him until he can make something to enable him to erect a better one; of a country where he can pasture his cow, his sheep, his horse, his hogs, etc., all for nothing; where snow never comes; where the soil never freezes; where the man who has the least bit of money-making tact is almost sure to get rich, or become independent; in short, of a country where he can live and ask but little or no odds of those who gripe their money; where he can shoulder his gun and go forth with a certainty of returning with meat for his family; where the lustrous rays of the sun, moon and stars are cheering to his heart, and afford him a greater delight than do the cart-wheel dollars give to the sordid and miserly man; where he can contemplate the bounties and beauties of nature with enjoyment, regardless of the dazzle and grandeur of fashionable life and empty show; and where, as I have

before said a man can be a man—not a dog; I say,
when I tell the poor man all this, and that this is the
place to live, I know he will not think that I am trying to deceive him. When I tell him that I have
swung the ax, the cradle, the scythe, the fork, the hoe,
the spade, and have stood by the plow, and have toiled
in the field year after year; have clipped the fleece
from thousands of the wooly tribe, and have done almost everything that the laboring man does in northern countries—he will admit that I ought to know
what is good for the poor man; that I ought to be
a competent judge of a country's advantages and suitableness for him; that I ought to feel an interest in
his well-being, since I have realized and know so well
his task—since I have realized and know so well the
stiffened joints that sometimes almost refuse to move
when he rises at the break of day to return to the field
to work on and lend his mite in the production of that
which clothes and feeds the rich, which warms and
nourishes the sick, and showers such blessedness upon
man. Yes, he will admit that I ought to know all
this, and undoubtedly do know it, and am telling the
truth. So, farewell poor man! with these, and a
thousand other things I might tell you, until I meet
you in western Texas. But you may say hold, for a
moment, and tell us why you are so poor, after being
so long in this fine country, where you say it is so
easy to become rich. This you have a right to ask,
and it is my duty to answer you, which I can do in a
few words. The writer happens to be one of those
whose disposition it was to climb Fortune's ladder by
skipping too many rounds for the purpose of going too
rapidly up, and, consequently, losing his hold, came
prostrate to the ground. And when coming to Texas,
after trying his fortune in different parts of the world,
instead of improving little advantages that lay before

him, instead of buying a few cattle, a small flock of
sheep, or something of the kind, and going gradually
but surely up, he misplaced his confidence and under-
took again to climb the quick way to a fortune, and
this time the ladder, whose ascent he would have handsomely made, proved deceitful and rotten. My read-
ers may not all understand this, but there are, perhaps,
a few who will, and that will answer the purpose.
When arriving in Texas the poor man should not be
discouraged, and suffer himself to think that there is
nothing here that he can do. He must remember that
he is from the same country where old Texans came
from, and he must pitch in at the best thing that offers. Let Texans know that he is neither "pepper nor
salt," "sponge-cake or dough," but rough-and-ready
for the work of the country. Pitch in at any price,
for awhile, and let 'em know what you are good for,
and you will soon be all right.

TEACHERS VS. SCHOOLS, CHURCHES, MINISTERS, ETC.

Common school teaching, in western Texas, is that
to which I would call the attention of the poor man of
education. The recent census of Texas shows a population of nearly half a million of people. Consequently the pupilage of the state is large and rapidly
increasing, which makes it an inviting country to the
teacher—a broad, expanding field for this fraternity.
The school teacher can here put his earnings into
stock, and have it attended to as well as though he
gave it his personal attention; and during vacation
he can ride among it and satisfy himself in regard to
the business and management of his cattle, sheep, or
whatever kind of stock he may have his money invested in. By laying out his surplus money in this
way, he would soon have an income from his cattle
that would equal his salary for teaching, and before

many years, with prudent management, he could take up his abode in some good grass region, with his hundreds, and possibly thousands of cattle around him.

I can imagine nothing more encouraging to the patient and perplexed school teacher, than to have an opportunity of investing his little surplus or savings in a way that it shall be rapidly compounding, or in a way to get the free use of a great natural pasture, upon which the increase of his stock will carry him on to wealth.

Let me ask the district teacher how he would like to have his brand upon cattle that are grazing on the commons, and all about him, the keeping of which might not cost him a cent, and the marking and branding of the increase of which he could pay for by the head, or give a portion of it for the branding, etc.— among which he might ride at leisure times upon his pony that might always be close by, staked out, or hoppled upon grass near the school-house. All this the teacher realizes in this country, and the stock-boys are glad to see him start his fortune and reap the benefits of the yielding earth in common with them. It is not unusual here to see a half-dozen or more horses staked upon grass near the school-house; and what is more encouraging and satisfactory to the friends of education than to see those horses, coming from the outskirts of the district, loaded down with healthy and happy children, on the way to school.

If the teacher prefers it, his investment might be in a flock of sheep, or a herd of mares, to be kept by some one not far from his place of teaching. In several instances I have known this course to be pursued by teachers, who would at times ride with the stock-boys, help drive and brand, and become acquainted with the business. And I presume, should I make a little inquiry, I could find out many here with fine properties who, in the commencement, pursued this same course.

It is not long since I knew two young men, brothers, to purchase five hundred head of cattle, paying a portion down and depending upon their salary as teachers and the few beeves they might have the next year to pay their notes for the balance.

Of course there are many high schools in Texas, good teachers of which are appreciated and well rewarded, and there is a disposition in the south to depend more upon itself for the education of its children. They prefer having schools near home rather than be compelled to send their sons and daughters north for an education. There reasons for this are many and sound, and this determination will be the origin of many private common and high schools and colleges which, of course, will multiply the demand for teachers of all kinds. Teachers of music can nowhere do better than here. Ornamental education of the different kinds is sought and well paid for in this country.

The school fund of Texas is very large, and there is always a great surplus for educational purposes in the treasury of the state. Our system of schools is very popular, and we boast of affording superior means of education to the many. In fact, our school system is claimed to be a model after, and an improvement upon, the school systems of the older states. This, I suppose, arises from there being people in Texas from all the different states of the Union, and the manifest disposition to introduce here anything that is good from any of the older states. The voice of New England is heard in Texas.

It is needless to say that the churches and religious societies in Texas exercise a powerful influence upon the morals of the country and lead many into the holy bonds of the Christian religion. Churches and places of worship are quite numerous and rapidly increasing, and our clergy are proud of their country and labor devoutly and with zeal in their cause. Our benevolent societies and institutions speak well for the hearts of our people.

It is not unusual to see the brand and mark of our ministers upon the cattle of our prairies, and many of them have fine stocks of different kind of animals which have frequently accumulated from little beginings. The generous stock-boy sometimes by way of compliment and as a commendable act, puts his minister's mark and brand upon one of his heifer calves. Of course all would look out for the minister's cattle; and, as he is so generously remembered, his stock is ever on the increase, and as a natural consequence becomes large and valuable, the proceeds of which afford him an easy support for his family and enables him to educate his children as he would wish to at home or abroad. One minister I know who is not only the shepherd of his flock in church, but the shepherd of his flock on the prairie—a beautiful flock of the woolly tribe. Often when working with a crowd of stock-boys I have known some one or more of them to brand all the motherless calves they might find on the prairie, and now and then a yearling that had left its mother, to some little orphan girl or boy.

I have nowhere mentioned that when a stock of cattle is neglected, and the calves get to be yearlings and leave their mothers before being branded, they are liable to be taken up and branded by any stock-grower who may find them. This is perfectly right and will make stock-growers look after their business in time.

KINDS OF LABOR IN DEMAND.

From the beginning of this work it has been the writer's intention to note down every description of

18

labor for which there is a demand in western Texas, also all the different vocations and branches of business in which men are engaged, but the want of space and time and the writer's neglect to make a memorandum of his observations, from time to time, upon these points renders it quite impossible for him to do so. As a general thing the different branches of business of a country indicate the kinds of labor wanted, and by reading this work the laborer of any kind would be pretty well qualified to judge for himself whether western Texas is the place for him or not, even though I should say nothing more upon the subject. I will, however, after adding several branches of business to those already mentioned, put down several kinds of labor for which it occurs to me there is a good demand in western Texas : Lumber-men with portable sawmills could nowhere do better than in the timbered sections of the country; good hotels and boarding houses do remarkably well here; good thorough farming, independent of the stock business, pays exceedingly well—half-way loose farming does not pay, for in this case thrifty weeds are sure to take the field. The livery business nowhere does better than in Texas—the prairie grass is free to the liveryman, which he can have merely for the price of cutting and drawing to his stable. The sale of northern wagons and carriages of all kinds is very extensive. It is enough to say that the pursuits of the towns generally of any civilized country, such as butchering, draying, blacksmithing and general mechanical business, pay well here. Laboring men about our coast-towns and wharfs, generally, get good pay for their services. Stage-drivers get from $20 to $50 per month, and many of them soon get into the stock-business or become speculators in horses, mules, etc. Horse, mule and ox-teamsters get from $20 to $35 per month, and-can accumulate by being economical and investing their savings in stock of some kind. Stock-drivers get from $20 to $40 per month, and soon begin to accumulate property in the way of stock, etc. Beef-buyers and drivers get from $40 to $125 per month, and with economy and good management can soon get rich. Northern and European sheepherders or shepherds get from $15 to $30 per month, and can get ahead by putting their savings in sheep. Sheepshearers get from four to six cents per head for shearing. Managers of large flocks of sheep get from $30 to $50 per month, and can get rich by investing their surplus means in sheep. Plantation overseers get from $300 to $1,000 per year, and many of them work their way up in the world. Clerks in mercantile and other establishments get from $250 to $2,500 per year. Laborers at general farming get from $15 to $25 per month. Ditching is done by the rod and pays the laborer well. There is a great want of servant girls in western Texas, and any number of good servant girls could get good situations at fine prices.

In conclusion, thousands of apt and handy mechanical and general laborers could find enough to do in Texas and would find it profitable to go there. Although railroads have progressed rather slowly thus far in western Texas, they are sure to be built and thread our country in all directions, and this will create a renewed demand for labor of all kinds. The constant emigration of wealthy and enterprising people is sure to bring about the extensive construction of railroads, which will open a wide field for all kinds of business and labor. It is thought by many intelligent men that a railroad reaching the Pacific will some day have an eastern terminus on the gulf coast of Texas. It would seem that such might be the case.

Indians, snakes, poisonous insects and musquitos

are supposed by some in the north to be the great
plagues of Texas. Along the bordering settlements
of Texas, at times, Indians are troublesome. But new
settlers seldom go where they would be likely to be
disturbed by them. In all the writer's travels, for
years, in western Texas he has never seen an Indian
here unless it was one who passed for a Mexican.
The opinion abroad in regard to Indians is entirely
wrong. They are only troublesome at those points
where new-comers would not be likely to settle.
Snakes and poisonous insects are quite plentiful in
parts of western Texas; but where cattle and hogs or
stock of any kind are kept they soon disappear. Hogs
devour them, stock-boys shoot them and they give way
to civilization. During the writer's six years residence
and travels in western Texas he has never known a
single individual bitten by a snake or a poisonous
insect. That they do bite and that some of them are
deadly poisonous, without ready relief, I suppose is
certain. But men are so seldom bitten by them, and
they so seldom die when bitten, that I can see no good
reason why there should be so much noise made about
them. The people of Texas think no more of snakes
and insects and give themselves no more uneasiness
about them than do the people of other countries. I
suppose the awful reports sent abroad from Texas
about them are from new-comers, and women principally, who no doubt have a perfect horror for and
loathe the snake or poisonous insect, as they picture
them by accident under their hoops or in some way in
their imaginations over and around their heads.
Musquitos along the coast of Texas and as far back
as the level country extends, are at times quite plentiful and to new-comers somewhat annoying. But they
too give way to civilization; as the country is settled
and is trampled by stock they diminish in number.

The settler who locates upon an elevated dry spot, at a reasonable distance from ponds of water or a dense forest, need never be troubled with musquitoes about his dwelling or anywhere within its vicinity, if he has stock around him to eat down the grass and tramp the soil.

HARD. TIMES AND MONEY MATTERS.

It is an interesting fact, that what is known in other states as hard times, is never known in Texas. To be sure, men get cramped in business, but it is from their own bad management, or some local cause, and not from a general stagnation in the business of the country. Although Texas imports largely of those articles that she will eventually export, which must necessarially act as a drain upon the country, yet money seems always to be plenty, and business uniformly active. I might give some of the reasons for this, but it is enough that it is so.

TEXAS ALMANAC.

Persons wishing to know more of western Texas than this work affords them, can, by addressing Mr. Richardson, of the *Galveston News*, Galveston, Texas, obtain an annual, statistical, and general history of the state, called the "Texas Almanac," together with a cheap map of the state.

This almanac gives a description of every county in the state, stating its agricultural capacity, and price of lands, the amount, price, and kind of stock raised in each county; the condition of schools, churches, railroads; and, in fact, a large amount of useful information pertaining to the state and its prospects. For general and correct information in regard to Texas, no one could do better than send for the Texas Almanac, which is issued at the beginning of every year, and should be in the hands of every one who thinks of going to Texas, or wants reliable information in regard to it.

WHO AND HOW TO GO TO WESTERN TEXAS.

To make a comfortable and respectable home in western Texas, there is nothing like as much required as in the north. A hundred and one things are used, in doors and out at the north, that are not really needed here. Therefore, whoever starts out for this part of the world, with a family, should take such, only, of their household things, farming utensils,—bulkly, heavy, and cumbersome articles,—as they may think will be really necessary here. It does not pay to move old, worn-out furniture, hardware, and the like, so far. So I would say to those who go to Texas—reduce your stock of movables as reasonably low as you can, and depend upon buying in Texas, when you find what you really need here. I do not mean by this that you should leave all your woolens and warm clothes behind, or your nice, nearly new cook-stove, or your favorite bureau and mirror; but simply that you should not take such trashy, half worn-out stuff as is not worth moving. Get what you can for such things as you will not need in Texas, bring it in your pocket, and invest it in stock and lands here. There are a plenty of families in the north who have enough about them that they would not need in Texas, which, if sold, would buy cattle, mares, sheep, and stock enough of some kind here to give a person a respectable and encouraging start in the world. There are thousands of families in the north whose circumstances are embarrassed, and who are constantly pushed to get along, whose movable property, in and about their houses alone, including silver, China ware, etc., over and above what would be needed in Texas, if turned into cash, would buy in this country a beautiful flock of sheep, a fine tract of land, and erect a comfortable dwelling upon it.

Think of the change, you who feel pressed and poor, yet with enough around you, more than you need, which, if turned into money, would make you rich, in the most delightful climate and beautiful country. How many fathers there are, who, if they knew how far their little properties would go in Texas, would sell out and find their way here immediately: how many there are who will tug along the path of life, and leave their children but little or nothing, while others will go to western Texas, invest the little they have and live out an easy decline of years, and leave all their children a fine property. Could the sons and daughters of many a family in those cold and snowy regions, only know how they would be delighted here upon the evergreen sod of Texas, and how wealthy they might get here, they would give the father no peace until he should "pull up stakes" and start for the Lone Star land.

I said this was a good country for the man who would retrench, or who is unable to keep pace with the prodigality of the times where he may be living. Are you the man whose property is groaning under the extravagance of empty show, and whose course must be changed in order to avoid the unreasonable demands of inexorable and unfeeling fashion, and its ultimate disastrous effects? To be plain, are you the man who must get away from where you are, in order to curtail your expenses and place your sinking means in some country where they will afford you a better income, and enable you to meet the necessities and requirements of a large and growing family, without being constantly harassed by creditors, with the prospect of finally surrendering your all in keeping up ap-

pearances in the circle in which your family is moving?
If so, sell out, settle up, get ready as best you can,
and come to western Texas. You can here provide
yourself with the best of lands, for a trifling amount,
and build you a spacious and comfortable house, and
all necessary improvements, with but a small outlay
of money, and be as free from the follies and whims
of fashionable life as you please; and yet you need
not be entirely secluded and shut out from good so
ciety, unless in your selection of a home you prefer so
to be. By looking through this country, any one who
is in pursuit of a home, whether a professional man,
merchant, or mechanic, can find the place that would
suit him, unless he might be more nice than wise, and
look for that which no new country ever affords. The
farmer or stock-grower can find a section that is good
for the raising of cattle, horses, sheep, and hogs, without his producing, if he prefers not, anything for them
to eat,—a section that is good for raising wheat, corn,
and almost every vegetable that grows, various delicious fruits, which need not be far away from a good
school. But on account of schools, society, religious
and other matters to which I shall now devote a few
pages, I shall advise a way of coming and settling in
western Texas that I believe will make the foreigner
overjoyed with the country, and result most gloriously
for himself and posterity.

There is one thing about settling in new countries
to which I would call the particular attention of the
emigrant, and that is the mistaken idea that friends
are to be found in distant lands to fill the place of
those of early life. I care not how beautiful the country, or what advantages it may offer to the settler, or
what kind of people and society he may there find, he
will not be as well satisfied with and as well contented
in such country, by leaving all his relatives and friends

of early life behind, as he would be if more or less of such friends or relatives were settlers with him. A person may start out and travel over the world alone, and not feel his separation from youthful friends so much when he carries with him the idea of some day returning to mingle again with those to whom he became attached in early life, memories of whom he cherishes in connection with thoughts and comings of the future. But when he goes alone, or even with his family, to settle down in some new country, among strangers entirely, he is too apt to feel a loss of that which he can in no way make up. Time may roll on, and years may go by, and he may return to the home of his birth, which, although he loves, he would not exchange for that of his adoption, yet he asks, where are the friends of my early days, with whom I used to caper and play? where the cheerful and intelligent girls, in whose company I once loved to be? where the good old people of my neighborhood? where the friends of my youth, those friends of my happy days, such as I have never since found, the loss of whom has left a vacancy in my heart, a dreaminess in my life? How often has the settler exclaimed, O for one good old-fashioned neighbor and friend! Therefore, I would not ask a person to leave behind that cluster of endearments that have forever entwined around his heart, and all his relatives and friends of old, to take up an abode in a distant country among strangers. Paradise itself, with all its enchantments, could not withstand the encroachments of feelings occasioned by the thoughts of leaving all the friends of early life, to accept an abode even in her most favored spot. Judging the feelings of others in this respect by my own, I am always glad to see parties of emigrants linked together not only by feelings of interest in and dependence upon each other, but by feelings, if possi-

19

ble, of solid friendship and kindred love. Such kind
of emigration is worth while. But to hear a person
relate that he has left everything that was dear to
him, friends, relatives, and all, perhaps across the
wide deep, or thousands of miles away, it makes me
sad, although he may have come to this fine country,
where his prospects may be ever so good, yet it is sad
to hear his tale of loneliness. A person of talent or
shining abilities, of property in abundance, or one who
is gifted in the way of getting into society, and can
always make himself agreeable to others, or, in other
words, one who can adapt himself to circumstances,
might not feel the force of these remarks, as would
those who are without these qualifications. As a general thing, the lonely emigrant or family, who settles
in a distant country, among strangers, forever mourn
their complete separation from relatives and friends
of early life.

There is something of still greater importance that
the lonely emigrant is too apt to feel the want of,—
that is a way to educate his children properly, and
give them the advantages of moral and religious examples and instruction. Strangers in new countries,
and in Texas particularly, do not seem inclined to settle near each other, but very often locate as far apart
as possible, for the purpose of gratifying their avarice,
and having a vast range for their stock, where, perhaps, one spear of grass in a million is not consumed
by their cattle. But relatives, friends, old acquaintances, and even those who go from the same section
of any country to a new one, are apt to settle with a
view to neighborhood schools, society, religious advantages, and many other inestimable interests. And
it is well known that when people settle in this way,
those feelings that have so long existed between them
become strengthened, and they learn to regard each

other as brothers, and their intimacy is a source of such happiness to them as they could not have attained by settling separately and among strangers. I would not be understood that the thousands of men and families who go alone into a new country, are never happy and contented; but that when they do so, they go without a peculiar source of happiness, for which they may ever after look in vain. I know the world is full of reputation, wealth, and steadfast friendship, that took root among strangers, in strange lands, yet who knows of the sadness occasioned by the thoughts of this separation from every one, and all, that was once dear to the possessors? who knows what it has cost them to do without a single friend of old?

I have noticed that settling among strangers is apt to create an indifference in regard to the education of children. Parents are too apt to say that "My children are not going to such a school, among strangers, and with such and such children. I will wait for a better opportunity." And from the simple fact of being among strangers, thousands of children are neglected during that period of their lives when all possible attention should be given to their improvement.

For these and many other reasons the writer is strongly in favor of party or company emigration and neighborhood settlements. Certain it is that when people of like peculiarities of society and life go to a new country, and take up near to each other, they are better qualified to appreciate and understand the excellencies of such country than would be the lonely emigrant, whose mind from the nature of things would be more or less occupied with that which renders, as it were, daylight in appearance too much like dark. Therefore come not alone but bring with you more or less of your old friends and western

Texas will prove to you as near to that paradise of
poetic and Bible renown as would any country in the
wide world. Come in a way that memories of the
past and cherished things of yore will not weaken
your judgment and ability to appreciate your present
surroundings. Bring the spirit with the body and
you can then understand,

THE BEAUTIES OF OUR LAND.

I do not mean to say that new countries should be
filled up by people all from the same country, but that
a few intimate friends or families, or people from the
same sections, of the same conditions of life, would
be happier settled near to each other than among
strangers in a new country. I said that people in
Texas are inclined to settle away from each other.
This is the case to a great extent with the stock-
growers of western Texas, and the reason for their so
doing, aside from their separation from their friends of
old and their forgetfulness of duty and disinclination
to society, is that their minds are so glutted with the
superabundance of the country that they are constantly gathering up their cattle from among other
peoples' stock, where perhaps the tops of the grass are
only eaten off, but not one hundredth part of it consumed, and pushing them far out upon ranges where
nothing but the Indian, wild horse, deer and the like
have for past ages made any pretension to possession
or consumption of the inexhaustible production, where
they can have it all to themselves and as little as possible to do, and too often smother their duty to their
children, society, and almost everything that belongs
to man, but property and money, or idleness and ease.
To be sure, they get upon their horses and go several
trips a year, for the purpose of branding their increase, amounting in all, perhaps to three or four

months' work, such as it is, and the balance of the
year is too often most wofully squandered or unprofit-
ably passed away.

I would not have the reader understand that these
remarks set forth the habits and condition of all stock-
growing communities in western Texas, but that there
is too great a disposition among our stock-growers to
settle far away from each other, which deprives them
of the advantages of schools and society, the cause
of which, to a great extent, is the want of intimate
acquaintance, early attachments, and like peculiarities
of life and raising.

There are a plenty of stock-growers in western Texas,
living some distance from a neighborhood or school,
who mount their children upon horses and they gallop
away to school; but some are too indifferent in regard
to schooling for this, and others live too far away to
send their children to school. Many send their children to towns to board and attend school, or to a
boarding-school; but this occurs too often after their
younger days are neglected.

Now I will suggest a way of emigrating to western
Texas, that would result most gloriously to the settler
and his posterity; and I can see no reason why it should
not be practicable. If I were a resident of an old,
densely-populated country, where perhaps I could find
nothing profitable for me to do, and should take it
into my head to go to western Texas, and should be
pleased with it, and prefer to make it my home, what
objection could there be to my returning and interesting with me, if possible, a half dozen or more of my
former friends, for the purpose of settling in that fine
country, in a way to be satisfied and contented? and
for our convenience and benefit, what could be more
becoming than to interest with us several mechanics
of different kinds, say a blacksmith, shoemaker, tin-

ner, gunsmith, wagon-maker, cooper, harness-maker,
tailor, millwright, carpenter, and possibly other mechanics; a merchant and physician, an attorney, a
good schoolmaster, a printer, and a minister of the
Gospel, and as many of the laboring class as the company might see fit to induce to join them? And after
getting together and appointing the right kind of prudent managers, should there be found a want of funds
to enable the enterprise to go forward, how would it
do for the managers of such company to communicate
to some gentleman of ability, "that a number of respectable citizens and families [of whatever place it
might be] have determined to go in a company to
western Texas for the purpose of settling there as
farmers, stock-growers, mechanics, merchants, etc.,
to improve the country and be useful to themselves
and mankind, that there are poor people in the company, and that it is in want of means to enable it to
go all together and settle down in a way to get along
and be satisfied as pioneers, and we as their managers
are authorized and instructed to request you to address the people of ——— on the subject of *emigration*, for the purpose of forwarding this work. Could
you make it convenient to interest, with your influence and talent, the people of ——— in this subject,
and let this company feel their obligation and grati-
tude to you for having rendered the assistance they so
much needed," etc.?

Could not something of this kind be done, and col-
lections taken up in this or a similar way, with perfect propriety, to enable poor people to emigrate with
those who are better off? Would not this be the way
to advance the work of civilization; to carry light to
benighted Mexico? Would it not be somewhat in
imitation of the great AUSTINS, the colonizers and
fathers of Texas? Were the noble Austins the last

of old Connecticut's sons who will brave the dangers
of the frontier and open up new fields of civilization,
and call out the usefulness of men? Would not a
man of mind be proud to sound his voice in such a
cause? would not his soul fill with eloquence when
considering such a subject? Would not the people of
any community be eager to listen to an able speech
and orator upon such an occasion? and would they
mind a quarter or a small admittance to the hearing
of such an address? Methinks I hear the voice of an
Everett, eloquently discoursing upon the expanding
importance of this great land, carefully lifting the vail
of the future, and prudently directing the emigrant
upon his course. Methinks I hear the voice of a great
and wise man commending this laudable scheme of
emigration. Methinks I see a group of intelligent
men earnestly considering the prospects of western
Texas and mineral Mexico, and they decide to come
and live in these money-making and happy regions.
The spirit of a Washington pervades our whole country, and the same God that watched over the battles
that won the liberties of America, is still watching
over this expanding confederacy, and it is to be hoped
will never abandon it to an unhappy fate.

A very good way for poor people to get to Texas, is
to get in with those who are taking stock there, either
by land or water. Go along and help drive or attend
to stock, and so work your way to the country. There
are many going in this way.

DIFFERENT ROUTES TO TEXAS.

Those who go to Texas from the southern states,
generally go by the way of New Orleans, and across
the gulf of Mexico, or by Red river to Shreeveport, or
some point on this river, where they leave it and cross
the country by land, both of which routes to Texas are

much traveled. There are different routes for those
who go from the north, east, and west. There is a
regular line of packets running between Boston and
Galveston, which affords a quick, comfortable, and
reasonable passage. There is also a good line of
packet ships from New York to Galveston, and there
is regular steamship communication between Galves:
ton and the ports of western Texas, Indianola or Lavacca, and Brazos-Santiago. There is also a regular
line of the smaller class of ships running between
New York, Indianola, and Lavacca, western Texas.
There are also schooners running from Boston and
New York, and vessels from Philadelphia to Galveston and western Texas. There is a quick steamship
and railroad route between New York, and New Orleans. Many northern people take this route to Texas,
and some take what is called the southern route, by
way of Washington, on to New Orleans, and across
the gulf. The last two routes are principally for pas-
sengers, and not so much for freight and luggage.
Others go the western route, and down the Mississippi
river, either to New Orleans or the mouth of Red
river, and thence on as above stated. The price of
passage from Cairo and St. Louis to New Orleans, is
from twelve to thirty dollars, according to circumstances. The distance from Cairo to New Orleans is
about a thousand miles. The price of passage across
the gulf, by steamship, from New Orleans to Galveston, is invariably fifteen dollars, and twenty dollars to
Powder Horn or Indianola, and I think about twenty-
five dollars to Brazos-Santiago.

There are two routes from New Orleans to the ports
of Galveston and Indianola—the inside and the outside route. The inside route takes you over about
seventy miles of railroad, extending from New Orleans to Burwix bay, thence by steamship across the

gulf. The outside route is performed entirely by
steamships, down the Mississippi river to its mouth,
and thence across the gulf. Some prefer one route,
and some the other. The price of passage over either
is the same. There is no change by the outside route,
and the ships are larger than those of the inside route.
The Burwix bay or inside route is several hours the
quickest. It will not be long before the Burwix bay
railroad will be extended on to Galveston and central
Texas.

Those who cross the Mississippi river at St. Louis,
above or below, and go by land to Texas, I am unable
to direct, further than to say that there are noted crossings at all the large rivers, and good routes are to be
found, of which any one can learn anywhere along
the Mississippi river. There are regular thorough-
fares across Missouri, Arkansas, and the Indian territory, to Texas, which are perfectly safe, and along
which animals get all the grazing they need, free of
expense. There are many going these overland routes
on through northern to western and southern Texas.
People going these routes with wagon and horses, or
oxen, can lay in and occasionally buy provision, camp
out, and travel very cheap. Sheep and all kinds of
stock, I learn, are being largely driven across to Texas
from the western states. The higher up the route the
better it is considered for stock-driving, as grass is
more plentiful, there is less timber, fewer settlements,
and the crossings of rivers are more shallow and easily
got over. The roads higher up the country are said
to be better. Some, who drive cattle from Texas
north, go entirely around Missouri, by going through
the Indian territory, Kansas, the corner of Nebraska,
into Iowa, and so on. Some drovers cut across the
upper or northern portion of Missouri.

It is said that forty thousand sheep, on their way to

Texas, passed through a small town last year (1859), on one of these overland routes. Probably not less than a hundred thousand sheep will be taken into Texas, from different points north of Texas, this year (1860). Let them go: that is the* place for them. I see it is stated that two hundred and fifty thousand sheep were brought out of Mexico into Texas in 1859; but this must be a mistake.

Many are the wool-growers who are now making their way to western Texas. The man who can make a raise of a pair of horses, or oxen, and wagon, and a small flock of sheep, had better join some friend, mix flocks, and find this way across the country to the sheep region of Texas, that is, if he would make a fortune at the business. The man of but little means could, if he chose, take his family in this way, and drive his sheep along with but a trifling additional expense. He could take in a wagon nearly all that a small family would require, at first, to keep house with in western Texas, or that portion of it where snow is seldom or never seen; where cellars, filled with vegetables for the winter, are not required; where houses, plastered and air-tight, are also not required; where a little open shanty will do until a better one, or a good house, can be built.

In going these overland routes to western Texas, a person may pass through the wheat region of the country, and no doubt many would be pleased with northern Texas, and would settle down before reaching their destination.

HOW TO FIND A LOCATION.

When arriving in western Texas from across the gulf of Mexico or any point at sea, unless a person may have friends in the country and knows to what point in the interior he is going, the questions will

naturally arise with him: " What shall I do ? Where
shall I go to find a location ? How am I to satisfy
myself in regard to this country ? And, possibly, he
may ask what am I to do with my family that they
may be comfortable and yet not bring a heavy expense
upon me, while I am engaged in exploring the
country to find what may seem to me a suitable location, for my business and my future abode, where I
could make it profitable and should be satisfied to live?
A family or a number of families arriving upon the
coast of Texas in this way, to accomplish these objects in a judicious and an economical manner should,
if their intention is not to live upon the coast, go a
little into the interior, where the nnoccupied country
is rolling and dry, where there is plenty of shade,
wood and water, and after camping upon some pleasant stream, in a way to get along comfortably, with
perhaps not more than one-fourth the expense of boarding at a hotel. I say after accomplishing this in a
judicious way, the gentlemen of the families or such
of them as may be best qualified and are agreed upon
for the purpose, after securing good, substantial and
gentle ponies, saddles and traveling equipage, coffee
and coffee-pots, tin-cups, sugar, dried meat, bacon,
hard biscuit or flour, and possibly a Mexican who can
talk your language to pack and lead your pack mule
or horse, to look after camping fixtures generally, and
do the cooking. I say again, after the first is accomplished and the last secured, the gentlemen agreed
upon, with a map of the state in their pockets and a
memorandum of what has been learned at hand,
should start out and give the country a good looking
over.

Those who intend wool-growing as their business
should, of course, go to the sheep raising sections, ex-
amine the ranges and different flocks of sheep, talk

with shepherds and proprietors, and be not afraid to push a little further on ; go up this creek, cross over and down that creek, make all necessary inquiry and when a good-looking unoccupied range is found, where lands are for sale, satisfy yourselves in regard to its suitableness for you—learn who has the title, for the owner may be a hundred miles away, learn as much of the title as possible, and be careful that you are not imposed upon by those who would not have you buy as well as those who might be anxious to sell. Continue your work in this way until you have found the place you want, and then either buy, lease, contract or make arrangements for a home upon it according to circumstances as I have repeatedly directed.

In looking out for ranges of any kind, whether for cattle, horses or sheep, a good hog-range will never come amiss. But if sheep-raising is the principal thing in view, do not surrender its claim to that of hogs or anything else. If a range for all kinds of stock is desired, a small section of the range at least should be quite rolling and dry. This, of course, should be for the sheep. For horses the country must be moderately rolling, and if it is hilly and mountainous even they will do well. For cattle, or Texas cattle at least, it matters not so much. I believe the stock-growers of western Texas, who make the most money at the cattle business, have their stock upon ranges near to the coast. But I would say to those who take Durham stock or northern cattle to Texas, not to attempt to keep them too near the coast on account of occasional wet seasons and musquitos.

Now, if the reader will carefully observe what I have said throughout this work, although some of it may seem of but little consequence, he will, if he settles in western Texas, be able to steer clear of many bad bargains and blunders that he might otherwise make.

There is one thing in regard to building spots in the lowlands of Texas to which I would call particular attention. When I speak of lowlands I do not wish to be understood as meaning wet or swampy lands, but the lands along the coast which are generally wide open prairies, much inclined to a level, but here and there slightly and sometimes considerably rolling, also, at greater or less distances, divided with streams and rivers, along which there is generally more or less timber. Now this section along the coast, which is an immense cattle range, has heretofore been considered, its river bottoms excepted, the poorest portion of the state, unless we except also the desolate plain in the far west. But this is a mistake. These lowlands will yet be found the most valuable in the state. I have no room to give my reasons why, but it is enough to say that they are rich, inexhaustibly rich, and are sure in time to be appreciated. What I am now at is this : When a person locates himself upon these coast-lands he should aim to secure a building spot that is somewhat sloping or rolling, and where if possible the sea-breeze can have a fair sweep— not behind a thicket of timber and underbrush, but an open spot where the water will readily run off. I do not mean by this a *hill* but a *sloping* or *rolling* spot. If these directions are observed and cistern-water used, after one or two year's occupation and acclimation is experienced, sickness and musquitos will be strangers to your house and surroundings. This subject of finding a location in western Texas, if rightly treated, would be very lengthy; I will, therefore, drop it with the few suggestions I have made and return to the camp of the families of those who went in pursuit of a place for a future home.

EMIGRANTS' CAMP.

Around its fires are seated upon chairs, boxes, blocks or whatever may be at hand, mothers and daughters, little children, and perhaps fathers and young men. They sit in the open air and talk of their recent distant homes, the land of their birth, and of scenes in the past. Perhaps, ere the sun had sunk in the west, the daughters of this group had returned from a stroll up the creek or the valley below, from whence they brought the flowers of winter time. The young men have returned from a hunting excursion, through the grassy forests or over the great prairie in the east—they met the prowling wolf, and gave him chase, and their hearts beat quick as their steeds dashed away and drew close upon the canine's heel. The whelp, exhausted, fell to the ground, and the happy crowd with shouts of joy gathered about. With a sneaking look the victim begged for mercy—but, alas, "thou art the curse of man and beast, and with convulsive jerk thou shalt stiffen and die as we batter your wicked head." Now, over the plain a herd of deer are seen, and like foolish boys they give them chase, and the deer outrun them in the race. They saw another herd and cautiously approaching brought some of its number to the ground. Thus while the talk goes on the sweet venison for supper is prepared and the merits of camping life are discussed. It is agreed that their change is a happy one, and that their new country is promising them a delightful future. Days and weeks go by and their camp begins to seem like a natural home—they feel that they are free from the restraints of artificial life, and are likely to do as they please. Nature becomes more their study and life seems unbounded and free. Now those who went to explore the country in pursuit of a place for a set

tlement having returned, they soon strike camp and
start off for the range of their future abode. Thus I
will leave the party to make their settlement and shed
its influence around, perhaps in the center of benighted Mexico.

SLAVERY.

Although I have seen a great deal of slavery as it
exists in the south, I have not acquired that practical
knowledge of it that I might have done. Much of my
time in Texas has been spent with that class of people who have but few and many of them no slaves at all,
and in sections where slavery is not considered profitable. But from the acquaintance I have with this
institution, I should say let it alone. Were it left entirely alone, in the opinion of the writer, labor in the
United States would find its true level. It is easy
enough to talk about the evils of slavery, and to agi-
tate with a view to its abolishment, and were there but
a few thousand slaves in the country they could be
set free and no great calamity would arise from it.
But when men talk about setting the millions of negroes in the south free, it is time we are talking about
ruining the south, and producing a great national calamity. What could be done with the slaves if liberated? Should they be left to work as free laborers
in the south? Let me say to those of this opinion
that when in Africa, not long after the liberation of
the slaves at Cape Colony, the writer put up at a
hotel kept by an intelligent English lady who had a
great deal of difficulty to get along with her household affairs in consequence of her slaves having been
set free.

She said that since the slaves of the colony had
been liberated, there was no dependence to be placed
in them; that they were a nuisance, and would not

work enough to keep from starving, and only at such times as they pleased. Sometimes the lady and her daughter would do the work of their large house, and again they could hire one of the liberated slaves and get along·very well until the hireling would·get drunk, or take a notion to lounge in the street. I saw a plenty of idle ones in gangs of five, ten, fifteen, and twenty, all over town, and they were saucy and impudent enough.

The lady told me that a farmer of her acquaintance, after giving up his slaves, attempted to hire them, and get along in this way. When his crop of oats was ripe, he went for his help, and found two of his men under an orange tree, with a jug of whisky. He made known his errand, and their answer was that they did not want to work; but after long persuasion and extravagant offers, they finally agreed to come and cut the farmer's oats, after they had eaten all the oranges off the tree, and drank up their jug of whisky.

What an orange and whisky orchard it would make of the south in exchange for its most beautiful cotton fields, if her slaves were liberated and left free in the country.

Now let us suppose that the slaves of the south were set free, and sent away to take care of themselves. My father once had a negro: they called him Jack. When sent out for a basket of chips, he would fall asleep while picking them up; when climbing a fence, he would sometimes get to the top, go to sleep and fall down. Jack was n't profitable without a whip behind him, and *he* was n't *niggers* enough to pay for an overseer; and for this reason he was either given away, or sent off to shirk for himself. At all events, the story runs that he went to riding horse on the canal—got asleep—fell in—and drowned, of course. Now, if the great mass of negroes in the south were

sent to think for themselves, in any part of the world,
would they not fall into the canal, or what would be
equally bad, get asleep while picking up their chips?
If slavery can live in contact with free labor, let it
live, and *peaceably* too. Slaves are human beings;
why turn them upon the world to starve? Go to the
cotton and sugar fields of the south and look about
you; ask yourselves where could these millions of
negroes be so happy, and where so useful to mankind?
Then consider and treat things according to circumstances, and think and talk of things that are practicable.

RELAXATION OF ENERGY.

I have somewhere said that the greatest objection to
this country is the easy means of support that it affords to men, which has a tendency to beget habits of
idleness. Some attribute the laziness of men in Texas
to the peculiar effects of the climate upon the system;
but I believe, and I ought to say, I know that such is
not the case. The most thrifty and robust young
men that I ever saw, were the anglo or white natives
of Australia, and if ever there were lazier white men
than the Australian stock-growers were, then I have
not seen them in my travels. The health of Australia is better than that of Texas, for one reason:—its
native growth of vegetation is not equal to one third
or fourth of that of Texas, and its trees shed a thin
scale of their bark instead of a mass of leaves; consequently, there is no vast decay of vegetable matter
as in Texas. Therefore, other things equal, the air
of Australia must be purer than that of Texas, when
first settled. But when the country around the settler,
almost anywhere in western Texas, is relieved of its
immense annual decay of vegetation, there is then, in
the opinion of the writer, no real cause for relaxation
of energy in the settler. Pure, wholesome air and
20

water, will never take away a person's energy, nor render him unfit to labor in any country; neither will it make him lazy. But a country that will afford a good living, and make a man rich, without his storing up but little for winter, neither for man nor beast, and is otherwise peculiarly easy for the occupant, would very naturally make him lazy; and to excuse himself, it does very well to say that a white man can't work in this climate. The truth is, men can work in Texas as well as in any country, and I sincerely believe that most of the time it is the most delightful climate to labor in that I have ever known, unless a person suffers himself to think that he is in a country where there is not much labor required of him, and indulges himself too much in this way until, perhaps, he thinks he can't labor. I am well acquainted with foreigners here who labor the year through at the cultivation of the soil, and they tell me that it is all nonsense to say that a man can't labor in Texas. That there is no necessity of his working so hard, is very true; but that he must for this reason become lazy and idle, is absurd. The industrious man who comes here from any country, can continue his industry as pleasantly and more profitably than in almost any other country.

ENCOURAGEMENT TO HOME INDUSTRY.

Texas has now under consideration a bill to encourage the establishment of home manufactories within her limits. It is couched in the following terms:

"*Be it enacted by the Legislature of the State of Texas:* That from and after the passage of this act, whenever any person or persons shall commence the construction of any manufacturing establishment, for the manufacture of silk, cotton, or woolen cloths, or for the purpose of manufacturing articles of use or ornament of iron, copper, or silver, from the native ores or native metals, he or they shall be entitled to receive from the state of Texas ten sections of land, of 640 acres each, for every $10,000 invested in said manufacturing establishment or establishments, upon the terms and conditions hereinafter prescribed."

At one dollar per acre, (should this bill become a law), there is offered $6,400 for every $10,000 invested in manufacturing of different kinds, upon certain conditions.

This certainly ought to encourage the emigration of foreign capitalists, and it seems to me that it might pay them to look into the matter and see whether it becomes a law or not, and what the conditions of this bill are. I am sorry to say that I have not got them at hand. They are no doubt favorable to the capitalist, and as there is certain to be a strong and continual emigration to Texas, those who accept this proposition from the state would be able to locate lands from which they could no doubt realize one dollar per acre at least, before long.

HOPELESSLY FALLEN.

I have stated that the disturbance by Cortinas and his followers upon the Rio Grande, would be of short duration. I did not mean to say by this that our difficulties with Mexico and her embittered factions were at an end, for I believe there never will be any permanent and lasting peace between that country and the United States, until she is in the hands of some other power, or becomes subject to our government in some way. I simply meant by saying that all would soon be quiet on the Rio Grande, that Cortinas and all outlaws in that quarter would be driven out of Texas, and that the state would take care of her own frontier in a way that people would be safe anywhere in the

settled portions of its limits. Statesmen may dream
and ponder, and they may exhaust their skill in
schemes of reconciliation; treaties may be made and
patched up, and confidence may be for a time somewhat restored; but all will be of no avail. Mexico's
bright days, if ever she had any, are gone; her peaceful sun hath sunk never to rise again. A brighter
sun than she ever had must transform her into a different sphere.

Seeing the recent accounts in regard to the contentions and hopeless condition of Mexico, I am induced
to add a few lines to what I have already said upon
the subject. I will now suppose that the Canadas on
the north of the United States, instead of being possessed as they are by a powerful and progressive people, were in the hands of a comparatively ignorant,
weak, and retrograding people, with a tottering government and the elements of self-destruction within
it, and that this country, instead of being a snowy,
freezing one, was one of a mild and pleasant climate,
and of a broad musquete surface, covered with horses,
mules, sheep, etc., abounding in the richest of mines
of almost every mineral, and in consequence of this
weakness and inability to take care of themselves,
they are taken into the United States, or under her
protection in some way, and their country opened to a
reciprocity of trade with her people, as are the Canadas
at present, and every body allowed to go into and
trade as best they could, on an equal footing with any
and all. I say, suppose that this might be the situation of the Canadas, how long would it be before the
Yankees on their borders or near to them would be
among them and have all the trade of the country in
their hands? and how long would it be before these
rich cultivating and musquete lands, these cattle,
horses, etc., would contribute to the wealth of these

Yankee merchants and speculators? Happen what will, the people of Mexico are probably to remain in their country until their race shall have become extinct or lose its identity, and they are to be consumers, and they are to labor in the cultivation of their more productive sections of country. And the Yankees, being superior merchants and tradesmen, farmers and speculators, to the Mexicans, should they settle in Mexico,—which they surely will,—would soon reap the profits of their trade, and make "ten strikes" at the purchase of their property and at the cultivation of their lands with the labor of the peons and otherwise.

I may be considered a little too fast about this, but it seems to me to require but little penetration to see about where this Mexican people and country are going, provided the United States remain a unit and continue to flourish. There is broad daylight examples before us to tell us how this thing will probably work, although it will take many ages to put Mexico where it would be a glorious thing, could she be to-day.

CHANCE.

There are no doubt many who would wonder that the lands of Texas are so cheap and so lavishingly bestowed upon capitalists, corporations, etc. There is so much of them that if, by giving a large portion of them away, capitalists could be induced to invest largely in manufacturing, and railroads could be extensively constructed, the balance of her lands, would be worth much more to the state than they all now are or ever would be without such encouragement. It is only from accident that Texas has so long escaped the attention of the business and intelligent world. Had her superior adaptation to sheep and wool-growing been known, and could she have been

occupied by a different people when Australia was
found to be so well adapted to this business, there
would no doubt now be at least thirty millions of
sheep within her limits, and other stock and business
in proportion, and many of the great chances now
offering to the world in Texas would have been improved long ago.

I will here state that the winter of 1859–60 has
been the most severe one ever known in Texas, and
the severity of this winter will no doubt be much
talked of; but if such a winter is only known once in
a long lifetime, and the stock upon our prairies generally live through it without the least attention, and
with but little loss, no one will be deterred from coming to Texas on account of such an unusual winter.

The death of bare-bellied Mexican sheep should not
deter people from coming to western Texas, as they
will die in an unusual cold snap, where improved
sheep and other stock would hardly feel the cold.

This winter will no doubt induce many stock-growers to cut a stock of hay to feed in case of emergency
hereafter. It is well enough for stock-growers in any
part of Texas to save a stack of prairie hay to feed
any animals that stay immediately about home where
the grass may be short, although it might not be
needed except for oxen, milch cows, work horses, or
something of the kind, one year in ten.

In writing a book of this kind, there are many, no
doubt, who would say nothing but nice things about
the country of which they might be writing; but I
have considered the dark with the bright side of my
subject, believing that no man of sense would expect
to read of a new country that could be honestly considered as without an objection. Men are raised differently, and are of different tastes, consequently no
new country would be appreciated or would suit every

body at first; but after living in western Texas a while, there are few who would leave it to live in any other country.

In conclusion, I will say that I have tried to treat my subject fairly, and that I have no interest in deceiving people in regard to Texas, neither have I any disposition to do so. I have written simply because I believe western Texas, all things considered, is the most delightful country I ever knew, and that there are tens and hundreds of thousands of people who would be much happier here than where they are; and furthermore, I believe a large emigration of the Anglo-Saxon or American race to this part of the world, would be of incalculable advantage to the country, particularly to the future of degraded Mexico.

WESTERN TEXAS,

THE

AUSTRALIA OF AMERICA;

OR

THE PLACE TO LIVE.

Must I remain forever here penniless and destitute? Is there no spot upon this wide-spread earth whereon I could live and accumulate a little to be called my own?

BY

A SIX YEARS' RESIDENT.

CINCINNATI:

FOR SALE BY E. MENDENHALL,

No. 10 West Fifth Street.

1860.